VENGEANCE FALLS

Avery West

Avery West

First edition, 2025

"Some rise by sin, and some by virtue fall."

– Measure for Measure, William Shakespeare

CHAPTER 1

A flash of lightning exposed the figure in the corner.

Her breath stopped as it took shape — Riley.

Beck wasn't surprised by the sight of her sister, who had a lifetime of turning up unannounced.

The blood.

That surprised her.

It covered Riley's clothes and hands, one of which trembled as it held a large black backpack. She whispered something, but Beck couldn't make it out.

And then Riley led her outside and showed her the body.

CHAPTER 2

Eighteen hours earlier

Beck checked the time and picked up her pace. St. Gerolamo Emiliani passed intermittently between the bars of the concrete-and-iron fence.

"Smells like breakfast," Father W shouted. Only a shock of white hair betrayed his seventy-seven years. In street clothes, his barrel chest and catcher's mitt hands could easily pass him off as a bouncer at any Fenway bar. He smiled at the sight of the shopping bag in Beck's hands, the paper warm and spotted with oil. Aromas of butter, brown sugar and syrupy berries complemented the fall air.

The children of "St. J's" were equally fixated. She could have been a seven-foot alien with three heads; their eyes would not have left the bag. Sister Lucinda blew her whistle, pausing the t-ball game. She was perturbed at the interruption but unable to stop the swarm from racing over. The other teachers and volunteers appeared grateful for the interruption as well.

"Cinnamon or corn?" Madeleine asked.

"Blueberry," Beck said. "But tell me you've had some protein today."

"You kidding? Lucinda the Lunatic won't let us leave the dining room until we eat all our eggs."

"Hey, keep it down."

"But you call her that all the time," Heather said, innocent Heather with a voice so high Beck was surprised dogs in the neighborhood weren't howling in response.

"Just eat." She passed out the muffins. Crumbs flew as the children thanked her.

"Ten minutes, then back to the field," Sister Lucinda called out, tossing the ball up and down. Unlike Father W, her physique was streamlined, like the drill sergeant in *Full Metal Jacket*.

"Nice to see her softening up."

"People go one of two ways after fifty," Father W said, a Haitian lineage seasoning his tone. "More centered, at

2

peace with their destiny, or regretful, dismayed at how it all turned out. Sister Lucinda's different; content but terrifying."

Beck stifled a laugh, fearful the t-ball would take her head off a second later. Father W grabbed a muffin. They sat on the concrete bench, the one with angels carved into its base, so worn down by the winters that only outlines of their chubby faces remained.

St. J's occupied eight square blocks north of Dyer's center. Not city blocks but Colonial cartways tarred over for modern travel. Beck could have traversed the campus – a church named after the patron saint of orphans, a dormitory, a patchy playground, a classroom hall and a 1930s Victorian – in under a minute. When keeping up on PiYo, anyway. Lack of exercise, thanks to a near-overwhelming workload, would blow that runtime out to a few minutes or more these days.

Her eyes scanned the chain-link fence circling the gabled Victorian – her childhood home. Warning signs foretold its demolition, a bleak reminder St. J's was part of a dying breed. For over a century, it had served as a home and learning oasis to underprivileged kids of all stripes and all faiths. Now, it was being carved up and sold to developers.

"Finally gonna do it, huh," she said.

"Must be done. The house is unsafe, and we need the cheddah."

"Cheddah? Really?"

"Priests can't be cool?"

"Not with blueberry stains on their shirt."

"Darnit." He licked his thumb and dabbed at the spot.

Her gaze traveled up the turret of the Victorian. Like a manor out of Hawthorne, the ten-thousand square feet were a maze of low-ceilinged rooms and dead-ends. A hardship grant from Yale had been her ticket out. Now graduated, she felt not a jot of nostalgia for the university; her college years enjoyable but focused, an all-business stop-off on the way to the rest of her life. Four years ago, though, she'd cried for three days after departing the timeworn house and its gloomy corridors, which never fully warmed in winter but somehow generated the heat of a coal-fired oven in the summer.

"The house may fall, but Mr. Gabriel will stand," Father W said. "How's our boy doing?"

She pulled out her cell and clicked on an app labeled MrG.

The program loaded and resolved into a lumberjack-type avatar. "Good morning, Beck."

"Morning, G. How's it going?"

"Excellent." His gaze angled over to Father W, his presence registered by the reverse-camera function triggered upon the app's startup. "*Bonjou, Papa.*"

Father W responded in Haitian Creole, the translation running across the bottom of the screen:

Nice to see you again, Mr. Gabriel.

You as well. You look younger every day.

As excited as she was by the continued evolution of Mr. G's natural language processing, the amazement in Father W's eyes thrilled Beck even more.

"We really should get going if we want to make the meeting," Mr. G said. "The travel time from your location to Paradigm is thirty-three minutes by T."

"I'll take a Lyft," she said.

"And I'll adjust the budget."

"You're such a stickler."

"I am what you made me," he said with a wink and a smile.

"Talk to you soon." Beck closed the app.

Father W issued a hearty laugh and threw his arm around her. "Incredible!"

"Pretty basic, believe it or not."

"Wizardry to a curmudgeon like me. From a painting to a…well, I'm not sure what to call him."

"A shepherd."

"Ah. Perfect."

She wasn't ready to go that far – as the primary engineer, there were always improvements to be made to MrG, an AI companion inspired by a mural on her bedroom wall up in the turret, waiting to be reduced to rubble.

A tiny figure crossed the playground – a boy with leaves clinging to his jeans and a too-big Red Sox cap obscuring his eyes.

"New arrival?"

"Jimmy Chen. DCF brought him in the night before last. His mother was killed coming home from work. Or she was killed *at* work; no one knows. A working lady."

"Where's dad?"

"They couldn't locate so much as a distant relative. His mum was knifed but made it all the way home before she succumbed. Probably didn't think her injury was as bad as it was. Jimmy sat next to her body for two days before they found him." Father W's words passed with compassion but also immediacy. In their world, extended grief was impractical. In their world, you ripped the band-aid off and got a move on. He lifted a muffin from the bag. "Go say hello."

She hesitated, then took the muffin and approached the boy. "Hey, Jimmy. Hungry?"

He showed no sign that he heard; just stared into the middle distance.

"My name's Beck. You like blueberries?"

The boy accepted the muffin and picked at the crumb topping, guiding morsels to his lips. "Are you going to take me away?" His voice was surprisingly low-pitched.

"No. Why?"

"People keep taking me places. The police station. The doctor's."

"They just want to know how you're feeling."

He dug deeper into the muffin but no longer ate. Blueberry and cake fell to the ground. His tiny fingers glistened with butter and turned purple from the mashed fruit. "My mom died."

"I know. I'm sorry."

"I don't have anywhere to go."

"You don't have to go anywhere. Father Winston's gonna look after you. Sister Lucinda, too. She can be scary, but this is their home. They'll take care of you as long as you need."

"How do you know?"

"Because they've been taking care of me my whole life." She recalled her first day thirteen years ago, the terror of being shunted to such a ghostly environment. She appreciated how vital a first day was and how every day felt like a first day to an orphan. "My old room's right up there."

"A couple kids were mean to me."

"Because they're sad. And scared. Madeleine's nice, though."

"She gave me an extra blanket when I got cold and sat beside my bed until I fell asleep."

"Sounds like her. Some kids leave. Others stay for years, like me. We call it St. J's, short for Saint Jerome's, which is easier to say than the Italian. For a while, I thought it was Saint Geronimo's. You'll be safe here."

He drove his thumb through the muffin. It fell apart, hunks spilling to the ground. He cried, too raw to process what was happening or why, crying for a mother who'd never return.

Beck didn't know what to do. Floods of emotion unsettled her. She glanced at Father W for help but felt Jimmy lean against her. Slowly, she eased her arm around his frail shoulders.

CHAPTER 3

"Sorry, I'm late." Beck fell into a chair, breathing hard after the sprint from the Lyft to the conference room.

Paradigm Ventures – the people betting on MrGabriel.com – sat around the top of the table, wearing the finest Newbury Street threads and typing on shiny, slimline laptops. Beck and her colleagues occupied the low end, wearing flannel, hoodies and sneakers, slouched behind laptops adorned with stickers of bands, *The Legend of Zelda* logos and snaps of the family pet. It amused her how the two groups always seemed to arrange themselves into adult and kiddie sections.

"Let's get started," someone said.

All eyes turned to the flatscreen. A video of Beck in the *Women in Tech* studio flickered to life, recorded yesterday and set to be released in a few hours.

"We were nomads," podcast-Beck said, gripping the photo of Ava Gideon, a mother who existed only in the picture, nowhere in her mind. "That's how my big sister describes it. All Riley remembers is a life of movement, job to job, starting with crop work down south before domestic service up here in New England. Our father was Jacob, who came and went with the seasons. Riley barely remembers him. Ava gave birth to me, then disappeared. Riley never them again."

Real-life-Beck reached into her pocket and extracted the photo. Her sister shared a lush set of reddish-brown locks with their mother, but only when not hacking her hair into a Goth cut or shaving off one side and dyeing the other platinum. Beck's hair grew straighter and darker. Riley was lean with gorgeous skin tones, Beck angular and pale, as if genetically fated to life behind a keyboard.

"Why carry a photo of the mother who abandoned you?" the host asked.

"It's a reminder of what my sister survived. The crime, the violence, the drugs. There were nights she slept in alleys and public parks. What Riley did for me after Ava took off…imagine being ten years old and handed your infant sister with no one to look after you."

"But you were fortunate, in a way."

"Very. Riley found St. Gerolamo's. Or maybe St. J's found us. But there are too many who aren't so lucky. Every year, twenty thousand minors age out of foster care with nowhere to go, no savings and no family. On any given day, another two to three million walk the streets without a home."

"Here, in the world's wealthiest country."

"Exactly. Then, there are all those children who do have parents or guardians yet still suffer horrible neglect and abuse. The numbers are staggering."

"What value a true parent brings."

"True parenting is priceless."

"And you think your tutorial app will help?"

"MrGabriel isn't a tutorial app. He's a shepherd. He's guided me through many challenging periods and even more sleepless nights. In a lot of ways, he still does."

"So he didn't begin life as an Artificially Intelligent application?"

Podcast-Beck grinned. "Hardly. His inspiration dates back to when I was a Lost One after Riley painted him on the wall behind my bed."

Real-life-Beck studied the faces around her for any sign of censure. She'd resisted doing the podcast, uncomfortable in the spotlight. Her strengths blossomed behind the scenes. The investment arrived almost accidentally via an engineering prize senior year after she, Amy and Eli – collaborators, BFFs – showcased a prototype for MrGabriel. Amy, a natural presenter, led the demo. Only after their professor sent it to Barbara Azakian, Managing Director of Paradigm Ventures, did the possibility of launching it as a proper business arise. A maelstrom of activity followed.

As did a heavy case of Impostor Syndrome. Beck tried to back out of the arrangement and, when that didn't work, push others to the forefront. However, Barbara insisted that Mr. G's success hinged on his origin story, the sisterly love that had born him.

"As you go, so goes Mr. Gabriel," she'd told Beck not five minutes after informing her of Paradigm's interest. "You are the matriarch and heavy lies the crown."

"Mr. G does offer learning modules," podcast-Beck continued. "He also reinforces social skills and positive habits like eating a balanced diet and brushing your teeth before bedtime. He can organize homework schedules while encouraging his flock to shut off the phone and go outside to exercise. As our network expands, users will set up playdates and leverage a recommendation engine to personalize the app. The goal is to promote personal growth and safety. Our company will drive revenue by licensing the app to child development groups. Schools. Medical and mental health facilities. Or just concerned, everyday parents. We will not profit by selling ads, plush toys or market research because we'll lose everyone's trust the second we do. And MrGabriel is all about trust."

"Computer science scholarship at Yale. Series A funding at twenty-two. Your story can inspire more than just Mr. Gabriel's users, Beck. Here at WIT, we're very concerned about the participation rates of women in STEM."

"Under thirty percent and falling. Lower for other underrepresented groups."

"Are you hoping to reverse the trend?"

"I'm just an engineer."

"Not anymore."

Those in the room laughed.

"It's gonna take all of us to bring about lasting change," podcast-Beck said, "but MrGabriel can – and will – represent."

"We appreciate your time."

"Thank you."

The video ended. A round of applause followed.

Amy reached over to grip Beck's forearm. Eli nodded rapidly in encouragement, causing his bangs to bounce off his forehead. Barbara smiled from across the room – high praise from the taciturn chiefess. Out of everyone, only she fully appreciated how daunted Beck had felt about the interview.

The head of Paradigm had faced multiple obstacles in her journey up the ranks of high finance, including a natural introversion not unlike Beck's.

The meeting turned to their presentation on Monday with the Boston School Committee, MrGabriel's most significant to date. Beck felt The Drift coming on – simultaneously in the moment and outside of it – a tendency sprung from her programmatic mind and unbound upbringing. Father W chalked it up to a unique way of committing key moments to memory. While challenging, the visit to St. J's had re-stoked her excitement. Watching kids like Madeleine as they ran and played despite what life kicked in their faces gave Beck a boost, while kids like Jimmy validated her decision to return to Dyer. She was on the cusp of giving them a companion who would never beat them, leave the stove on, or forget their birthday. It was undeniably a moment worthy of The Drift.

The meeting ended. Everyone filed out of the conference room. Thirty-three employees looked over, anticipating an update. Beck did what she always did: she turned to Amy.

"Just wanted to let you all know," her friend said. "Happy hour is mandatory."

No doubt the cheers could be heard out on the corners of Dyer.

CHAPTER 4

She paused at the dead-end. The street didn't always terminate here. Long ago, it housed a subway access. The city welded the entrance shut after decommissioning the line. When the St. J kids grew bored playing hide 'n seek inside the Victorian, they designated a couple of blocks as an outdoor arena. You couldn't fully enter a building. The only legal concealments were within exterior nooks, behind parked vehicles, dumpsters and mailboxes and under whatever shrubbery fronted the tenements. The disused subway entrance, cracked ajar by climate and time, had been Beck's favorite hiding spot. Just tiny enough to squeeze inside, she wasn't breaking the rules because she didn't progress beyond the entrance. She cherished rules and hated cheaters. Also, she was terrified by the fathomless tunnel beneath her.

She shouldn't have been out alone, but Boston's late-night hums and buzzy stillness always relaxed her. Made her feel like she had an entire kingdom to herself.

Also, she needed to walk off the booze.

"Happy hour, my ass."

I'm sorry, Beck, I don't understand your last statement, Mr. G said through her Bluetooth earbud. *Are you feeling irregular?*

She snickered. Mr. G remained phone-based for now. Near-term innovation included integrations with smart devices – watches, earpieces, cameras, glasses and clothing – to relay environmental cues and vital signs to the app. She'd been testing wearable tech for over a year: the mini WiFi camera clipped to her collar, her FitBit and the earbud, so accustomed to Mr. G's voice in her head that she sometimes forgot he was watching. "Just wondering why they call it happy hour since it usually lasts way longer than sixty minutes, and the next day is far from happy."

The origination of the term happy hour—

"I'm good, G. I don't need a history lesson, and I know exactly where I'm going."

I'm glad to hear it because the forecast calls for thundershowers.

She crossed Silversmith Green. Everything was closed except for the Kleen-o-Mat, its track lights flickering over lonely machines. She strolled past The Meeting House, the first public building in a town named in honor of Mary Dyer, a Quaker martyr hanged for refusing to bow to Puritan patriarchy. As the noose slipped around her neck, they offered her clemency *if* she repented. "I came to do the will of my Father," she claimed, "and in obedience to His will, I stand even to the death."

Given more chances to recant, she chose to swing.

Thunder preceded a sprinkling of rain. She relished the numbing drops against the stomach-acid burn of alcohol and chili cheese fries and an unnecessary but totally delicious detour out to Golden Temple for a bowl of hot 'n sour. Then, the water began to fall in pleats. Icing off a drunk was one thing; risking pneumonia another. No cabs at this hour, and by the time a Lyft showed up...

She took off as lightning coursed over the city, charting a direct course over side streets, courtyards and alleyways, a sopping mess by the time she reached her block. She darted between the cars, glancing up at her loft—

Movement.

Skidding through a puddle, she caught herself on a light pole.

Her living room curtain had moved.

She was sure of it.

"Did you see that?"

See what?

"The shade. Over the front window. When I looked up, it settled back into position, like someone inside had just let go."

I am unable to reply.

She hated it when Mr. G went into robot mode.

The storm bore down more intensely.

"Stop being ridiculous and get inside before Zeus barbecues your ass," she said.

Beck—

"Forget it. Heavy drinking followed by a sprint run through the rain...I'm exhausted, and my mind is playing tricks on me. No need to respond."

She jogged into her building, three stories of white brick, its best days dating back to the Roosevelt Administration – Teddy, not Franklin. Beck occupied the third floor, Amy the second, the only inhabitants, the first floor a hollowed-out home for critters they dared not think about. If her window shade moved, it was likely because of the unceasing drafts inside her unit. The loft had been the only rental in her price range. Paradigm's investment budgeted for decent salaries, bonuses triggered by financial milestones and the startup's Holiest of Holies – the option – but Beck's fellowship had only covered basic tuition. She'd incurred a fair amount of debt despite living like a miser and doing work-study. Her bank and credit card statements made her eyes bleed. Amy could have afforded better but refused to let Beck dwell in a house of horrors alone. The lofts were large, the location ideal – four blocks from MrGabriel's HQ – and the roof deck big enough to support a few chairs and a cooler of refreshments. What else did they need?

"Heat would be nice," she said, ascending the stairs.

You set the thermostat to seventy-five to offset the drafts.

"Drafts. Right. More like hurricanes."

Humorous understatement?

"You're getting smarter every day, G."

Thank you.

The staircase faded into black. There were no lights in the communal areas, another deficiency of the aged structure. She moved by memory more than sight. On the second level, she knocked softly on Amy's door. Then loudly. A memory teased Beck, a visual of her friend climbing into a car and riding off somewhere. She considered using her emergency key but decided against it: happy hour had also hammered Amy. Beck's distilled delusions did not constitute an emergency or justify rousting her friend.

She continued up to the third floor. Unlocked the deadbolt and doorknob lock and entered her loft. She shook off the rain and locked the door behind her, entering the living area.

A flash of lightning exposed the figure in the corner.

Her breath stopped as it took shape—

Riley.

Beck wasn't surprised by the sight of her sister, who had a lifetime of turning up unannounced.

The blood.

That surprised her.

It covered Riley's clothes and hands, one of which trembled as it held a large black backpack. She whispered something, but Beck couldn't make it out.

And then Riley led her outside and showed her the body.

CHAPTER 5

The garage sat across a narrow, unpaved path, a stiff wind away from collapse. Mud squished up around its foundation. Upon arrival, Riley didn't know what smeared the windows. Then she'd seen it as some kind of chalky grit and reminded herself arachnophobia was the least of her concerns.

Upstairs, after enduring Beck's frantic check, she couldn't summon the energy to explain that her injuries were more profound, deeper, and in places not made up of flesh and bone. So she'd run back down, crying as she led Beck through the downpour. A pinched, ugly cry.

She thrust the garage door open, scraping it across concrete studded with mossy green fluff. Tommy's car, an early 70s GTO, once black, now withered a spotted gray, filled the space. A friend once gave him grief about its condition, a tease that escalated into a rollicking brawl – a fight over something as stupid as a car. Not the car, he'd said, respect. Only a slightly less ridiculous reason for a face-buster, she'd though.

Beck opened the passenger door on Tommy's corpse. Riley averted her eyes. She couldn't look at him again. He was too wrecked. Beck put a hand over her mouth, whispered something regretful, almost like a prayer, then eased the door shut. She returned to Riley, who was busy rubbing snot from her upper lip. She saw herself through Beck's eyes: a disgusting mess. Nothing new there, except tonight's wretchedness wasn't a comedown from a bender but a straight-up fright fest.

"It's not what you think…"

"I don't know what to think." Beck glanced down at the backpack and opened the flap to expose the bricks of money in thick rubber bands.

A hundred grand, Riley wanted to tell her but felt herself losing power. She slid to the floor, palming the welt on the crown of her head as the garage did a tilt-a-whirl. Beck took out her cell. Riley clamped her hand over it. "Don't."

"Why? What did you do this time?"

CHAPTER 6

"Whaddya mean, what did I do?" Riley half-shouted.

Beck kept her gaze steady.

"I didn't kill him! How can you even ask?"

Voicing all the plausible answers—

her sister stole from Tommy

she and Tommy stole from someone else, someone armed to the
teeth.

she and Tommy were using again.

any combination of the above

—would only complicate matters. She escorted Riley
back up to her loft. Her sister clutched the backpack to her
chest, looking determined never to let go. In the bathroom, she
swabbed Riley's wound. While inflamed, the cut was narrow
and already scabbed over – the blood covering Riley had
spouted solely from Tommy. Beck fought her gorge at the
memory, grabbed an ice pack from the freezer and then led her
sister to the bedroom. She wrapped a comforter around her
and set the pack on the inflammation.

"You can put that down now."

Riley set the backpack on the floor. Then grabbed
Beck's hand. "Thank you."

Beck nodded, caught between anger and empathy,
uncertain how to express either. "Tell me."

"Z Stratton...he shot Tommy."

"Who's Z Stratton?"

Zachary Stratton—

"G, it's okay. I got this."

"What?" Riley asked.

—currently trending at the top spot in Boston news.

"Send me the results," Beck said.

"Who are you talking to?"

Done.

Beck swiped her cell to life. Mr. G had compiled
several sources in the Links section of the app. Stratton's name
was everywhere. Boston X. An Apple News blurb. Patch. She
chose a Breaking News link from WCVB. The video shook,
diffused by rain and the blurs of police bars. A Chyron blared,

"Shootout Sparks Manhunt." She recognized the building in the background: Round Midnight. Tommy's nightclub. The one Riley managed.

The video cut to a drenched beat reporter: "The search for Zachary Stratton continues in the wake of a deadly shooting. Early eyewitness accounts describe Stratton and his crew exchanging gunfire with a second as-yet-unidentified party, possibly a rival gang."

A mugshot of a white male with a doll's eyes appeared in the corner of the screen. Z Stratton was hairless, his face, head, cheeks, chin and neck scraped bare. Nicks and cuts pockmarked his face as if he'd groomed himself with broken glass. The report mentioned several dead and injured. Stratton had slipped away in the melee.

"I'm calling the police," Beck said.

"No—"

"I'm not letting you get away with this."

"With what—"

"Messing up my life!" Beck's shout bounced off the brick walls. "Do you know how hard I've worked to get here? To figure out who I am? My life is simple now. I finally understand who I am and where I'm going. I don't need all your…shit!"

"No one knows how hard you've worked more than me. I'm sorry, but can you please slow down so I can catch my breath?"

Beck scanned the articles and shook her head, knowing she should be dialing the police, that she'd already waited too long. "What happened?"

"I don't know. Somebody conked me on the head. I woke up just as Tommy pulled me off the floor and told me to run. It was a war zone. We jumped in his car, but he…he was bleeding all over the place…I didn't know what to do! I floored it and got out of there."

"Are you clean?"

"Yes—"

"Look me in the eye."

"I'm clean. Five months. Ever since your graduation—"

"If you're clean and haven't done anything wrong, why can't I call the police?"

"All I need is a couple of hours."

"Whose money is this?"

Her sister rubbed her eyes.

"Where's your purse? It wasn't in the car."

"I don't know."

She rooted around into Riley's pockets—

"What are you— stop it—"

She found Riley's phone and held it up for Face ID to unlock, then clicked through emails, texts, call history and social media apps. Nothing unusual, nothing to provide additional insight into her sister's latest disaster. She tossed it back. "Last chance."

"I told you everything."

"I don't believe you."

Beck's phone buzzed. Startled, she nearly dropped it. The call connected from the box at the front door. She answered and hurried to the window.

"Rebecca Gideon?" a man shouted into the speaker, then held something aloft. It glistened a pale gold in the rain.

No need to call the cops. They're already here.

Detective Henry Washington wasn't surprised by the sight of Tommy's body. He slid on gloves, checked the ignition and pulled down the visors. "Keys?"

"If they're not in the car, Riley must have them," Beck said, adding, "She needs a hospital."

"This your garage?"

"Abandoned. Detective, did you hear me? My sister's in rough shape."

"Then why haven't you already called?"

Because this is Dyer, she nearly replied, a neighborhood that didn't exactly foster a kumbaya with the cops. Out here, you considered all potential outcomes before making a move. She'd wanted to understand the circumstances propelling Riley to her home, but all she'd done was stir up more chaos. "I was just getting ready to when you buzzed."

He took out a Leatherman multi-tool. Beck owned one. It made Swiss Army knives look like kindergarten shears. He picked up a chunk of concrete dislodged from the wall, unfolded the pliers, and positioned them around the trunk lock. Three powerful strikes from the concrete drove the tips into the metal. He twisted. The lock tore out like a cork. How Tommy would have reacted to such brutal treatment…it might have been a beater, but he loved his car.

Washington raised the trunk on warped hinges. Cast his flashlight inside, into all the crevices around the tire-changing kit. He pulled up the mat to check underneath, then closed the lid with more than an ounce of frustration. He tapped his phone, requesting "medical aid and transport" at Beck's address.

"Thank you," she said.

He unlocked the rear door and peered under the seats. "How did you know she was here?"

"You're her only family. She tell you what happened?"

"She said Zachary Stratton killed Tommy."

Washington peered over the roof of the GTO. "She said those words exactly."

Beck nodded and rubbed her eyes. Lack of sleep and residual alcohol threatened to narcotize her. "Can you tell me what happened at the club?"

He didn't; he just turned back to the car, to Tommy's body, and extracted a phone. Held it up to a lifeless gaze, then pressed one of Tommy's stiff fingers on the button. The cell remained locked. The detective slipped it into his pocket.

"I'd like to know what's going on."

"So would I." He swung the door shut. Read the distress on her face and softened. "I'll tell you everything, Ms. Gideon, but I have to talk to your sister right now."

His calm nearly put Beck at ease…only nearly because there was still a cop questioning her, a dead man parked outside her home and her sister unable to prove her innocence. It would be a long time before Beck felt at ease again.

CHAPTER 7

"Elevator's shot, sorry," Beck said.

The detective appeared bone-weary as they labored up the stairs, depositing rainwater with each step. "The biggest manhunt since the Marathon bombers, and Riley runs to you instead of us...why?"

"Because it's what she does. She gets in trouble and wants me to bail her out."

"And Tommy Hain?"

"When I was younger, he was like an eccentric uncle. I figured he and Riley might get married someday."

"But."

"They were terrible for each other. Codependent. Probably why they never got together, you know, romantically. Tommy was every girl's dream. He loved my sister, and she loved him, but they never moved out of the friend zone. Just another example of her flaky nature, I guess."

"Any idea when Tommy partnered with Stratton?"

"Partnered?"

"You don't know."

"We're not close anymore."

"I wouldn't be so sure." Washington paused to catch his breath. "He was like an uncle. Your sister seeks you out right after he's gunned down. Maybe you know more than you think, Ms. Gideon."

Her head tightened at the way he manipulated her statements. "I haven't seen her or Tommy in five months. And please, enough with the Ms. Gideon crap. It's Beck." She continued the climb.

"Why five months?"

"They were out of their gourds at my graduation. Completely embarrassed me in front of my friends and professors." She realized she sounded harsh, given Tommy's death. So be it. She didn't want to be within a hundred miles of whatever dumpster they'd lit on fire.

"Did Tommy have any other residences?"

"As far as I know, only the one above his club."

"He ever come here?"

"No."

"Did your sister?"

"Tonight was the first time."

"She store anything here? Clothes, knickknacks, boxes? Did she or Tommy ever give you anything for safekeeping?"

Beck recalled the backpack, considered its contents, and decided to let him see it for himself. All she wanted was for Washington to get Riley to the hospital and out of her life. "Nothing."

"Does the name Martin mean anything?"

"I don't know any Martin."

"Stratton?"

"First time I heard his name was twenty minutes ago."

The detective caught his breath as they reached the third-floor landing. "Tommy was pushing Stratton's drugs through Round Midnight. And Z Stratton, Beck, is a straight nightmare. If your sister says he pulled the trigger, I believe her. But I need to hear her say it."

"She's in the bedroom." Beck opened the door and led Washington around a stack of boxes and shelves containing MrGabriel designs and iterations.

"Congrats, by the way."

"You know about my startup?"

"Read about it on the way over." He admired the clay bust of MrGabriel Amy had sculpted and painted in exquisite detail.

"It's this way," she said, leading him to her bedroom.

Her empty bedroom. "Riley?"

She reversed course and flicked on the light in the bathroom.

Ran out to the kitchen.

The living area.

No Riley.

She tapped her earbud. "Call Riley."

Dialing Riley Gideon.

Voicemail picked up.

"What the hell?" Beck said. "Where did you go? Call me back right now."

Should I try the number at Round Midnight?

"Now's not the time to play games, Ms. Gideon," Washington said.

Ms. Gideon again. "I'm not playing any games. She couldn't have gone far, the condition she's in. I'll find her." She turned towards the front door—

The detective's hand gripped her arm. "You're not going anywhere."

"Hey—"

"You two think you can play me?"

"I don't—"

"Where's the money?"

Beck looked around for the backpack until it hit her. "How do you know about the money?"

He slammed her into the wall. As her senses struggled to catch up to the moment, one of the detective's hands wrapped around her throat and pushed her up on her tiptoes. "Don't fuck with me!"

In the blink of an eye, Detective Henry Washington had transformed. Gone was the wearied, put-upon cop. In his place, a raging menace leaned close. She'd faced predatory gazes such as his before, staying out too late, fighting off the grabby boys on the bottom floor of the Victorian. Degrading stares and commands that made her feel like a piece of meat.

Mr. G spoke again, but the blood rushing in her ears drowned out his words.

"She tossed the briefcase a quarter mile from here," the detective said. "Finally realized I was tracking it, I guess." His free hand used the door to lever open the Leatherman's blade – serrated, capable of sawing through frozen steak – and set it against her lips. "For every lie, I cut me a piece."

Beck, who is this man?

Her loft started to gray out at the edges.

Is he hurting you? Your heart rate is highly elevated.

"Where's the money? Where's your sister?" Washington's grip relaxed just enough for her to respond.

But the answer came from over his shoulder: "Right here."

He spun around—

Riley doused him in the face with a clear liquid. He grunted, releasing Beck. The rubbing alcohol landed in front of her. Her sister and the detective fought and barreled into her, trapping her against the wall. Riley grabbed the detective's knife hand and used all her weight to scrape it down against the jagged brick. The Leatherman fell. She reached for his sidearm but had expended the element of surprise. His hands clamped over hers as the handgun cleared its holster. They danced away, allowing Beck to move—

A crack.

Not thunder. Louder.

Heat flared through Beck's left arm. An invisible force spun her around. She didn't feel anything at first but watched, incredulous, as blood seeped into her shirt sleeve.

Shot.

She'd been shot.

Now, the pain.

Beck!

"Call—"

Riley and Washington's grappling forms careened into her again. She fell, so focused on cradling her arm her head bounced off the floor. The earbud popped free. Their feet stomped over, on and around her, Beck caught up in their scrum. She snared the Leatherman in her good hand and lurched upwards with a shout, slashing at the detective's arms. The gun clattered away. He drove Riley against the wall. Her watery gaze found Beck. Her mouth moved—

Run.

Growing up, when trouble found them, Beck followed Riley's lead. Her sister was the fighter, the schemer, the first to react. Now was not the time to disregard her directive. Beck stumbled towards the front door. What else could she do? She lacked Riley's physical gifts—

Her foot kicked the gun across the hallway. She scampered after it, but Washington leaped onto her back, collapsing them both in a tangle. She tried to squirm away. He flipped her over. Cocked a fist—

Something shattered against his head. Shards sprayed out. He fell, revealing Riley, the remains of the MrGabriel bust in her hand. Washington tackled her.

Beck crawled into the darkened hallway, probing. Metal grazed her fingertips. She seized the gun. Raised it in both hands, blood oozing along her fingers. She'd never held a firearm before.

The detective prepared to bash Riley's head against the hardwood.

Beck squeezed the trigger. The shot flung her arm back, nearly causing the gun to fly out of her grasp. The bullet thudded into the brick over the cop's head. She stood, gun quaking. Washington yanked Riley to her feet, one arm under her chin, positioning her between him and the smoking barrel.

"Let her go!"

Instead, Washington pushed her sister forward. Beck backpedaled. Lightning strobes turned her loft into a funhouse. She reached the storeroom, its double doors ajar. The collapsible ladder was down, the hatch above open, the passage Riley had used to break in and then momentarily escape. Beck scuttled up, glancing back to see Washington toss her sister aside and give chase.

The bolt on the exterior door of the antechamber above had been pried free, the structure rocking in the rioting wind. Washington clamored up after her. She ran out onto the roof deck. She should have waited for him to show himself, but she had no confidence she could hit the broad side of her building, never mind an executioner prowling after her in a thunderstorm.

Onto the roof itself, the tarpaper slick beneath her sneakers. She veered away from the fire escape, the obvious route. An idea had occurred to her with a moderate chance of success, certainly more significant than her gunning down or outrunning the detective. She targeted the L-shaped HVAC unit. Waited long enough for Washington to see her, then ran around it, out of sight, and leaped onto the cross-section of vents.

He sped after her, his alcohol-stung eyes and the surges of lightning causing him to overlook the hole in the roof as he turned the corner. The owner had warned Beck and Amy never to step off the deck and to avoid the area where the controls for the mothballed elevator had been removed. Traffic cones ringed the weak spot, but the detective tripped over the cones and ran straight out onto the damaged section Beck had just leaped over. Degraded tiles fell apart like soggy newspapers as the roof above the empty shaft disappeared beneath him. He caught the edge of an I-beam. Hands slicked by rain slapped across the steel as he steadily lost the fight against gravity.

His eyes glazed in mortal terror. "Help."

Atop the HVAC housing, Beck looked for something to extend to him. Reacting. Not considering what would happen if she pulled him to safety.

And then he was gone.

Without a sound, sucked down into the pit.

CHAPTER 8

Riley brought Beck back inside the loft, forcing herself into action despite the wobble in her step. Her head thrummed, her equilibrium seesawed, but she managed to help Beck remove her sweater to expose the split skin and muscle, her biceps like a piece of overripe fruit dropped on a sidewalk.

"Oh, Beck…" She pressed a hand to her mouth, wanting to make a fist and shove it through her stupid head for bringing a maniac into their lives. Beck looked delirious, about to slip over. Riley had encountered plenty of people on the edge, been there herself, stupefied by drugs and violence. She knew how tough it was to return from a breakdown. She slid her fingers into Beck's left hand. "Squeeze."

The response was firm enough to suggest no significant bone or nerve damage.

Thanks to Winston's army medic training, Father W and Sister Lucinda had taught their charges how to survive. A local doctor stocked St. J's with prescriptions, trusting Father and Sister to use them only in crises. Many orphans lacked good healthcare; the state-sponsored plans barely covered an allergy shot. Public clinics were dingy and overrun and offered little long-term follow-up. So Father W and Sister taught their protectorates how to remove splinters, apply the Heimlich on themselves and others, perform CPR, splint broken bones, and more. Holy preppers, Riley called 'em, but took to the lessons rigorously, anticipating a future requiring a higher degree of self-preservation.

She and Beck were healthy, but a survey of their closets and vanities would have suggested the Gideons were the sickest people on earth. Z Packs. Albuterol inhalers. Tetracycline and amoxicillin. Ambien for when the ghosts in their heads kept them awake. Tamiflu. Doses of Paxlovid thanks to the planet's latest torment and enough bandages, gauze, ice packs, athletic tape, antiseptics, swabs, trauma shears, scalpels, PVC gloves and tweezers to patch up the Bruins.

She could do this. She'd stitched Tommy up often enough. Opening a suture kit, she told Beck to sit on the closed toilet and rest her arm on the edge of the sink. Then washed her hands with water hot enough to fog the mirror. She slipped on gloves, flushed Beck's wound with saline and prepared the skin stapler. "Tylenol kick in?"

Beck shrugged. Riley had made her swallow three tabs as soon as they came downstairs. It wasn't gonna do shit, but it was the most potent stuff on hand. Beck eschewed the Oxy and Vicodin Riley stocked up on. She pinched the split meat around the gunshot wound and clicked the stapler twice to pin the skin together.

Beck's scream kicked her back from the edge and into the very unpleasant here and now.

"Almost done." Riley clicked the stapler three more times.

"No…iodine…"

"I know. You don't have to remind me." There was a temptation to apply antiseptics to an open wound, but chemicals can burn exposed skin and impede healing. "Even beat to hell, you're a know-it-all." Said with a smile, but Beck kept her head hung. Riley wrapped a bandage over the incision, peeled off the gloves, and held up the amoxicillin. "Every four hours. Don't forget."

Beck nodded, then looked up. "You came back."

Riley had been five steps from gone, about to bolt back down the fire escape and jump in the GTO, when it occurred to her that she'd left Beck all alone to deal with the consequences of her and Tommy's actions. The consideration made her pause long enough to hear the cop shouting at Beck.

So she turned around and ran back faster than she'd run away.

Because for the first time in a long time, Beck needed her.

CHAPTER 9

Her sister's black-dyed hair hung in wet strands, half-covering a pair of eyes even more recessed than the last time Beck had seen her. She and Riley were so different, the attritions spiritual, reduced by choices made, not time passed. "You came back," she said again.

"Come here." Riley eased her arms around her. "Relax."

"I am."

"Breathe."

"You know I don't like..." She squirmed in Riley's embrace, fighting the enclosure, pulling away from the fabric of her sister's damp blouse.

"It's okay. You're okay."

Slowly, Beck's resistance faded, replaced by a near-paralyzing surrender. She sobbed, hating herself for such a stark release, but the only way to expel a riot of misery.

So close.

So close to dying.

Washington's hand around her throat. She gagged, still feeling it tighten.

The knife.

The fight.

His filthy grip on her, his breath rapid and excited. The sheer physical offense.

Running.

His fear before he fell.

It was too overwhelming to process, with no sensible way for her to parse the attack into workable segments. Her hands found Riley, pushing her away and pulling her closer at the same time. A minute passed, the only sound her big sister's heartbeat.

Finally, Riley released her and grabbed a towel to dry her hair. "Is he dead?"

"I..."

"It's important."

"I think so."

"We gotta be sure. Wait here."

"No."

"You're in no condition—"

"Neither are you." Beck forced herself up. "Besides, there's no way I'm staying up here by myself."

Riley pocketed Washington's gun and pulled out four fresh PVC gloves. In the storeroom, she selected a hammer and a rechargeable flashlight. They went out the door, down to floor two, where Beck again put her ear on Amy's door. Although fossilized, the building was constructed in an era of brick, concrete, and steel. Sound didn't travel well, and the storm would have drowned out any excess.

"Who's there?" her sister whispered.

"Amy."

"Nothing?"

Beck shook her head, grateful she hadn't dragged her best friend into the confrontation. They continued to the basement. Beck and Amy had only been down here once after the owner boasted about the extra storage – they'd vowed never to return. Grime blacked out the windows, whose loose frames leaked enough water to cover the floor. The boiler rattled like a middle-school percussion section as four-legged somethings scampered out of the flashlight's beam.

They slipped on their gloves. Beck needed help to cover her left hand. Her arm was an electric rod on the verge of bursting.

Her sister approached the elevator doors. A metal strip covered the seam. She worked the claw of the hammer under the ribbon. It bowed easily. Consistent with other renovations, the material was low-grade. "You're sure he's…"

"No, but he won't be setting any land speed records."

The rivets holding the strip pinged off the floor. Riley handed the strip to Beck, who set the flashlight down and wielded the twisted metal in her good hand like a machete. Her sister inserted the claw between the doors and jimmied it back and forth until she could slip her shoulder inside. She drew the detective's gun and used the left side of her body to push the doors apart. If Washington were alive, this was the moment he would—

There was no attack.

No sound at all except the falling rain.

Riley cast the light on the detective's face, his eyes rolled up, vacant.

The owner hadn't merely retired the elevator; he'd dismantled the entire unit, causing Washington to fall onto the upturned rebar and gear works. Beck's stomach threatened to add to the dreadful scene. Riley searched his pockets. Came out with a small leather holder and a wallet.

"Do you know him?" Beck asked.

"No."

"He said you discarded a briefcase. What does that mean?"

"I have no idea."

"Will you please stop lying to me?"

Riley glanced over and sighed. "Tommy got mixed up in something."

"Stratton. Drugs."

"I don't know all the details, but it came to a head tonight." Her sister shut her eyes as if to stave off a ghastly memory.

"If you had to guess about Washington…"

"He's gotta work for Tommy's family."

"He's a cop."

"You don't get where they are without shitheads in high places."

Beck matched up the information between the license from his wallet and the police ID in the holder of Henry D. Washington, resident of Rutland Street in the South End.

"I know you got questions," Riley said, "but we gotta take care of him first." She stuffed the wallet and holder back into the detective's pockets. Found two cell phones – Tommy's and one Beck assumed was the cop's. "His phone's off."

"He faked a call to the paramedics. He wanted us all to himself."

"And if you don't spring the trap, it's us they're peeling off the ground."

Beck collapsed onto the stairs, sending shockwaves up her body.

Her sister walked over, setting her hands on Beck's shoulders. "I'm gonna make this right. We need the police, but I don't want you involved."

"Little late for that."

"No. Your part ends right now. You got too much to lose. Help me do this, and you're out."

"Do what?"

"Get rid of this sonofabitch."

Beck wanted to tell her to stop. She wanted to call in reinforcements and turn herself over to the people who managed the seedier sides of life, but she was too tired, stunned, and scared of whatever unknowns connected to the night's events. Images of the podcast interview, the people at Mr. Gabriel, Amy and Eli, Barbara and Paradigm ran through her head, all the fantastic, scary but exciting moments captured in The Drift over the past five months.

It probably wasn't the right choice to follow Riley's plan, but it was the easiest.

The next few minutes unfolded like a gory dream. They detached Washington's body from the gear works. Riley pushed the elevator doors closed and used the hammer to pound the strip back in place over the seam. Beck somehow exceeded the last vestiges of strength to help carry the detective up to the rear entrance. Her sister reversed the GTO out of the garage. They loaded the cop into the back seat. Beck checked the dashboard: 4:31 am.

Nothing good happens after midnight, Father W used to say.

Understatement of the year, she thought.

The next thing Beck knew, she was back upstairs in bed. "What are you going to do?"

"Whatever it takes."

Her sister's last words before the night took over.

CHAPTER 10

Riley avoided looking directly at the bodies slumped next to and behind her. She didn't want to consider Tommy's leather jacket, his worn-out Bruno Maglis, the silver thumb ring he habitually tapped against any surface. To any passing motorists – thankfully limited at this hour – she hoped Tommy and Washington would appear to be sleeping.

She sped out of Dyer on local roads to avoid traffic cams. She'd snagged a hoodie from Beck's closet and pulled the strings tight, concealing her face. Her fingerprints were already all over the car from running Tommy's errands. She was more concerned about any prints, hair, skin or blood left on the cop. Hopefully, her plan would eliminate them.

She hadn't exactly lied to Beck – dishonesty wasn't Haley's comet in Riley's universe; lying to Beck, to anyone, came second nature – but she hadn't been entirely truthful, either. She put no faith in any agency or system. One of her earliest encounters with the police occurred at St. J's when two bulls started citing the girls for petty offenses like "sauntering and loitering." To prevent drug deals from going down, they claimed. Riley and her St. J sisters knew the patrol officers meant "going down" in an entirely different context. The longer the St. J girls held out, the more the two leches wrote up violations, everything from noise complaints to improper trash disposal. The situation ended after Father W turned to an old friend for help, Tommy's powerful grandfather, Francis Hain. Less than twenty-four hours later, the department reassigned the cops who never showed their faces in Dyer again.

That was the system, the engine driving it all. All these salute-the-flag, weepy civic duty clichés were wholegrain horseshit. You either had juice or you knew someone who had juice. If godly folks like Father W and Sister Lucinda could get pushed around, people like Riley didn't stand a chance of landing a fair deal. Castoffs were just numbers on the city's balance sheet, and John Q public wasn't the most empathetic bunch these days. Parishioners used to pack Father W's church for Sunday service and high holidays. How many of the sanctified ever walked across campus to bring one of his orphans home? Foster care was a paid gig. How many considered loving the unloved for free?

Not many.

Then there was Tommy's family. What would they do to avenge their fallen, even if reckless, son? Tommy's old man, Carlow, was about to become mayor. She'd already passed two of the bastard's billboards, the golden boy likened to another great Massachusetts son, John Fitzgerald Kennedy. Her passion for Tommy was the inverse of her loathing for the Hains. Her only defense would be, "Wasn't me, no way, I loved the guy."

Did she? they'd wonder.

Did she genuinely love him, or was she just another hanger-on taking advantage of Tommy's kind heart? Yeah, he was the black sheep, but they'd tried to get him help, only to watch riffraff like Riley Gideon drag him down.

She needed time, a distraction.

Hopefully, Beck wouldn't turn stupid and blow the whistle. Riley didn't think she would. Beck had the luxury of believing in the system; it served her well.

Turning onto Adams, she passed through Milton, a busy thoroughfare studded with cameras, but the only way to get where she was going. They used to come down here on sunny afternoons to hang out on the grassy atolls. Far enough from Dyer to feel like a legitimate getaway. A realm of baby strollers, buff dudes slinging frisbees and college crews rowing past zillionaire homes. Where she and Beck ate grinders from Molinari's and talked about buying apartments in the North End, meeting a restauranteur, falling in love, having babies and getting fat on the family biz. Where Riley did her best to excite Beck about the future and tell her anything was possible given her big brain and strength of spirit.

Where she told Beck to follow all the life lessons Riley had shunned.

From Adams, she turned onto a narrow, tree-lined street and headed towards the river.

CHAPTER 11

There was no describing the agony. Beck loosened the bandage. The skin around the staples had reformed but glistened like gelatin. She tried to recall the last twelve hours but could only produce mental snapshots from a distance, the kind she assembled during The Drift.

Running home through the rain.

Riley's shocking appearance.

Tommy's corpse.

The fight with Washington.

A flash from the gun.

The roof.

The basement.

Cramming the detective's body into Tommy's car.

Emotion remained elusive: the rush of outfoxing Washington, the irrational impulse to save the man who'd just tried to murder her and Riley, the sting of antiseptic, the revulsion of disinterring the dead cop. Was he married? Did he have children? Despite growing up at St. J's, Beck had never fully bought into a universal morality. She hoped to be pleasantly surprised after the final curtain but accepted Father W's emphasis on virtue because life was tenuous, making it essential to live the time given as productively and humanely as possible. And yet, while she didn't strike the final blow, she had unquestionably lured Washington to his end.

The worst sins are those committed for the right reasons – another Father W chestnut.

She'd wanted to survive, and she'd been willing to exchange Washington's life for hers. Understandable, but she wondered how much of herself she'd sacrificed in the barter.

She reached for her phone. A scrap of paper under it floated to the floor. She picked it up, recognizing her sister's scrawl:

If anyone asks, you haven't seen or talked to me in months. Not even Father W can know. Get rid of the slugs and burn this note. Leave no trace. Protecting you has always been my job. I'm sorry I got so shitty at it. –r

It did not read like the note of someone about to confess to the police.

It read like Riley Gideon, Ph.D. in Complicating Life.

Someone buzzed downstairs. Cops. It had to be. If she didn't answer, would they bust the door down?

"Yes?" she said, voice stuccoed with rheum. It took a second to process Eli's voice. She told him she wasn't feeling well.

"Did you see the news?" he yelled. "Open up!"

She tapped nine to unlock the door. Eli had a spare key; he'd let himself in if so concerned. Her left arm issued a deep ache as she pulled on a sweater. At the front door, she heard Eli stomping up the stairs, his gait ungainly, one leg an inch shorter than the other, enough to jinx him with a permanent side-to-side sway. She opened up as he dashed over the final stair.

"It's Tommy!" He ran into the living area, picked up the remote and clicked the TV to life.

A DMV photo of Thomas Hain shimmered onscreen, followed by pics from Round Midnight. The images ran haphazardly in Beck's overtaxed brain. She fell onto the couch as the special report cut to the Neponset River, crowds gawking from the banks.

A crane lifted Tommy's GTO out of the river.

Bodies found within.

Bodies.

CHAPTER 12

The Neponset wasn't a deep or rapid waterway. A rowing team braving the autumnal temps had noted an odd ripple in the current, then a metallic glint just below the surface. Upon closer inspection, they saw the rear bumper of the GTO just below the surface, not ten feet from an elevated shoreline off of which, the reporter surmised, the car had launched itself. White sheets lined the marshy edge of the river. A police chopper cleared the skies above the scene, but not before one intrepid hawk snapped the license plate and identified the car's owner, igniting the airwaves.

The news cut between the river salvage and the home of Carlow Hain, Tommy's father and projected runaway winner of the Mayoral election in two weeks. A ratings godsend on an otherwise slow Saturday, the national networks started picking up the story, but Beck barely noticed, dialing and texting Riley repeatedly.

"I'm sure she's okay," Eli said in that benign tone people use when they suspect the opposite.

After another round of voicemails, Beck wanted to throw her phone against the wall. "I need coffee." She turned too quickly and banged her bad arm on one of the brick columns that demarcated the kitchen area. She howled and grabbed at the stapled skin.

"What's wrong?"

"Nothing. I fell last night and hurt my arm. Can you...?" She motioned to the coffeemaker on the counter.

"Sure, but what do you mean you fell? Where?"

"On my way home from the pub."

He paused on his way to the kitchen. "Did you drop that, too?"

The remains of the MrGabriel bust, the one Riley had smashed over Washington's head, piled up at the mouth of the hallway.

Get rid of the slugs and burn this note. Leave no trace – Riley's instructions.

Beck grabbed the dustpan and brush from the closet, her arm screaking at the movement. "Yeah. I can't even remember why I picked it up. I was loaded just like everyone else." She swept up the fragments, avoiding his gaze, feeling his eyes on her as he fired up the brew.

"I'm sorry. Assuming Tommy is…I know he's a friend. Or used to be."

"We don't know anything yet." She glanced at the front wall. Amidst all the brick-and-mortar hid the bullet she fired at Washington. Granules of displaced cement dotted the floorboard. And then there was the round fired through her arm somewhere near her bedroom—

"Beck?"

She'd Drifted again. "Sorry. I'm just…"

"I can go if you want to be alone."

Unlike Beck, Eli had a hard time masking his feelings. Amy used to joke about him crushing on Beck until they realized how much it tormented him. The closest he came to acting on his attraction was one late night after they completed a shared assignment for Discrete Mathematics. They celebrated with a bottle of Boones Blue Hawaiian, the rotgut sparking a look in his eyes that was anything but discreet. He kissed her and instantly apologized. She tried to tell him it was no big deal, but the sudden intrusion threw her as well, causing her to babble as she pulled away, making him feel even worse.

It wasn't the physical affinity that unsettled her but the feelings prompting it. She expected disappointment, if not outright disaster. When something good and life-affirming came along, she immediately started prepping for its departure, abandonment a fear and an expectation. Father W and Sister Lucinda battled those demons as best they could, and Beck had made significant progress thanks to Amy and Eli's friendship, but romance? Forget it. A baffling equation she'd yet to broach.

"I'm glad you're here," she said.

And she was. Over the past four years, she'd opened up to him and Amy more than anyone except Riley and Father W. As the news droned on, Eli's simple kindness and loyalty threatened to bust the truth out of her. But how would she even start such a conversation?

Guess what? My lunatic sister and her equally unstable partner pissed off a drug dealer. As a result, we killed a dirty cop and/or professional assassin, so I'm pretending not to know anything while Riley does what Riley does, which is to make everything exponentially worse. Assuming she's not under one of those sheets next to the river. Hungry? How 'bout Chinese?

She carried the bits of clay to the trashcan. As she stepped on the control to raise the lid, she heard Eli suck in a breath. He stood on the bathroom's threshold, staring at the bloody gauze, now a deep rust color, littered across the floor. She dropped the dustpan and brush into the can and ran over.

"I forgot to— Told you I fell. Hang on." She shoved him out of the way and slammed the door. Plucked the dirty swabs off the tiles, threw them in the toilet, hit the plunger, and watched them spin down the tube.

— and then Washington was gone, without a sound, sucked down into the pit —

She tossed the staple gun into the suture kit and stowed it under the sink. Her torn and stained blouse sagged across the edge of the tub. Balling it up, she flung it into the hamper.

"My first felony." The words leaped out of her.

"What?" Eli asked from the other side of the door.

"Nothing. I'm—"

Destroying evidence? Committing obstruction? Something equally egregious, according to all the cop shows and movies she'd ever seen. For one so disparaging of Riley's unknown and undoubtedly crazy-ass plan, Beck was doing a damn fine job of perpetuating it.

Once a Dyer girl…

"Stop it," she told herself. The old-world creeds of her hometown didn't apply. She wasn't backsliding into Riley and Tommy's netherworld, but shielding Eli, Amy and MrGabriel from it. After all, there was no evidence to prove self-defense. The default setting didn't enable Mr. G to record. He only responded to commands. In the future, Beck envisioned scenarios Mr. G *reacted* to without user directives. Had the app been so enabled, she'd already possess the evidence to prove Washington's murderous intent: Mr. G would be the witness. However, audio and video files ate up memory, and privacy concerns about unauthorized recording needed to be reconciled. Thus, the decision to let users choose when to record – a product decision that didn't address the use case of, what if someone's trying to murder you and you want to chronicle the homicide?

Washington's gun and Leatherman were missing. Riley must have taken both, along with the cash. Beck washed her hands and checked the mirror, stunned at the person staring back. Her eyes were ringed in shadow, and her hair flared out in wispy strands around a sallow complexion. She looked many years older. She looked like Riley. Cold water restored color to her cheeks. She tied her hair into a ponytail. Double-checked for additional indications of last night's hostilities, then opened the door.

"That was a lot of blood," Eli said.

"Looked worse than it was. I cut my arm when I fell."

"Maybe I should take you to—"

"I said, I'm fine!"

He nodded and retreated into the living area. Beck wanted to apologize and spill her guts.

But someone started pounding on the front door.

CHAPTER 13

Washington was dead. So was Tommy.

Another text from the client filled his cell screen:

Where are you?

He ignored it and pushed the Chevy POS faster through Brighton. POS indeed stood for Piece of Shit, anointed after he purchased it in cash from a used dealer up in Danvers. It wasn't the first time, nor would it be the last, Jordan Lear bought a cheap, rundown vehicle to fit an alias. It came with the territory of being a specialist who dealt in the rarest of commodities: the truth. Jordan was an expert at mining people's deepest and darkest. Hence, the cover he adopted for each new job. Overkill? He used to consider the possibility, but after what went down last night…

The only two criteria his customers valued were success and discretion. His cover fueled success because it left no trail back to the client. Discretion he cultivated by working alone. As a general rule, he considered humanity disreputable. He didn't hire a partner because he'd never met anyone trustworthy. But on days like today, he wished he had someone to watch his back.

The police had finally confirmed Detective Henry Washington and Thomas Corbin Hain's deaths. Boston was ablaze. Media clamored at the ramparts of police headquarters. Jordan had spent most of the day watching the recovery down at the Neponset from a safe distance through binoculars. At least, he assumed it was secure.

Another text. Another call.

He appreciated his client's urgency, but Jordan needed to safeguard the goods – all the intel he'd assembled on the Gideon sisters, Hain, Stratton and Washington.

He parked in front of a hydrant. Checked the load on his Colt Commander – the most stopping power in his arsenal – slid it into his under-the-shoulder harness, and exited the POS. A three-quarter jacket, button-down, jeans and Chuck Taylors blended him into the crowd. He jogged up the exterior stairwell to the residence he rented in cash from a guy who lived in the basement like some bridge troll, unlocked the door and entered.

Someone had ransacked the apartment.

Trouble. Jordan sensed it too late, scrambling for his piece as someone shouldered him from behind. A curved knife glinted as it swung forward and rested on Jordan's jumping carotid. A second hand extricated the Colt and cast it aside.

"Where is it?" The words hissed in his ear, low, grunted.

Jordan said nothing, afraid to move, afraid to breathe under the blade. As the attacker's face pressed into the back of his skull, he felt the grainy fiber of a ski mask.

"What. Do. You. Have?" the attacker asked. "Photos. Files. Recordings."

"I got no idea what you're talking about."

"You've been running down Tommy Hain for months. Which means you know about his deal with Stratton. Which means you got plenty on Riley and her sister, Beck."

"Who?"

"I won't ask again, Jordan."

"My name's John."

"Johnny, Jordy, whoever. Last chance."

"I'm telling you, you got the wrong guy!"

"And that's the wrong answer."

The blade rammed into Jordan's spine.

CHAPTER 14

Slow down, Winston thought. At his age, a trip and fall would delay him and risk considerable damage, but Beck wasn't responding to any of his calls or messages. Sister and the children were water painting on easels on the side lawn. Usually, he loved watching their imaginations spring to life, but he didn't want to explain why he was in such a hurry, so he avoided eye contact.

He climbed into the church van and cued the remote to open the garage door. The Econoline featured three rows of bench seats to shuttle groups for doctor's appointments and shopping trips. Sister usually took the wheel because Winston, for all his merits, was an abysmal driver. Vehicles in proximity caused him to overcompensate with gas-guzzling starts and queasy stops. She once wondered if his driving inadequacy stemmed from post-war anxiety. He told her he'd dedicated his life to letting go and letting God; commanding fast-moving tonnage was outside his comfort zone. He reversed into the street without running anyone over, dropped the van in gear and drove as slowly as his escalating tension allowed through the narrow lanes of Dyer.

He parked at a meter around the corner from Beck's loft. A few residents strolled along the sidewalks. A pair of young parents at the corner failed to even acknowledge his greeting, their attention attuned across the street.

To the police cars in front of Beck's building.

Winston jogged as fast as he could, ignoring the tightness in his chest, produced either by the cold sucked into his lungs or something far more problematic. He pushed on without concern over any potential stumble. He hadn't been this confident in his steps in decades.

A young blue idled at the front door, holding it ajar but positioned to monitor who went in or out.

"Everything okay?" Winston asked.

"Far as we know," the officer said.

"I'm paying a house call."

"Name?"

"Rebecca Gideon." The cop's eyebrows arched. The constriction in Winston's chest intensified. "Is she okay? What happened?"

"She's fine. Just talking to one of our detectives."

"I must see her."

"What's so urgent?"

"Is she under arrest?"

"No."

"Then I don't need your permission." These were not the words of Father Winston Ismera but Winnie, the kid who used to strut the blocks of Lynn with attitude to spare. He pushed past the officer.

"She's not up there, Father."

CHAPTER 15

Beck wondered if Detective Underhill had intentionally positioned her out in the open amidst the babble of voices and telephones. Civilians occupied every compass point, a few cuffed, others escorted vigorously by the elbow and still more idling, waiting to share their statements about Round Midnight and the super-heated fallout. After leading her inside the homicide unit at One Schroeder, the detective had indicated a chair in the eye of the hurricane and promptly disappeared.

Thirty minutes passed. Thirty minutes for the hue and cry to wrack her brain. Thirty minutes to suffer the acrid humidity of the room. She slipped out of her flannel, then noticed an amoeba of blood on her sleeve and shrugged it back on.

They know, they know, they know.

She tried to calm herself. Touched the earbud under her hair. "Hey, G."

Good morning, Beck. Are you okay? Geolocation returns a match to Boston Police headquarters.

"I'm alright." She swallowed a shaky breath. "Just wanted to hear a friendly voice."

I'm happy to oblige. I'm not detecting a camera today.

"Forgot. I left in a bit of a rush."

Maybe a coffee and cheese Danish from Lewek's will help. Should I preorder?

She grinned. "Thank you, no."

A cry went up. A patrolwoman tried to calm a disheveled man yanking his hair with both fists as he bellowed, "Too much, too much!"

"First time in a police station?"

"Of course it is," Beck said. "You should know that." She turned around and realized it wasn't Mr. G speaking, but Underhill.

"Should I?"

"Sorry, I didn't— I'm sure you've checked my record by now."

He sat down, offering no apology for his vanishing act. She'd been on high alert since his request to "come down and answer a few questions." An "informal chat." After all, she wanted to locate her sister, right? A patrolman remained behind to question Eli. She didn't believe Underhill would have been so apparent – parking police cars out front, showing up in broad daylight, calling the owner to come down and unlock the front door – if he intended to murder her. To refuse would have raised suspicion.

The detective differed from Henry Washington. For starters, he was noticeably younger and a bit slovenly. His hair hung to his collar and appeared styled with a few five-fingered swipes. He plunged his hands into his suit coat and walked with a noticeable slouch. A picture of indifference. Beck suspected it was a ploy to loosen tongues.

A TV in the corner updated the action on the Neponset.

"The currents aren't too powerful," Underhill said. "We would have found Riley by now if she'd remained in the car."

"Remained?"

"Preliminary forensics suggest Hain and Washington were dead before they hit the water. Someone placed a large rock on the accelerator, put the gearshift in drive and sunk the car."

Before she could ask why he believed Riley rigged the GTO, Underhill unleashed a stream of questions. She tried to respond and maintain an air of concerned innocence. When was the last time she saw Riley? Why weren't the two sisters close? Riley makes dumb decisions. So why did Beck invite her and Tommy to graduation? How surprised was she really that they showed up loaded?

Inquiries similar to Washington's before he revealed his true self. Beck assessed her answers for any giveaway, but spontaneity was not her strong suit. She functioned best when able to relax, contemplate and evaluate.

"You knew Tommy well?" Underhill asked.

"I guess."

"You guess?" His forehead barely narrowed, his eyes on low heat.

She wondered if he could manage any facial expressions at all. "Yes, I knew him. He was more involved in my life when I was younger. And Riley works at Round Midnight. Well, worked."

The newscast interspersed shots of the nightclub cordoned off by police tape.

"What about this man?" The detective turned his monitor around on a photo of Henry Washington in his dress blues, looking every bit the fallen hero.

"He's the police officer they found in Tommy's car, right?" She tried to unclench her fists. Unsuccessful, she buried them between her legs.

"Seen him before?"

"No."

"Not at the club? Around your sister or Tommy?"

"I've only been to the club twice. It wasn't my scene."

He flicked through a stack of notes. "Where's your sister, Rebecca?"

The repeat query caught her off-guard. A typical cop tactic, she supposed, asking the same question to see if the answer changed, filling a natural break in the conversation with a fast injection. Yeah, this guy's air of disinterest was unquestionably a ploy.

I can text you Riley's address if you need it.

Mr. G only responds when directly addressed or when detecting uncertainty or urgency in the user's words. Sometimes, though, his participation was randomized, which, she supposed, mimicked human behavior. She considered these interjections mysterious and a distinction of AI's learning capacity, but now they threatened to distract her.

"I told you, she hasn't gotten back to me," she said.

"And you're not concerned."

"Of course, I'm concerned," she fired back, falling into another trap, his phrasing implying she wasn't worried about her sister's fate.

Underhill was putting her on the defensive.

"I know," she said.

He looked up. "Know what?"

She pinched the inside of her thighs, realizing she'd addressed her inner thoughts out loud.

"Are you or are you not worried about your sister?"

"I'm worried because Tommy was her friend. But Riley isn't involved in any of this." She gestured at the TV.

"Did you consider heading down to Roslindale?"

"Yes."

Riley lives at 201 Wiggin Street.

"No, no, wait—"

"You don't know where your sister lives?"

"The North End. Two-Oh-One Wiggin Street. A basement unit."

Underhill's stare held for a few beats. "How is she connected to Tommy's death?"

"I just said—"

"You haven't seen her in several months. Given her history, how can you be certain she isn't involved? Court-mandated drug testing. Petty theft. Robbery. One count of check forgery."

"I know her history better than anyone. I've told you everything I can."

"Except where she is."

"Why are you so focused on her? Many people knew Tommy."

"By people, I supposed you mean fellow addicts and joyriders because it doesn't appear his family had anything to do with him for a long time."

Beck's frayed nerves, the pounding in her arm and the collective sweat stench conspired to knock loose a few tears. She dried them quickly.

"Why hasn't she called you back?" the detective asked.

"I don't know."

"Would she come to you if she was in trouble?"

"Probably."

"Did she?"

"No—"

"I've fought with my siblings before. I don't think I've ever ignored them for five months."

More tears broke through. Mr. G's questions faded behind a hum of overloaded mental circuitry. The urge to confess, if for no other reason than to break Underhill's impassive stare and escape this hellhole, gathered force. It would be so easy to just lay it all out for him.

A hand fell gently on her shoulder. "Beck."

She looked up. Father W stared down, bushy white brows knotted in concern. An apparition, she thought, another defense mechanism. Then he grinned. She felt her breath return. He grabbed an empty chair and slid it over.

"What are you doing?" Underhill asked.

"Father Ismera. I'm counseling Rebecca."

"Unless the BAR association's handing out clerical collars…"

"This isn't a formal inquest. It can't be because she's sitting out here and not in an interview room." He turned to Beck. "Did he read you your rights?"

"No."

Father W returned to the detective. "Then a priest is just as acceptable as a lawyer. Besides, you'll want to hear what I have to say."

"Really."

"Beck is in no way connected to the murders, the club, any of it."

"How can you be so sure?"

"Because I know who killed Tommy and why."

Beck felt the floor drop away.

The detective straightened his slouch. "Excuse me?"

"Zachary Stratton murdered Tommy Hain over a debt of a hundred thousand dollars," Father W said, "a debt accumulated from trafficking narcotics."

He knows about the money.

How does he know about the money?

Underhill set his phone down and turned on the recorder. "Can you please repeat that, Father?"

CHAPTER 16

Three days earlier

"I'm a dead man," Tommy said, hunched over in the pew, fingering a bruise around his right eye.

Winston's spirit sunk. The cycle of iniquity was unending. The reckless behavior, the immorality, the tribal hatred. People cited various areas of progress, but all he saw was a world tumbling further from enlightenment. Individuals might be capable of humility and compassion, but the collective failed faster each new day. He sympathized with Tommy even as the young man's compulsions exasperated him. Winston wanted to hug him. Wanted to throttle him. But all he could do was advise him, which didn't feel remotely adequate. "The police—"

"Forget the police. They'd want me to testify, and I'm not gonna spend the rest of my life looking out for whoever Stratton hires to make me regret it. If I can come up with the cash, I can swing a deal."

"Not from a man like him. He will never stop taking from you."

Tommy stood up, wincing from the beating he suffered.

"What about your family?" Winston asked.

"They're the reason I'm in this mess."

"Nevertheless—"

"I already asked. Months ago. Made me sick to my stomach, but I tried, and if just one of those pricks had come through, I wouldn't have needed Stratton. All they care about is my father's campaign."

"What can I do?"

"You can start by writing a check."

"Tommy."

"What? You got the school, the church. Maybe some rich parishioner. Everyone trusts you. Tell them it's for a new refrigerator or something. It's just a loan. I'll pay it back. You know I'm good for it."

"The Diocese manages our expenses. And if any wealthy parishioners remained, we wouldn't be selling off our land. I have some savings. Maybe we can work out a repayment plan."

"Repayment plan? Look at this." He pointed to his eye. "I've been living in my car since Stratton and his goons knocked me around, Winnie. He's not a loan shark. He's a killer. How the fuck can I make this any clearer?"

Winston shot to his feet. "Father W to you, and you can start by watching your tongue in this house! After everything we've been through, at least respect my position!"

Tommy held up his hands. "Sorry. I'm sorry. I do respect you. You've been more like a father to me than anyone. I'm just lost...and scared."

"Then take shelter here while we figure this out."

"There is no shelter, Father. Stratton isn't afraid of you or my family or anyone. I got two days, or I'm all done."

CHAPTER 17

Beck sat in astonishment as Father W recounted the story.

"Did you loan him the money?" Underhill asked.

"I could not loan him what I did not have. I begged him to go to the police, but he didn't believe he'd survive Stratton's reprisal. He became frustrated, angry, and took off. I called repeatedly. Even went down to his club and apartment. Nobody had seen him. A couple of days later, one of the older children ran inside after taking out the trash, scared by a man running through the back alley. We teach them all about stranger danger. I went outside to check and thought I saw his car pulling away. He'd told me he'd been living in it, hiding from Stratton. The alley is well concealed. I shouted his name, hoping he'd return to accept my help, but he kept driving. The next day, he was gone…" His eyes welled up. He pulled out a handkerchief to dab them dry.

"Wait here," Underhill said and rushed to a group of plainclothes personnel inside a glass office. They bore the grim expressions of seniority pissed the rank and file hadn't solved the crime yet. The detective appeared deferential, an eager student trying to impress the dean, so different from the sleepy-eyed slouch he'd presented to Beck.

"Why didn't you tell me?" she whispered.

"You have more important matters to attend to."

"What about the cop? Did Tommy mention this Washington guy?"

"No…You really don't know where Riley is?"

She shook her head, the deception expressed quickly, too easily, considering she'd spent her entire life telling Father W the truth.

"Good. Do not get involved. If Riley turns up, call the police or me."

She nodded.

"I need to hear you say it, Beck. Promise me you'll stay as far away from this as possible."

"I promise."

The suits walked out with Underhill and led Father W into a conference room. Just before the door closed, he told Beck not to worry, a sentiment he'd expressed too many times to approximate. Feeling unworthy of his fidelity, she trudged into a darkening day. Mr. G ordered a Lyft. She told him to leave a twenty percent tip after the ride, then closed her eyes.

Beck, we're home.

His voice pulled her from a dreamless sleep. She thanked the driver and ran up to the second floor of her building. Knocked on the door and let herself in.

Amy ran over. "I'm going to hug you. Don't freak."

Beck laughed and nodded but had to swallow back a scream as her friend compressed her wound. She glanced at Eli, his expression circumspect, most likely contemplating the mess in her loft in combination with the sudden arrival of the police.

"You shouldn't have gone down there," Amy said, stepping back.

"I don't have anything to hide." She was so tired she nearly laughed at the absurdity of the statement.

"They come snooping around again, call Barbara or Paradigm's lawyer, Lyle. Don't let them tie you up in your sister's mess."

The advice didn't surprise Beck. Amy was the center beam, holding everyone else up. Nothing to worry about 'til there's something to worry about, and even then, she resolved glitches swiftly and without excess sentiment. It was why they got along so well – her style was akin to Beck's rip-the-band-aid-off approach.

However, Beck wondered how Amy's patrician control would hold up if she knew about the war waged just twenty feet above her loft. "Where were you?"

"I went home after the bar. I had to get up early to help Mom prep for brunch tomorrow. Only the Tennysons need forty-eight hours to plan for eggs benedict and mimosas. Don't you remember?"

"Eh, it's a bit foggy."

"Four Stone-Cold Stingers will do that to you."

This was why they hadn't walked home together after happy hour: Amy had ventured to her family's place in Wellesley. The information prompted more details of the night to return—

Amy climbing into a Lyft, "off to see the Fresh Princes and Princesses."

Feeling distressed at her absence – Beck hated staying in the building alone.

A taxi ride for a bowl of hot 'n sour at Golden Temple.

The long walk back to and around Dyer.

Pandemonium.

"What happened in your loft?" Amy asked.

Beck jolted.

"Eli said you took a tumble."

"It's nothing," but she wondered what else he told her.

"I'm sorry about Tommy. And I hope Riley's okay."

"Thanks."

"I think a round of piña coladas will do all of us wonders. Eli, how about a few of your famous egg sandwiches?"

"Are they famous?" Beck asked as they entered the kitchen, needing Eli to say something, anything, to gauge his mindset.

"Famous enough for Amy to send me calendar invites to come over and make them."

"I thought you appreciated structure and scheduling," Amy said.

"The invite was for every day of the year with no expiration date." He rolled his eyes at Beck and gathered ingredients from the fridge. Any suspicion appeared to have diminished. At the very least, he hadn't speculated to Amy about the disarray upstairs, the fractured bust or the bloody bandages.

Relieved, Beck grabbed a stool as Amy fired up the blender. The tension of Riley's unknown fate remained, but the company of her friends took the edge off. She thanked Gaia and all the gods for planting these two in her life. Eli was a problem-solver who ranked other people's problems above his own, gifted with leadership skills but happier as part of a team. Amy was a contradiction: a money-whiz who found solace in creative abstractions, a junk-food junkie who maintained a lean repose with a fierce regimen that made PiYo look like a stroll on the beach and a lady to the manor born resolved to succeed without dipping into the family fortune. Her portfolio manager father could have funded MrGabriel out of his Newport vacation budget. Eli had suggested presenting to him, only to be rebuffed by the arch of Amy's eyebrow.

Contemplating her friends' virtues made Beck feel rotten for lying, for being a Dyer girl who would do anything, say anything, and use anyone to move from one moment to the next.

Amy filled three tumblers with colada.

Beck tried not to drain the glass. The sweet sting sent a welcome freeze down her center. She turned to Eli. "What did the cop ask?"

"How well I knew Riley and Tommy. If I'd ever seen this detective before. I told them I don't know any police officers, and we went to Round Midnight once for a Christmas party, but only once. Do you know where she is?"

"No clue. I assume neither of you ran into her."

"Haven't seen her since Commencement," Amy said. "You were never keen on us hanging out with her or her clique. Is it weird you haven't heard from her?"

"That wasn't the first time we fell out, but it was the first time I didn't make the move to reconcile. Tough love, I thought. She needed to get clean to be part of my life."

"You did everything possible. People like Riley don't change unless they want to. I know. Wellesley's got enough functioning addicts to cast a dozen *Real Housewives*."

"I always feared their lifestyle would lead to one or both of them dying young. It's hard to process now that it's happened."

Eli laid out his sandwiches on paper towels. Amy chastised him for not using plates. She grabbed the flatware she'd made in a pottery class. "This isn't a frat house."

"As if I was ever in a frat, Miss Haversham."

They finished their meals. Amy poured refills. They returned to the TV area. Amy clicked to a college football game, an avid sports fan. Beck and Eli – avidly not – typically fired off questions to annoy her. Today, they watched in silence.

Beck leaned back on the couch, trying to empty her head and Drift. Her cell chirped. She didn't recognize the number and hit talk, expecting to hear the voice of the police. "Hello?"

"The jackboots gone?" Riley asked.

Beck sat up, feeling everything at once: consolation her sister was alive, apprehension her friends would realize she'd lied about everything, anger over Riley's insane decision to drive Tommy's car into the river. "Sorry, not interested." She disconnected. "Friggin' spammers."

"You haven't registered on Do Not Call?" Eli asked.

The phone vibrated in her hand. She read the text.
need to c u

"Man, now they're texting." As she typed the word 'where,' she said, "Unsubscribe."

Riley's response came back a second later.
hide 'n seek

CHAPTER 18

Claiming exhaustion, Beck said she was going upstairs to rest. She ran down and out the rear exit. Avoiding the main roads, one eye out for the police, she slipped through the cracked opening of the abandoned subway depot and descended a swaying staircase. Her cell light cut a narrow slice out of the black. Too narrow. She became stuck in place, breathing hard.

A light glowed up ahead. Riley appeared, the backpack slung over her shoulder.

Beck resisted an urge to leap on her sister and choke her. She followed her into what looked like a maintenance room; the door wrenched off its hinges. Inside, a sleeping bag, two 7-Eleven carryalls and the remains of a convenience store meal lay scattered. "You slept down here?"

"I figured the cops were looking. I dumped my phone and got a prepaid." Riley waved the disposable cell. "You okay?"

"Um, no, far from it. You have to come forward. Despite your river trick, the cops aren't just gonna forget about you. Even if you and Tommy weren't friends, you were the manager at Round Midnight, which sounds less like a music club and more like the tour bus for Mötley Crüe."

"I didn't know how bad it was until this week, I swear."

Fatigue rolled over Beck. She dropped onto the sleeping bag. "Don't swear. Just tell me."

"The pandemic wasted the club. Afterward, we had a tough time booking acts, even those bar bands who play crappy cover tunes and get the crowd dancing and eager to buy watered-down drinks. Without music…well, people didn't hit us up for the mozzarella sticks. We brought in DJs. Got desperate enough to host Trivia Nights. Nothing worked. A few days ago, Tommy started pounding on my door at the crack of ass. Soon as I let him in, I know he's in trouble. Again. That one of his dodgy schemes has backfired. Again. His hair was standing straight up, and you know Tommy. He spent more time primping and preening than you and I ever imagined. Had an enormous bruise over one eye. He was talking so fast I thought he was using again."

"You were using," Beck said, "both of you."

Tommy Hain's proximity could be intoxicating. His boundless energy had created some fun times back in the day. On what should have been the biggest day of her life, though, she'd noticed a prominent gray in his stubble and webs of blood in his eyes. Once blindingly handsome, the hard life had eroded his appeal; like Riley, he was calendar-young but withered by indulgence.

"After Commencement, after we ruined your day, we got clean. We were tired of the heartache."

"But."

"Not all the bad choices went away." Riley chewed her cuticles. "He said he owed. Big time."

"Stratton."

"Creep started hanging around the club over the summer. Garden variety lowlife, I assumed. But he ran with a pretty scary entourage. I didn't know Tommy had struck a deal, not until he showed up at my place beat to hell, askin' me how much we could scrape together. I laughed. I kept the books. We were so far in the red it was almost purple."

The words were too familiar, too customary. Did her sister even register their emptiness anymore? Tommy's first year at Andover, he was at the top of his class, "wicked smart." Then he and Riley thought it would be fun to go joyriding in one of the three-wheelers used by the school's landscaping crew. The joy came crashing down the second they plowed through the front of a Dairy Queen loaded on Kool-Aid and Everclear. Expelled and sentenced to community service, Tommy vowed to turn it around. So did Riley. Many promises followed over the years, all unfulfilled. Instead, they fell in with the ramshackle rich, the broken scions of prominent families dedicated to a life well-narcotized. They graduated from boozy sweet drinks to drugs: pills, then meth, then God knows what, and began to beg, borrow and steal to fund their habit. Tommy's sister finally forced him into the finest therapy money could buy, while Riley suffered through public detox perdition and a stint out in MCI Framingham. He finished a one-year hospitality program at BU and exploited his surname to land primo gigs at five-star hotels and restaurants. He hired Riley whenever possible. Temptations resurfaced. If one fell off the wagon, the other jumped off in solidarity. Still, Tommy forged enough connections to launch Round Midnight, a callback to yesteryear's clubs, the kind even Father W reminisced about from his pre-ecclesiastical days, like the Boston Tea Party, Cantone's and the infamous Bunratty's. It was Tommy's last and most promising chance, save for one inescapable truth: Tommy was even worse at business than he was at living well.

"Everyone came to my birthdays," he once told Riley and Beck in her room at the Victorian, sullen and feverish from an eight-ball comedown. "Remember how I threw the best parties, Riles? You would have loved them, Beck…except I don't think any of those bastards were my friends. I don't think I had any real friends until the two of you."

The Hains owned property on the North and South Shore, down the Cape and in faraway cities like Dublin, Zurich and Prague. Tommy's grandfather had converted a fabled crime syndicate into a legitimate construction company. At the same time, his father seemed to own every shipping liner on the Atlantic and had turned his attention to politics. Tommy Hain should not have turned up jitterbugging in Riley's basement studio, indebted to a drug dealer.

And Beck should not be sitting in a deserted subway line after being shot because of their latest gambit. "What went wrong? How did Tommy and Stratton end up at odds?"

"Stratton runs his biz like a damned consignment. You buy wholesale, sell at a markup, keep the margin."

"You were selling directly?"

"Not me! I told you, I didn't know about the drugs until Tommy came to me with problems way bigger than being late on the heating bill."

Beck doubted that. How could any of this have gone on without Riley's awareness?

"The bartenders and security guys did the pushing," her sister continued. "Tommy said it was only supposed to be short term. High-grade product to attract high-grade clientele."

"Right, because that's exactly what high-grade clients want – to be photographed partying at an opium den. Zip right to the top of TikTok, assuming you're not swept up in a raid. Exactly how did this ingenious plan go awry?"

"Despite the uptick in attendance, it wasn't the right crowd, if you know what I mean."

"I can guess."

"We got a few newcomers, people who threw the cash around, but not nearly enough to cover the obligation to Stratton, who kept shipping. Monthly dues, he called them."

"Why not just return the unsold inventory?"

"It's not Amazon Prime, Beck. He wanted his money, not the product."

Even during her worst moments, her sister projected defiance. Beck made decisions based on logic. Riley charged headlong into a quandary. This was the first time she recalled seeing her sister so defeated, so diminished. She couldn't imagine the depth of loss she felt over Tommy's death.

"Stratton gave Tommy forty-eight hours to make good," Riley said. "Thirty grand…I know how it sounds, Beck, but he was trying to do the right thing. He hooked up with Stratton only so he and I could finally start over. He said to me, Beck's made it. You don't have to worry about her anymore. He figured we could hit the road to palm trees and sun in six months like I always dreamed about. When he fell behind, he offered Stratton the club. Stratton agreed…if Tommy paid him a hundred thousand."

"You just said thirty."

"Thirty for the drugs. Stratton called the additional amount a drop-out penalty. A hundred grand and the deed to Round Midnight in two days or else." Her sister ran her hand under her nose. "I was so mad when Tommy told me I wanted to throw his ass out."

"Why didn't you?"

CHAPTER 19

Beck will never understand, Riley thought. As much as Tommy infuriated her, she would never have given up on him, just as he'd never given up on her. Their link went beyond love, honor-bound long ago. "He was my Tommy," was the only answer she could give.

"So you two were finally gonna hit the road after all these years of never getting married, never living together, never even calling each other boyfriend and girlfriend."

"Sometimes, there are too many memories binding you up. Getting out of here might have finally freed us. Now, we'll never know."

"Where did Tommy get the money?"

"No idea."

"Why did Stratton shoot him if he was about to settle the bill?"

"Same answer. I was at the club. I received an alert from the security app that our back door was open. I went to check it out, and somebody brained me. Tommy found me. All I could hear were gunshots and people screaming. We ran for our lives and...well, you know the rest."

"You're positive Stratton shot him."

"Hundred percent. Asshole was popping off caps like it was the Fourth of July."

Beck stood, rubbing her injured arm. "I should have stopped you. The coverup is just as much my fault as yours...but it's not too late. Father W confirmed the debt."

"What?"

"Tommy approached Winston about a loan. The police know all about the arrangement."

"Okay, but I don't see how that changes things. Cops were already tracking that animal down."

"You're the star witness. You saw him shoot Tommy. You can put Stratton away forever."

"He's a cop killer, Beck. Know what happens to cop killers in this city? In any city? Stratton's toast. It's just a matter of time. And you're out. Like I promised. All you gotta do is play dumb and stay mum."

"I can't live like this. Not for tonight, not for another minute." Beck gripped herself, staring at the floor, disconnecting like she did when shit got too real.

"Yes, you can. You don't have a choice." She tried not to lose it. Beck was brilliant but soft, so used to everyone singing her praises – acing school, racking up those gold stars. Riley believed when the chips were down, you came out swinging. "Your fancy new friends and fans can't protect you. Not the way I protected you. What, you're having a moral dilemma? Don't. People like Stratton and the Hains don't bat a goddamn eyelash when they torch some poor fool who gets in their way. Washington deserved every ounce of pain and terror he felt the entire way down the elevator shaft, and I hope very soon, Stratton feels a million times more."

"So, what are you going to do?"

"For now, disappear."

"A hundred grand's a lot, but it's not forever money."

"I know. That's why I asked you to come down here. I need to know if there's any way to get it in one of those finance apps without anyone noticing."

Beck stared at her for a minute. "What?"

"You know, like under a fake name."

Beck laughed, but there was no amusement in it. "You really are crazy. Hate to disappoint you, Riles, but they didn't cover money laundering in school. Maybe in the MBA program."

"Alright—"

"What do you think happens if you run?"

"What do you think happens if our fight with Washington comes out? You had all day to bare your soul, but you kept your mouth shut. Why?" Off her silence, Riley continued: "Don't know? Can't even hazard a guess? Let me help you out." She stamped her hand in the air as if laying out a headline: "Tech's latest star slays hero cop. Probably not the best marketing campaign. You did what you had to do to protect what's yours. Because of what I taught you. Trust. No one."

"How can you stand there and give me advice? This is all your fault!"

"Which is why I'm trying to fix it. And in case you haven't noticed, it's working. All you gotta do is dig out those slugs and dump 'em in the sewer. Then you're done. Safe and sound and back to your pampered little life."

"Don't be a bitch."

"I'm done being collateral damage, Beck. If you can't help me, fine, but I'm playing their game now."

"Who are you even talking about? Whose game?"

"Everybody's!" Riley's anger finally jumped the barricade. "Every asshole who lorded over us. Every guy who cruised the school and called us whores for not taking twenty bucks to blow 'em. All the cool kids who whispered behind our backs and pretended to be our friends. The bastards who have dictated our lives since the beginning. Hate me all you want, but eventually, you'll see I'm right. If you want to blow it up, go 'head. I can't stop you. But I don't think you'd survive the night in jail."

"They'll think you're a fugitive."

"I am a fugitive." Riley gathered her belongings. "Always have been." She hugged Beck with one arm and kissed the top of her head. "Don't spoil a good goodbye. I love you."

"Wait—"

She ran out, taking the light with her. She heard Beck trying to follow, but Riley knew the depths of the bygone subway line better than anyone.

Within seconds, she was gone.

CHAPTER 20

The nightmare unfolded in supernal bursts of violence and oblivion—

Mr. G, hunched over, stared into a void. Beck called his name, but he faded into the empty horizon, never looking back.

Another figure materialized: Tommy, doing a disjointed walk, like a marionette, face covered by a sheet of blood.

Finally, Riley, who used a knife to carve off pieces of her body. She advanced, eyes rolled back to their whites, and drove the blade into Beck's stomach.

"Beck!" a voice called.

Her sister drove her deeper into the murk, entombing her into darkness. She swung her arms—

"*Beck!*"

Her eyes shot open. Her hands swatted up against Amy, who was trying to keep her from falling onto the floor.

"It's me! Stop!"

"Amy? Oh my God, are you…?"

"I'm fine. So are you." She untangled the twisted blanket. "Man, you're stronger than you look. Who did you think I was?"

Beck didn't even try to explain. She barely remembered the trek home from the abandoned subway.

"You're burning up. Did you take something?"

"Not since yesterday. It's in the bathroom." She walked over and pounded an array of pills. "Maybe I should shower."

Amy waved under her nose. "No maybe about it. I'll get you some clothes."

In the shower, Beck rinsed her biceps, biting her lip, then sat on the cracked floor of the tub until the stream went cold. Afterward, she redressed the gash and slipped into the flannel, sweatpants, and wool socks Amy had delivered. She glided across the floorboards out to the living area. Outside the front door, Amy conversed with a large man whose jawline was as squared off as his haircut. He marched downstairs before she closed the door.

"Who's he?" Beck asked.

"Dad's driver. He's kind of on loan." Amy retrieved a tray of lemon tea and wheat toast with orange marmalade – Beck's favorite. She set it down on the aged Seward trunk purchased at a pawnshop, now serving as a coffee table/storage center/gaming area. On Sundays, Beck and her friends gathered around the trunk to advance their *League of Legends* campaign or play epic rounds of hearts and Texas Hold 'Em, betting loose change or Goetze's caramel creams.

"You look nice."

Amy wore a form-fitting black turtleneck, burgundy slacks and sneakers. "Brunch with Mummy and the ladies, remember?"

Beck remembered. A small blessing. Heading out to Wellesley Friday night had kept her friend away during the faceoff with Washington. It explained the sneakers: Amy's small defiance against the mannered class. "Want some?"

"You think I jammed up eight slices just for you?"

They nibbled on the toast. "Not as good as brunch, I bet."

"You kidding? A thousand times better. Because of the company."

Beck smiled. "So why is your father's driver on loan?"

Before Amy could answer, their phones began dinging with texts from Barbara Azakian requesting their presence.

Immediately.

CHAPTER 21

It took Beck twenty minutes to get into some semblance of presentability. Amy introduced her to Darren, who looked more like a Marine than a chauffeur. He drove them to the Financial District. His eyes never stopped scanning the surrounding roads until they arrived at One Federal, home to many of Boston's most influential firms: AON, Credit Suisse, J.P. Morgan, U.S. Bank.

And Paradigm Ventures.

Beck tried to tamp down her nervousness. Paradigm was their collaborator, mentor and sponsor, and over the last few months, Barbara and her team had even become friends. This was their second home. Inside, the people of MrGabriel were always welcome.

Inside, Detective Underhill waited.

Eli showed up ten minutes later, bounding into the waiting area. Judging from his attire, Barbara's summons had interrupted his morning bike ride. He said nothing, reading Amy and Beck's trepidation.

Becks' mind raced as she watched Underhill chat with Barbara and the management team inside her corner office. What had brought the detective here? What had changed? Had Riley done something even worse? She perused the news. The only new nugget was "confirmation" of Tommy's debt to Stratton and a "pipeline of drugs" moving through Round Midnight. Father W went unnamed as the source. A search on Riley's name returned a user forum dedicated to Boston nightlife. The comments jumped out:

WTF! Tommy's dead?!?! Guy was a l-e-g-e-n-d

T Hain hanging with this skank? GTFO.

awful club. that riley bitch walked around like she owned the place.

good riddance

Wading through the cruel thoughts of strangers was like pushing on a loose tooth, but Beck had to admit they weren't entirely inaccurate. She kept scanning blogs and articles, a digital tsunami of facts, speculation and outrageous conspiracy theories.

"Beck?" Barbara stood outside her office.

An image of Mary Dyer striding to the gallows popped into her head as they entered; however, this was not a march of defiance or in service to any nobler cause. Paradigm's attorney, Lyle, and Isaac Ling, head of HR, flanked Barbara at the head of the table. Beck hadn't noticed Underhill's departure, consumed by her internet scrounging.

"You know how much we care about you and everyone at MrGabriel," Barbara started. "Our belief in the app is unwavering, and we will get through this, but you should have informed us about what was happening. Interviews with the police – concerning a homicide, no less – and we don't receive a single phone call? That is simply unacceptable."

"Frankly, you're lucky we're not enacting the morals clause and asking all three of you to step down," Lyle said.

In extreme circumstances, Paradigm could remove or suspend any member of MrGabriel, even Beck. The threat was well-conveyed. And they didn't even know the half of it.

"You're right. I felt overwhelmed. Heartbroken. Tommy wasn't a bad guy. I wouldn't be sitting here today without him and my sister."

"I'm sorry for your loss," Barbara said, "but all the more reason to keep us in the loop."

"What did the detective say?"

"He wanted to know if we'd ever seen Tommy or Riley around MrGabriel."

"He also inquired about your access to capital," Lyle said. "They're trying to trace money in your sister's possession. A hundred thousand dollars. The amount Tommy owed this Stratton degenerate."

"And he thinks we gave it to him?" Amy asked, incredulous, her fire returning, always the first to rise to a challenge. "It's not like we have a pot of gold in the back room for whoever wanders in."

"It's about perception," Barbara said. "A drug dealer and murder associated – no matter how tangentially – with the creator of an app designed for children is not a connotation we can afford."

She was right, of course. Soon, the same columnists celebrating their rise would eagerly cover their fall or at least land a few blows to the whiz kids from Yale. This was the era of trial by social media and the almighty click. You only needed to be mentioned in the same area code of impropriety to find yourself at the wrong end of the firing range. If the whole truth ever came out…sayonara.

"So what do we do?" Eli asked.

"I'll make sure the School Committee focuses solely on the app," Barbara said. "I'm having dinner with the chair tonight. I'll confirm that these events involve a family member no longer in contact with Beck or anyone else."

Beck managed to nod along with her friends.

"From this point forward, though, redirect all correspondence – media requests, police inquests, tweets, emails, voicemails – to my office. Am I clear?"

Another round of nods.

"Finally, I need to know if there's anything else you're holding back."

Amy and Eli shook their heads, but Barbara's eyes never left Beck.

"Nothing."

On the drive home, Amy told them she was again spending the night at her parents' place. Eli asked if they wanted to grab dinner before she left. Beck said she wanted to rest and practice tomorrow's pitch to the School Committee. Outside her building, she hugged her friends and moved inside as fast as her injuries allowed so they wouldn't see her crying. She fumbled her keys, entered her loft, and prepared for an early sacktime. She donned a worn Chatham sweatshirt, purchased years back on a Cape trip that soured when Riley got drunk and went off with some pumped-up gym rat from The Squire, leaving Beck to eat alone in the motel room. Before she slipped it on, she checked her arm, fearing the worst. Yep, all kinds of bad. The slash puffed up and down like some crimson parasite.

She summoned Mr. G. "I think I already know, but what are the signs of infection?"

He rattled off the symptoms.

"Okay, I pretty much check all those boxes."

Do you want me to find the nearest urgent care center or emergency room?

"No, just modify the reminder on the antibiotics to every two hours." She ventured to the bathroom and downed the amoxicillin with two acetaminophen chasers. The real miracle would be if her liver didn't go on strike. She fell into bed. "Wake me up at 3 AM."

She hated herself. She'd been gifted two for-life friends after growing up without any except for her guardians. Unconditional love was invaluable, and Beck had deceived both Amy and Eli, as well as their benefactor. In a lifetime haunted by periods of intense isolation, she couldn't remember another when she felt so alone.

There was only one thing left to do.

Mr. G woke her by escalating the volume on Nate Smith's "Retold."

She splashed cold water on her face.

Located Riley's note.

And burned it over the stove.

Deleted the text from her sister's burner and the number from her recent list. The provider had a record of the call but would require a warrant to share the information. If Beck reached the point where the cops were serving warrants, an unknown call from a prepaid burner would be the least of her troubles.

She located the two bullets fired through her arm and at Washington. Pulled on winter gloves and used pliers to avoid touching the slugs, wrenching them out of the scarred brick and laying them onto a napkin, which she balled up and stuffed into her pocket. Then finished cleaning the loft.

Her winter coat and ski cap were too hot for fall but concealed her well. She trod down the stairs and let herself into Amy's apartment. Rolled out her e-bike and relocked the unit. It took all of Beck's limited strength to navigate the bike down the stairs without letting it slip out of her hands.

Outside, the wind sliced and gusted. She tightened the hood and set the bike to maximum assistance. She could have ridden to Savin Hill in under thirty minutes at this hour, but she chose side streets and even pedaled across a few parks, erupting clouds of dried leaves in her wake. Streaking past the Vietnam Memorial, she reached the water's edge and set the kickstand. She flung the balled-up bullets as far as she could. The napkin came apart, disgorging the slugs before it hit the water and dissolved. The two hunks of lead didn't even make a splash. She climbed on the bike and followed another serpentine course back to Dyer.

Her sister hadn't been wrong when she called out Beck's self-preservation; she'd been considering the repercussions on MrGabriel almost from the second Riley had turned up covered in blood. What else could she tell the cops? Or Barbara? Or her friends? If any evidence remained at the bottom of the elevator shaft, it would only prove Henry Washington died in her building, not that he first tried to kill Beck and her sister. Only Z Stratton could fill in the blanks, and the entire Boston law enforcement apparatus was mobilized against him. Her part in this whole ordeal was finished. She needed to get back to work, now more motivated than ever to develop a platform to shepherd Lost Ones like her.

A true mission.

Many had done far worse to protect far less.

"Half a truth is often a great lie."

– Ben Franklin

CHAPTER 22

"Twenty-five liners. Hundreds of ports and harbors on every shoreline. Three thousand employees…all union."

The crowd laughed and applauded. A few dozen "hands" stamped their feet as cameras rolled, committing the speech to digital posterity. The quip served as an unsubtle reminder Carlow Hain was good people, a worker even though he was the founder, principal shareholder and CEO of Hillary Maritime, the fastest-growing titan in 3PL.

Third-party logistics. A fancy term for moving and storage. Supply-chain management as a discipline and art form. A trillion-dollar industry with growth rates exceeding whole economies. Carlow and his wife Olivia had purchased an underperforming fleet seventeen years ago and modernized it with software, predictive analytics and increased coverage, birthing one of the principal freight, warehousing and distribution companies on the high seas.

The union shout-out helped, further bolstered by his dress – a starched white button-down, cuffs rolled to the elbows, tucked into jeans that wouldn't set you back more than $29.99 at TJ Maxx. A brilliant line in a brilliant speech; he caught the author's gaze on the exposed second floor – Olivia returned a subtle nod.

Carlow returned to the mic: "I named my company after Edmund Hillary, the first explorer to reach the top of Everest and set foot on both the North and South Poles, a living testament to a fearless, know-no-bounds philosophy. Maritime companies can sail under the flags of other nations. It saves money and avoids many regulations."

He hesitated, letting the setup cook. "Hillary's different. Our vessels proudly sail under one flag, and one flag only: the flag of the United States—"

The crowd's roar drowned out "of America." Olivia had predicted the response and instructed him to pick up tempo and volume to capitalize on the momentum.

"Now I want to bring that same fearless, know-no-bounds philosophy to the city I love, which is why I have just submitted my statement of candidacy to be the next Mayor of Boston!"

The cheers multiplied—

Carlow shut off the replay with a click of his mouse. He typically loved revisiting his campaign announcement, the pride and excitement he felt. A new beginning. A vision extending beyond mayorship into the Governor's mansion, and from there, who knew? The dynamism of his campaign had expanded all summer to where he was ahead by ten points in the polls by fall – four months from dark horse to frontrunner. Four months to re-energize a city and an entire region, for as Boston went, so did New England.

Four months for it all to fall apart.

A five-minute exchange on his front stoop was all it took. The second he glimpsed the cheap ties and belt badges through the sidelights of his foyer, he sensed calamity.

Tommy.

Who else. Carlow wasn't surprised, not solely because of his oldest son's delinquent tendencies, but because they shared a surname: Hain. The source of all their suffering as well as their success. Carlow couldn't escape it, nor could anyone in his family. No matter how many lives they touched and provided for, they'd continue to pay the price of an insidious legacy. None deserved the burden. It wasn't fair, and Carlow wondered when The Hain Curse would come for him.

"You need to get up." She spoke from the doorway. Unlike Carlow, Olivia didn't wear her emotions on her sleeve. "Do you hear me?"

"Yeah."

"There's too much to do." She flowed into the room, shawl and dress pants blowing around her skeletal frame. She peered out the window where the media with whom they'd enjoyed a love affair for two decades gathered. The vampires sipped coffee and leaned on their vehicles, settling in.

"He's dead, Olivia."

"Yes, our son is dead. He made all the wrong decisions, and now he's gone. But we have two other children, thousands of workers with families of their own and an entire city depending on us. On you, Carlow. There will be time to grieve. Just not today."

His phone rang. He slapped at it until it stopped.

"You can't keep ignoring him," she said.

"I know."

She headed out, her gusting wardrobe making it appear as if she was floating. "Then get off your ass and clean yourself up. We need to talk to that sonofabitch father of yours."

CHAPTER 23

"Joan is lost," Beck said, pointing to the large monitor on her left. "After being separated from her mother during a shopping trip to Copley, she's wandered outside to try to find her."

The Boston School Committee bounced their eyes between Beck and the screen. She wondered if they could see the sweat coursing down her body or feel the heat radiating off her skin. Her fever had returned. The prospect of returning to work had felt like a non-starter. She'd swigged all her meds with a tumbler of OJ and Emergen-C, thinking, *yeah, this will do it; a fizzy dose of raspberry-flavored vitamins and antioxidants is absolutely the best way to treat a gunshot wound.*

Push forward, she told herself. This was why she'd decided to clean her loft and remove the bullets. Her work. Her mission. She re-buttoned her sportcoat, the underarms of her blouse soaked, and focused all her energy on the presentation. The monitor conveyed a live stream from Joan, another Yalie friend eager to strap on a Go-Pro and act out the part of a Lost One.

"Hello, Joan!" a voice called out. On the monitor, Joan held up a cell displaying an avatar with the regality of a queen and the smile of your favorite elementary school teacher.

"Hi," Joan replied, imitating a child's voice in a believable rendition that cracked everyone up.

"This is Miz Ariel," Beck noted, "our female counterpoint to Mr. G."

"What about non-binary?" a committee member asked.

Amy spun her tablet around to exhibit a series of avatars. "All our shepherds are fully configurable, offering a range of design choices to reflect any child's culture, lifestyle and identity."

Onscreen, Miz Ariel remarked, "You look lost."

"I can't find my mommy."

"Wait, how does it know she's lost?" another member asked.

"Hold," Eli whispered across his connection to Joan.

74

Beck explained: "Parents can use MrGabriel's calendar function to schedule events and appointments: test dates, dance class, a visit to Santa or, like Joan, a shopping trip with her mother. Miz Ariel has been tracking Joan's movements using our geolocation service and calculated that she's stepped outside the mall."

"How does it, or she, or *whatever*, know Joan's mother isn't standing right next to her?"

"Because Joan has been asking if anyone has seen her mother for the last five minutes. None of the responses from passers-by returned a match to the mother's voice-print."

A few committee members nodded, impressed by the functionality of boundary breeches and voice-print analysis.

"Continue," Eli told Joan.

Miz Ariel appeared on the monitor with a reassuring look. "I know you're scared. Everything will be okay. Let's call Mom."

The app dialed "Mom" from the list of contacts on Joan's cell.

Voicemail.

"It seems she is busy," Miz Ariel said. "Let's try Daddy."

Another call to the contact listed as "Dad."

Another voicemail.

"Parents of the year," a young woman on the committee commented, cueing more laughter.

Beck used a tissue to dab at beads of sweat on her brow and sipped ice water, hoping that if the committee read any distress, they'd chalk it up to nerves. "MrGabriel's decision trees are designed to address many crises."

"Okay, Joan, here's what I want you to do," Miz Ariel said. "Do you see the store with the big red letters?"

"No."

"Don't worry, I can show you. Hold me up so we can see each other."

On the monitor, Joan lifted her phone. The screen diverged, one half displaying Miz Ariel, the other the street before them.

"Whoa," the committee chair said. "What just happened?"

"The app has assumed control of the phone's camera and split the screen so Miz Ariel can show Joan the best way forward," Eli said.

Digital markers highlighted a CVS fifty feet ahead.

"Do you see the letters now?" Miz Ariel asked.

"Yes," Joan replied.

"Walk towards them and wait for Mr. Farmington to come out and meet you."

Joan's phone dialed CVS. A male voice answered. Miz Ariel explained the situation in a few brief sentences and asked for a password. The man responded, "Butterflies," and stepped out of the store a few seconds later. "Hi, Joan. I'm Mr. Farmington."

A photo of "Mr. Farmington" appeared on the app. Facial recognition processed his live image and scripted a green checkmark, matching the image to the young man standing before Joan.

"Mr. Farmington will help you now," Miz Ariel said, "but don't worry, I'll be right here the whole time if you need me or just want to talk."

The young man – Jack, a new hire in MrGabriel's customer success department – held the door open for Joan to enter.

"Our Lost One has arrived at a Safe Space, and our system has confirmed the intervention of a Guardian," Beck said, "part of a network of approved shelters and support personnel."

"Thank you, Joan," Eli said into his microphone. "Great job."

The monitor cut out, ending the video chat.

"How are you vetting Safe Spaces and Guardians?" the committee chair asked.

Amy outlined the ten-point screening process adapted from clearance procedures for highly sensitive occupations. "In an unresponsive parent or emergency scenario, MrGabriel will search for the nearest police or fire station, ER, Safe Space or

Guardian. It will dial 911 and share the location with the dispatcher. Or execute all those actions simultaneously. We are also looking at integrating with AMBER Alert. The aim is to help the child as fast as possible."

"I hope you've all had a chance to listen to the podcast," Barbara said from her seat at the far end of the table, lending her presence but allowing Beck, Amy, and Eli to run the show. "Beck was a foundling herself. After her sister sought refuge at St. Gerolamo's, Beck was brought to Faulkner Hospital, where they established her as a ward of the state. We have already contacted the Department of Children and Families to integrate into their oversight of lost or neglected children. Nearly half a million kids go missing each year. Twenty-three hundred a day. MrGabriel is truly a shepherd."

Beck stood, trying not to lose her balance. "Are there any questions?"

"I guess what we want to know is how the heck it does all this?" a member asked.

"Magic," Beck said. Thankfully, the joke landed. "Sometimes it can seem like magic, which is why nobody knows whether to be excited or terrified by the prospect of AI. Nobody can escape the term. It's part of our lexicon now, but it's important to understand that it is simply another resource. A tool. And just like you can swing a hammer to build a house, you can swing one to tear it down. You're all familiar with the sobering statistics on device usage in younger generations. The bullying. The psychological damage from assessing self-worth based on likes and comments. In a population now more connected than ever, people have never felt more alone, leading to higher rates of depression and even suicide. You also know there's no going back. The digital ship has sailed. We believe MrGabriel can ensure it's at least sailing in the right direction."

A round of applause followed. Beck thanked the committee, ready to wrap it up and make a break for the brisk air outside.

"No app can raise a child."

It took her a second to register the comment. "I'm sorry?"

A gentleman with a few wisps of white hair above each ear – a former superintendent, if she recalled – directed a disapproving gaze in Beck's direction, nearly a scowl. "I know you're trying to sell something here, but you speak of this thing like it can assume the role of a parent."

"He's not a thing—"

"Program. App. Whatever. I agree he's a resource, potentially a tool, but aren't we doubling down on the problems you cited? This committee cannot stand before parents and teachers and tell them the fake man on the phone is now the solution to all of our child-nurturing problems."

She tensed at his disparaging tone and struggled to control hers. "I don't think we suggested he solved all the problems, but certainly some."

"I feel you are overstating your value prop. There are time-tested approaches to teaching and parenting a machine will never replicate."

"Change can be scary, I agree—"

"This isn't about change," the man said, leaning forward, elbows on the table, every bit the authoritarian, adopting a how-dare-you-disagree-with-me pose. A "table-pounder," Beck called them, using volume to drown out differences of opinion. "You are not a trained clinician. You are not a psychologist. You did not complete a degree in education. Are you at least a parent?"

"I am not."

"Do you plan on having children of your own someday?"

Beck felt her illness intensifying under his barrage. "I haven't decided."

"Yet you stand here presenting a protocol for child development."

"MrGabriel was designed to address issues I saw all around me growing up—"

"You were brighter than most and cared for by Father Ismera and the staff at St. Gerolamo. Human beings, Ms.

Gideon, not programs. I don't believe an app would have made a difference in your life or the lives of the other children at St. J's…Certainly not in the life of your sister Riley."

Bastard.

Asshole.

Mother—

Barbara jumped in before Beck jumped over the podium. "Curt, I already discussed this issue with Analise—"

"Yes, I heard about your dinner, Barbara. A personal engagement, I assume. Not official business, as none of the other members were in attendance." He returned to Beck. "I'm not holding your sister against you; simply using her as an example. Do you think MrGabriel could have kept her on the righteous path?"

"Riley is the one who first drew him on—"

"I'm aware of the story. A cartoon painted to provide imaginary comfort to a child. My inquiry concerns your application: would it have saved your sister? I hope you're not suggesting MrGabriel can replace a flesh-and-blood parent?"

"I'm not suggesting it; I'm stating it outright."

"Well, now, that's just—"

"Let me finish." His eyes rounded out. Clearly, it had been a long time since anyone dared to *tell* him something, but Beck didn't give him a chance to scold her again. "Mr. G has been with me my whole life. He's with me now. I wrote the first line of code over a decade ago, and I've been cultivating him ever since. AI operates by identifying patterns in enormous datasets at speeds no human could process, meaning MrGabriel can store a repository of every event in a child's life and then aggregate, predict, and rank guidance based solely on generating a positive outcome. Most of us operate by instinct and personal bias. Feelings. Moreso than anyone I've ever met except Father W, MrGabriel is designed to listen. He takes it all: grief, heartache, regret, anger, sadness and never forgets a detail, interrupts or sits in judgment. If these time-tested theories of teaching and parenting you mentioned are so foolproof, I wonder why the world is in such a story state. The answer, 'That's how it's always been,' doesn't seem adequate anymore. MrGabriel may be the first app where consistent usage is beneficial because the more he gets to know you, the more adept he is at guiding you. He will always have a child's best interest at heart. I'm not sure we can say the same about every asshole who decides to have a kid."

The room fell silent.

There were no more questions.

As they left Bolling Municipal, Barbara asked Beck to ride with her. Amy and Eli tossed her a pair of concerned looks as she entered the waiting Bentley. The heavy vehicle melded into traffic, the thick frame shutting out virtually all city noise.

"I'm sorry," Beck said.

"For what?"

"Losing my cool."

Barbara grinned. "Passion counts. Always. Don't worry about Carl. He is an asshole."

Beck issued a startled laugh. "I didn't come across as too testy?"

"Well, your blood pressure could have launched a satellite, but no one could have delivered that level of vigor."

"Somehow, I think you would have managed."

"Management is one thing, authenticity another." Barbara poured them Evian from the center refrigerator. "MrGabriel's target demo doesn't live in Back Bay, Brookline or Wellesley. He's a nice-to-have for families who can afford daycare, private schools and au pairs. No matter where I am or how busy, my daughters see and hear me say, 'I love you,' each night before they close their eyes. Not every child is so fortunate. You built him for places like Dyer. I invested in you as much as I did the technology."

"I hope I didn't blow it."

"You didn't. They're accustomed to tough conversations." She set a hand on Beck's knee, which, for Barbara Azakian, was a cloudburst of empathy. "Now. Are there any recent developments concerning your sister?"

"None. You'd be the first to know."

"That's what I like to hear."

They clinked glasses and sipped the cool, clear water.

CHAPTER 24

The beach rolled by on his right. Carlow peered between the dunes to glimpse his boyhood home. In Celtic myth, *Annwn* is a land of eternal youth where disease has been eradicated, and no one goes hungry thanks to an endless bounty of food and wine. On the North Shore, *Annwn* is a half-acre compound constructed a century ago by Nathaniel "Natty" Hain as a symbol of inspiration and triumph – not to mention a refuge from the FBI disrupting his liquor, gambling and guns trade. After Natty was gunned down one dreary St. Patrick's Day a week before Carlow's birth, his father inherited *Annwn*. The walls remained, but these days, you were more likely to see the mansion in *Architectural Digest* or on the news for hosting high-profile fundraisers.

A security guard opened the gate. The Town Car curled up the sandstone path. The dunegrass separating the main grounds from the beach whipped in the wind. A second guard opened Olivia's door and extended his arm. She politely waved it away. Carlow exited and drew in the ocean air through his nose; the briny scent soothed him. Above the massive oaken front door, a chunk of Connemara marble bore the family crest, engraved with a typical Irish blessing:

May the roof above never fall in, and those beneath never fall out.

Inside, Da's housekeeper slid their overcoats over her arm. She whispered condolences. Carlow and Olivia's daughter Susan rushed forward, eyes red from crying. She hugged her mother, then nearly leaped into Carlow's arms. Always one to dress to the nines, her rumpled sweater and frayed jeans bespoke a profound sadness. No one had been as close to or as patient with Tommy as Susan. She'd organized the interventions, helped him paint and renovate Round Midnight, and predicted runaway success even after the business fell off to keep him distracted from his vices. Despite her busy life and intense post-grad studies at Tufts, she always made time for Tommy.

"I should have checked in with him more often," she said.

"Don't blame yourself. You did everything you could." Carlow wiped away her tears.

Susan led him and Olivia into a great room large enough to have once hosted a rainy-day soccer match between Carlow and his two brothers until Mam called a ceiling-shaking stop to it. A jukebox rested at the far end behind a billiards table. The *Star Wars* pinball machine Da brought home one Christmas sat dormant in the opposite corner. An 80-inch TV replayed the interview Carlow and Olivia had granted an hour earlier before slipping out of the city.

The Hain extended family filled the room – nephews, nieces, cousins, in-laws. One by one, they expressed their sympathies. Olivia soaked them up with the grace of a forlorn queen. Carlow accepted the embraces, but the words rang hollow, uninformed. Most of these people weren't alive during the treacherous years when Da carried on Natty's criminality. After two stretches behind bars, Da went legit with Hain Developers. What organized crime pulled off in Vegas, his father replicated in Boston, converting illicit gains into a real estate and construction megalith, inspiring Carlow to manifest his ambitions through Hillary Maritime. Construction and shipping. One could not have picked two industries with more checkered pasts, but having so many cards stacked against them made Carlow intensely proud of their achievements.

And yet, the legacy of Natty Hain endured in one regard: with startling regularity, a Hain perished in extraordinary circumstances and many before their time.

The Hain Curse.

After a terrible Red Sox season, some wag once wrote the team had as much chance to go to the World Series the following year as "a Hain does of dying peacefully in their sleep."

These descendants worked for Hain Developers or Hillary, accustomed to seats on the fifty-yard line at Gillette and invitations to the Governor's tent during the Head of the Charles. To them, *Annwn* was paradise. Tommy's death was their first encounter with the Curse. An existential fear filled their gazes and tucked in just behind their words.

"Carlow. Liv." Owen clomped across the den, cheeks even ruddier, belly even rounder than the last time Carlow saw him. His brother's pylon arms engulfed him, then swallowed up Olivia more gently so as not to snap her in two. "I'm so sorry."

They shed a few tears, leaning on one another.

"Da wants to see us, okay?" Owen said. He phrased most everything as a question, even when there was no option to decline.

Carlow followed him out. Olivia trailed them as the senior execs fell in line.

Owen held them all back with a half-smile. "Just the boys, yuh?"

The execs returned to their seats without objection.

Olivia scowled like Medusa.

The library framed an ocean view through an oval, blue-tinted window. A fire blazed inside a hearth so large Carlow and Owen could have entered it with barely a stoop. The stone featured etchings of sprites, imps, clovers and winding vines; folklore was everywhere inside *Annwn*. Shelves overstuffed with books and periodicals rose from floor to thirty-foot ceiling. As a kid, Carlow used to paw excitedly through the collection, drawn in by the colorful texts of real and imagined lands. He'd often find his Da by the fireplace with a photo album in his lap, paging through amber-tinged captures of his ancestry.

One album now rested on an end table next to a club chair; the horrid news must have sparked a pang of reminiscence. But the chair was empty. Carlow's father stood over his desk, surveying the newspapers he made his housekeeper purchase every day, his loathing of technology – particularly mobiles and the internet – an enduring trait. He glanced up as his sons approached.

Francis Cathal Hain.

Son of Natty Hain, mobster, smuggler, butcher.

Majority owner and founder of Hain Developers.

An enigma to those who wondered if he'd genuinely renounced his felonious ways.

Da.

He came around and embraced Carlow. "My poor boy."

Despite efforts to buck up, Carlow began to cry. Da waited for him to regain control before he patted him on the cheek and walked over to the wet bar to pour three shots of Dead Rabbit. They drank to Tommy's memory.

Then Da sat down and dove in. "Did you know?"

"No."

"Why didn't he tell you about the debt?"

"I guess…" Carlow cleared his throat. "I guess he thought I wouldn't bail him out again."

"He was probably right."

Harsh but true. If Tommy had asked for cash to clear a narc liability, God help him, Carlow would have tossed him right back into the street.

"This Stratton bastard ain't long for this world, yuh?" Owen said.

Da sipped. "Right before the election. What a cock-up."

"I'm not thinking about the election," Carlow said.

"You should be. Your opponent is, and people are already speculating. They'll use anything. I don't have to tell you." His father picked up a newspaper and let it drop. "Another dead Hain. Tigers don't change their spots. The chum is in the water, boys." He went to the bar for a refill.

"I shoulda done more, Carlow," Owen said. "I'm sorry."

It took a few seconds to interpret his brother's words. "What are you talking about?"

"Tommy hit me up at the barbecue."

"What barbecue?"

"The Fourth. Right here. Your big campaign fundraiser."

Carlow slid forward in his chair. "Why didn't you tell me?"

"He said it was for the club. Business was down. It's down for everyone, right? He didn't say nothin' about drugs, and it wasn't the first time he came around with his hand out, yeah? I figured the last thing you and Pop needed was another of his distractions. I've been sending him a couple of grand every month. I didn't hear wind of it again, so I figured he was all set. I didn't get into details, okay?"

Carlow's anger rose. His fat slob of a brother had known about Tommy's troubles for four months and hadn't said a peep. So much had happened since then, so many things Carlow wished he had done differently – particularly this past week. He was about to tear into his brother when Da's quiet tone slipped in.

"Details…the details are where the devil lives." His father returned to stand in front of his sons, sipped his drink, set it on the desk and walloped Owen across the face, hard enough to rock his oldest child's head back, the flesh on flesh louder than the crack of logs in the hearth.

Carlow recoiled at the sight of his brother, a grown man less than a year from his sixtieth birthday, being thumped like a misbehaving child.

"You absolute *gobshite*," Da hissed, eyes liquid in fury. "You don't turn your back on family. Have I taught you nothing, ya fucking donkey?" He jabbed his stick-like forefinger at Owen. "One who don't ask a family member with a history if he's in deeper trouble because, ya know, *details*, and the other—" he flicked his thumb at Carlow, "—with no idea what his kid's mixed up in, sittin' here sobbing like a wee girl. If any of you dumb monkey cunts talked to me other than when you want something, none of this woulda happened." He swiped his glass off the desk and threw it at the bar, where it bounced between the bottles and split in two.

"Pop, I'm—"

"Shut your mouth, Owen. Better yet, take your lard ass into the kitchen and find something to stuff down your gullet. It's all you're good for."

Owen remained in his chair.

Da lasered a look. "Now."

Owen stood, the welt on his left cheek bulging, and lumbered out of the room.

It took Da a few minutes to calm down. "Why did Tommy hate us so much?"

"He didn't—"

"Course he did. Disrespected us, anyway, which is its own kind of hate. Despite the clouds we set him on, he preferred the gutter."

"He made his own choices. Each more terrible than the last. And it's not like he felt comfortable coming to you, either."

The disgust on Da's face pinned Carlow to his chair. "Because he was your lad. Your flesh and blood. Your responsibility. Imagine if I'd let you dangle."

"What's that supposed to mean?"

"I guess you think your razor-like business sense secured all those favorable contracts. The arrogance! Your customers, partners and vendors signed as fast as they could push the quill because you're a Hain. Because you're my boy, and don't ya ever forget it."

"How can I?" Carlow said. He glanced at the photograph in the center of the mantel. A position of honor. Snapped twenty-some years ago. Da's favorite picture: he and his three sons on the dock off *Annwn*'s shores.

Yes, his *three* sons – Owen, Carlow and David, the hallowed prince no one was ever allowed to forget. David would have turned fifty-five this year if not for the Hain Curse. Da loved to make grand speculations about his youngest had precious David not perished in a car crash that nearly ended Carlow's life as well. Did Da ever get on his bony knees and thank the Good Lord for sparing one of his sons? No. The carbuncle would have swapped Carlow – or Owen or any family member – for David in a heartbeat.

Da sunk into his chair with a weary exhalation.

"I did everything I could for Tommy," Carlow said, voice shaking, the damnable tears threatening to return. "Don't make this about something else." He stood up and marched for the door.

"Son," Da said with nary a hint of iron. If anything, he sounded worn out. "Come back."

Carlow returned to his seat.

"Focus on the campaign," his father said. "I'll see to Tommy's affairs. Things are already in motion."

"What do you know?"

"I said, leave it. Whatever comes, you may need to distance yourself."

"Impossible with our last name."

Da grinned. "Get out there and keep crowing about change. The bad times ended with Natty and me. No one's gonna be surprised if it turns out I'm still a pissant little gangster who only understands violence and vengeance. You're the new day. Stay righteous." He came around and sat on the desk. "People don't follow weakness, son; they follow strength. They need to be comforted. Get out there and show them the grieving father but also the crusading mayor who's gonna find his son's killer. Be sympathetic. Be strong. If it gets Biblical, I'll be the one to send the plagues. Now stand up and give your Da a hug."

CHAPTER 25

Beck returned to her loft and slept through the afternoon. It helped. Her arm was now a bluesy Joss Stone tune rather than a jet-fueled Dorothy. She cleaned up and microwaved leftover tortilla soup from Trader Joe's, feeling energized after the presentation and limo ride with Barbara, who had left three messages of positive news about her follow-up with the Committee, asshole Curt's grousing notwithstanding. Beck emailed Eli and the engineering leads, inviting them to Barstool Brew, an artisanal coffee joint that transformed into an organic cocktail lounge at night. The email referenced a new spur of Mr. G's roadmap: wearable tech integrations. Beck was excited to share her vision. She put in the earbud, clipped on the camera and FitBit, and headed for the front door.

Her cell buzzed.

Father W.

She sent it to voicemail.

Now her phone dinged with a text. Most likely, he wanted to ask about the School Committee meeting – news she'd be eager to share at any other time – but Beck couldn't imagine how the conversation wouldn't eventually turn to Tommy and Riley.

Another ding.

She stepped outside and finally took her phone out to read the text.

they found riley

CHAPTER 26

"New Hampshire?" Beck looked from Father W to Sister Lucinda to Detective Underhill. They hadn't exactly found Riley but tracked a part of her movement.

"Near Mount Sunapee," the detective said. "Witness saw her clear as day. Sounds like she and Tommy were regulars. They liked to rent this one cabin near the Lake. The witness who recognized her is the campground manager."

"If you say so."

"You didn't know they went up there?"

"She might have mentioned it, but I told you, we—"

"—haven't talked in months, yeah."

Beck ignored his skepticism. "So she's in New Hampshire."

"Nope. She came back."

"I don't understand."

"Neither do I."

"Detective, you asked me to bring Beck over here," Father W said. "I think it's time you stopped playing games and told us why."

She detected a slight slur in Father's words. So did Sister Lucinda and Underhill, judging by their gazes. It was Monday evening, the night Father treated himself to episodes of *Grantchester* or another BBC mystery. She wondered if he'd also treated himself to a few snifters of Bakara.

"Riley steals a car and slips our net," Underhill said. "Makes it a hundred miles north, a few hours from the Canadian border…then drives straight back. Dumps the car in Malden and falls off the radar again. Footage shows her lugging a heavy backpack, which I assume holds this hundred grand we keep hearing about. Seems odd. I mean, she got away. Why come back?" Off their silence, he asked Beck: "You're positive you haven't spoken to her?"

Beck unlocked her phone and held it out. "See for yourself."

Underhill hesitated. Glanced at the phone. At Father and Sister. "That won't be necessary."

She pocketed her cell. Although she'd wiped her sister's burner information, she was grateful he declined to scour her accounts.

"It's a simple question," he said. "With every cop from Fairmount Hill to Eastie looking for her, why did Riley return?"

"We don't have any idea," Father W said.

Underhill passed his sleepy gaze across each of them and back again. "Well. If you think of one, you know where to find me." He walked off, climbed into his car, and stared at Beck as he drove away.

By the time they reached his room, Father W was half-asleep.

Up close, Beck smelled the scent of rum masked with Listerine strips. "I can take him from here," she told Sister Lucinda, who nodded and headed for her bedroom. Beck eased Father W onto his bed.

"Beck," he whispered.

"I'm right here."

He grinned and nodded at the earbud under her hair. "So's he."

"Always."

"Is he looking after you?"

"That is his only priority."

"Wonderful. I'm not sure I'm good at it anymore."

"Don't say that." He appeared to be on the precipice of sharing something heavy, inhibitions loosened by the Bakara. "What is it, Winnie?"

He issued a long stream of air through his nose. "Nothing. Come by tomorrow. The children always love it when you visit...so do I."

"It's a date."

He fell onto his pillow. Muttered something in Haitian, then passed out.

She pulled the blanket over him and shut off the light.

CHAPTER 27

Outside her building, Darren waited in the Range Rover. Beck waved. He didn't even blink. She ran up into Amy's loft, where Beck found her and Eli sipping coffee.

"Is your driver going to sit out there all night?" Before she even finished asking, she sensed a charge in the air. "What's up?"

"I'm leaving," Amy said. "The 'rents are freaking out. Some official busybody called Pops about the police paying a visit. They want me to come home. They know we have nothing to do with…whatever…but they need peace of mind until this all blows over. And, uh, Eli's coming with me."

Eli stared into his coffee.

"Sure, yeah, whatever." Beck struggled to sound casual, supportive. She knew how much it pained Amy to fall back on family affluence, but the Tennysons sensed a disturbance in the congregation. A drama of murder and drugs even remotely associated with their daughter was enough to dispatch a knight errant to bring her back behind the castle walls.

"There's something else," Amy said, showing Beck her cell. A performance app filled the screen.

"What's that?"

"Fitness tracker for my e-bike."

Uh-oh.

"Yeah, I meant to tell you, I borrowed it," Beck said.

"At three-thirty in the morning?"

Shit.

Shit, shit, shit.

"I couldn't sleep."

Amy nodded. Threw a look at Eli.

"I told her about the bandages and the broken bust," he said, his words coming out in a rush.

So it wasn't just the Tennysons who sensed a disturbance in the congregation – her two best friends had been reexamining recent events, and who could blame them? The disarray of her apartment the morning after Tommy's extravagant demise. Riley's disappearance. Police interrogations. An inexplicable bike ride in the witching hour.

Beck wondered how hard Amy had to work to convince Eli to take shelter. Probably not very. After all, they'd been friends first. It took almost all of first year before the shy girl from Dyer let anyone in. A part of Beck always resented their history, which was irrational because she was the one to resist their overtures. "I told you I was drunk."

"I found you thrashing around like the little girl in The Exorcist," Amy said. "You almost knocked my head off. I can't imagine what was going on inside your head to make you so crazy...but it sucks you won't tell us."

"You think I'm lying?"

"Are you?"

"No!"

"If something is going on you don't want Barbara or anyone at Paradigm to know, you can tell us."

"Yeah, we got your back," Eli added. "Always."

They waited for her to respond, but she couldn't make them understand without endangering herself and the company.

She'd cleaned the apartment, dumped the evidence, and lied to the police.

She'd made her choice.

"Riley's disappearance has rocked me pretty hard. I hate her, I love her, I don't know if I can live without her. I'm trying to pretend it's no big deal, but there's a lot of baggage here!" She bit off her emotion. "And Tommy...there were days I looked forward to his visits as much as Riley. I'm pissed off and devastated they couldn't get it together...and I feel like I made it all worse by ignoring my sister."

As much as it didn't convey the complete story, at least these were her true feelings.

"Then you should stay with us, too," Amy said.

The invite felt obligatory. The last thing the Tennysons wanted was Beck anywhere nearby. "I'll be fine. I need to rest...But you believe me, right?"

Eli nodded and stared back into his coffee.

"Of course," Amy said.

They were terrible liars.

She waved as Darren whisked her friends away. As tired as she was, sleep would be no easy feat. Also, she didn't want to deal with another harrowing series of nightmares. When stressed, Beck turned to three diversions: fantasy novels, fantasy games and work. She ran up to grab her laptop, came back down, and started a quick march.

Dyer rolled up the sidewalks after nine. Other than the Jeannie James Pub, Barstool Brew and the Kleen-o-Mat, no other business catered to a late-night crowd. The empty blocks calmed her. She unlocked the front door of MrGabriel's HQ, a former bakery, and entered the security code. Eli routinely claimed he could still smell the yeast. Paradigm's budget allowed for swankier digs, but Beck and her friends had flipped for the high ceilings and used the money to renovate instead of renting some frilly McOffice. She typically found answers to one problem while working on another. She moved down the central aisle towards the sticky notes of tasks on the engineering wall, intending to knock out a bunch while her subconscious mulled over the implication of Riley's return to the lion's den.

It was no surprise that the place was deserted. Attendance was hybrid-based: three days a week in the office; the rest of the time, people worked from home. Beck, Amy and Eli didn't care where the job got done as long as the teams delivered the desired quality on time. Beck could have worked in her loft, but HQ never failed to inspire. It was a testament to how far they'd come in such a short time. Like the empty blocks outside, the solitude relaxed her. Also, her desk was set at the proper height, shiny and clean, with everything in its proper place.

"Hey, G, please start the coffee."

The coffeemaker is offline.

She angled into the kitchen and flicked a light switch: the room remained shaded. She turned to scan the work area. Usually, the interior looked like a Christmas tree, pockmarked with the lights and diodes of phones, computers, and other devices. Right now, the interior ran away from her in gray-scale.

"Is the power out?" she asked, feeling like an idiot – obviously, the power was out. The security system ran off the grid, and the streetlights outside were aglow. Only HQ was down, and in her near-Drift contemplation of the office, she hadn't noticed until now.

There have been no reports of outages in our area.

Shuffle.

She pivoted again. She couldn't identify the sound except to say it implied movement.

"Tell me you heard that," she whispered.

Yes.

"Any idea what it is?"

A scuffle of sound.

She gritted her teeth. Mr. G was a shepherd, an ever-present observer, an encyclopedic genius with unfailing recall and a blazingly fast predictor. However, he was about as advanced as a sock in moments requiring creativity and an ability to reason in the abstract.

The team had found evidence of late-night visitations: trash pulled from the cans, disappearing fruits and snacks left on a counter or desk. In an antiquated city like Boston, it didn't matter how many new walls and foundations you built – the earth below belonged to creatures hearty enough to survive a nuclear holocaust. Chances were, Beck had just stumbled across an enterprising varmint who thought the bipeds had all gone home for the night.

Another part of her – the Dyer girl – told her to run.

She reversed direction, choosing the closer exit in the back—

A dull glow in the server room slowed her down. The door stood open. Usually, someone locked it. The silence was noticeable; the servers and ventilation system to keep them cool made a racket even with the door closed. Maybe their IT director learned about the outage and came in to check on her machines. Beck called her name and peeked into the room.

A laptop rested on a rack, running on its battery, screen lit up, wired into an idle server.

Shuffle.

This time, behind her.

CHAPTER 28

Thirty-nine hours earlier

Jordan said nothing, afraid to move, afraid to breathe under the blade. As the attacker's face pressed into the back of his skull, he felt the grainy fiber of a ski mask.

"What. Do. You. Have?" the attacker asked. "Pictures. Files. Recordings."

"I got no idea what you're talking about."

"You've been running down Tommy Hain for months. Which means you know about his deal with Stratton. Which means you got plenty on Riley and her sister, Beck."

"Who?"

"I won't ask again, Jordan."

"My name's John."

"Johnny, Jordy, whoever. Last chance."

"I'm telling you, you got the wrong guy!"

"And that's the wrong answer."

The blade rammed into Jordan's spine.

The impact blazed across his lower back, but his body armor saved him. The attacker cried out. A curved knife fell to the floor – a Karambit, Jordan noted, a close-quarters weapon designed to inflict devastating damage. He kicked it away and spun around. The attacker's hand gushed, balled up in pain. It must have been propelled along the Karambit's edge. Driving a knife into Kevlar was like stabbing concrete. He right-hooked the attacker's jaw, then dove across the floorboards after his gun, rolling over, forefinger disconnecting the safety—

The attacker hurtled down the stairs, Karambit in his good hand.

Jordan jumped up to give chase and immediately fell as a pang in his back arced down his legs and out to the tips of his toes.

Paralyzed. You're paralyzed.

No, he could move. Barely. He'd been an ace soccer player as a young man and once landed square on his ass trying to show off a bicycle kick, damaging his lower spine. The injury ended his sporting aspirations and plagued him into adulthood, particularly after a strenuous workout or idle stretches at his desk. The knife strike had re-stoked the affliction a hundredfold. He locked himself into position and waited for the voltage to recede. Gingerly, he sat up. Wriggled his toes. Used the counter as leverage to stand. A million pins and needles pricked his legs. He climbed onto the kitchen counter to reach the ceiling. Pushing aside a panel, he located a rope tied to a water pipe. Reeling it forward, he heard the package slide out of its hiding spot. The bubble wrap crackled as he pulled it into view. He crammed the package under his arm—

—and plunged off the counter as his legs gave out again. The currents returned, his backbone pulsing hard enough to make him probe under the Kevlar to see if the attacker had broken skin after all. He felt the distended area, his fingers moistened with sweat, not blood. He limped out.

If he could snap his fingers and teleport to the top of the Himalayas, he'd snap his damn fingers. Except the parties involved were powerbrokers who'd track him down no matter how long it took. Running was out of the question. He needed to identify the person who'd signed his death note. He tottered out to the street, gripping the Colt inside his sleeve. Collapsed inside the POS and peeled open the bubble wrap to inspect the laptop. It appeared intact. He messaged his client that he was on his way.

After I stop at my haven and hide the goods, he thought, connecting a USB cable to the computer to download the surveillance from his phone.

Henry Washington had been exposed.

And now, so was Jordan.

CHAPTER 29

The intruder's glove clinched her mouth closed. "Don't scream."

Beck nodded.

He pulled his hand away.

She screamed.

Then made a break for it. Unfortunately, someone could have clocked her speed with a sundial. The intruder's arms encircled her waist.

"Mr. G, call nine—!"

The glove clamped over her mouth again. "Stop."

She swung her laptop bag. He swatted it out of her hand. They stumbled into a cubicle littered with wires, monitors, keyboards and CPUs, bouncing painfully off the metal edges of the equipment before hitting the floor. The man shouted and grabbed his lower back but dropped his weight on her. His free hand pried her earbud out, then extracted her phone and slid it aside. His eyes narrowed on the mini WiFi camera, plucked that off and threw it away over the cubes. Finally, he used both hands to pin her shoulders.

She didn't scream, too busy trying to catch her breath.

"Bad timing, Beck," he said, as if it was her fault she'd interrupted his burglary.

The implication of the external laptop and power outage hit her – the intruder was trying to hack MrGabriel. The system was most vulnerable when it booted up. He'd cut the power and the battery backup and connected his laptop, which must have contained a hacking tool to access the operating system when he restored the juice.

"Look at me," he said, leaning close, filling her vision.

—Washington pushed her up on her tiptoes—

"Look at me."

She did, trying not to pass out under his assault. He was in his mid to late twenties, not much older than Beck. A tiny scar over his left eye disappeared under his hairline, unnoticeable except at such a close range. In any other scenario, she'd consider him handsome. Everything else about him – drab clothing, upturned collar, black watch cap –

suggested a man of concealment who liked to move unnoticed and fade from memory. Only his eyes gave him away: intense and inescapable.

"You don't know me, do you?"

She shook her head.

He held up his phone with one hand. A video played of a car in the rain. It took a few seconds for Beck to recognize herself on the recording.

And Riley.

Loading Henry Washington's corpse into the GTO.

He sat up, letting his butt keep her legs pinned, and rubbed his lower back again. "Tell me everything. And I already know about the debt to Stratton, so consider your words carefully. Where's your sister? Where's the money? And just how deep are you?"

She had to tell him something substantial…at least enough to ponder while her fingers tugged on the cable of a fallen keyboard. "She wanted me to help her deposit the money under an alias."

It had the desired effect; the intruder's eyes shifted slightly to the right as he considered the information. She whipped the keyboard into the side of his head. Letters flew through the air. He fell to one side. Hefting the keyboard with both hands, she sat up and slammed it down against the base of his spine, the area he'd been massaging. His eyes opened wide, his body rigid. She pounded the spot again; his shout filled the office. She grabbed his phone, but he held on, howling, not words, just rage and pain. They rose to their feet, fighting over his cell. He tore it from her, but the effort caused him to trip backward over the equipment. She snatched her cell off the floor and fled to the back door. Used her hip to ram the emergency crossbar.

And raced out into the night as the fire alarm blared to life.

CHAPTER 30

The sun broke orange and blue. Beck squinted at the stained glass window above the church chancel. She shivered, her jacket a skimpy blanket. St. J's did not house enough residents or attract enough parishioners to form a choir, so the raised space mainly consisted of dust and yellowed hymnals. She crawled out from under the risers. Her phone trilled repeatedly with texts and voicemails. She checked the time and discovered she'd slept the morning away.

Slept? More like fallen under a hex. There was no respite, only coarse fatigue. She'd considered running to Father W last night and even calling Underhill, but she didn't think she'd be able to withstand their scrutiny.

Or defend her decisions.

Father W used to preach about slippery slopes. She did her best not to recall the lesson.

The most recent voicemail reverberated in Amy's voice: "Where. Are. You. You're not home, you're not at work, and you're not responding. I get it if you're mad, but at least tell me you're okay."

She navigated to her friend's initial contact, a text:

Hey. Fire alarm at HQ. False alarm. Lisa went over. FD said a power outage might have triggered it. Everything's fine. c u in the morn.

Everything's fine? What about the mess caused by her brawl with the intruder? Had he cleaned up any signs of disorder? Why?

She texted Amy and told her she was at urgent care because her arm had started to hurt again. No worries. She wasn't mad and would check in later.

Bruises from the fight with the intruder partnered up with the burn of the gunshot wound to produce waves of discomfort as she pulled on her jacket. "You there?" she said into her phone.

Good morning, Beck. Are you okay? Last night, I thought I heard you shout. Were you having a nightmare? Also, it appears the Bluetooth earpiece and WiFi camera are offline.

"I'm fine."

Yeah, right. The intruder possessed dead-to-right evidence about Washington but hadn't brought it to the police. Instead, he broke in to hack MrGabriel's core system. He also paused to see if she recognized him when face-to-face. Both implied a desire for information. Was he a colleague of Washington's, Stratton's, Tommy's or some unidentified party?

"No external tech today. Please respond to my unanswered texts and messages. Use the reply I just sent to Amy."

Will do.

Beck found herself frustrated by a problem with insufficient conditions and substantiates. Only one person could help her fill in the equation. She texted the number of the burner her sister had used, hoping Riley hadn't tossed it yet.

where r you

She stared at the words and then added,

I need you

CHAPTER 31

"Our family is in pain," Carlow said. "Our only consolation is the knowledge that Tommy is in better hands."

Reporters filled the seats and lined the walls in Hillary Maritime's auditorium, a room usually reserved for company town halls and the holiday talent show.

He felt their hunger as they waited out the prepared statement, eager to tear into the meaty drama. "I know you have questions. Olivia and I will make ourselves available as much as we can. I hope I can count on you to respect our family's privacy as we grieve."

Olivia held his hand behind the podium.

First up was a reporter from the *Globe*. "Mr. and Mrs. Hain, I think I speak for everyone here in extending our profound condolences."

"Thank you," Carlow said.

"Can you provide any additional details concerning the death of your son?"

"It's not the death of our son," Olivia said, "it's the murder of our son. It was no accident. Somebody shot Tommy and dumped him, callously, into a river."

"Was he selling drugs for Z Stratton?" a voice called out from the back row.

"I know that's an outrageous meme circulating right now," Carlow said, "but the police haven't shown us any evidence to support it."

"They haven't? Even as the next mayor?" The question echoed from their left, the reporter holding up his phone to record, the starburst of the camera light dazzling.

"My focus is on my family, not the campaign. I have not received nor would I expect any unauthorized access. I have complete faith in the Boston Police."

"Police logs show a history of trouble at Round Midnight. Fights, noise complaints, citations for serving underage patrons."

"I missed your question."

"Was the club in trouble?"

"Not to my knowledge."

But he did tell my useless brother, Carlow thought in a flash of irritability.

"Was he using again?" another reporter called out.

The room hushed at the crass nature of the question.

Olivia's hand tensed, but her voice remained neutral. "If you're asking if Tommy had lapsed in his recovery, the answer is no."

"Not to your knowledge," the speaker said, an eager little porker in a bow tie and beard that made Carlow want to march over and shove his entitled little phone up his entitled little ass.

"My son was not using drugs," Olivia said. "We met for dinner last week. He had just passed the six-month mark for sobriety. I could not have been prouder." Her eyes welled up. "I wonder if you will have the courage to note as much in your blog, young man."

The porker slid back in his chair, as so many did when faced with Olivia Hain's displeasure. Carlow admired her control. Neither of them had seen Tommy in months. There'd certainly been no dinner or any discussion of his sobriety. So wrapped up in the race, Carlow had reached a point where he figured no news was good news when it came to Tommy.

Until this week, when it all changed for the worse.

"Have you spoken to your father about this latest loss?" someone called out.

"Latest," Carlow said. "I assume you're talking about the Hain Curse."

"It is a topic of conversation."

"Of callous speculation and mythical nonsense, you mean. But fine, let's talk about it." He released Olivia's hand and approached the front row of reporters. "Rivals gunned down my grandfather the year I was born. A car accident claimed my brother David. Now Tommy. Our family has lost others. Names and faces I barely recall. I've never made excuses for Nathaniel Hain or his criminal ventures. I never met the man. Nor have I made excuses for my father's actions before he rededicated his life to building rather than destroying. I am not my grandfather, nor am I the version of

Francis Hain before he found deliverance. Instead, I follow in the footsteps of my Da, the man who put his arms around me as I cried for my son…Redemption isn't popular these days, and it's downright impossible in this age of cancellation. I realize many believe the Hains deserve any hardship that comes our way. That it's karma. I say addiction is a disease, and if my son was unlawful, I will be the first to admit it. But as for the Hain Curse…well, let me tell you a story…

"My brother David wasn't drunk the night we crashed. I was. Blackout drunk. He was driving me home like a good, loving brother. It was New Year's Eve. I don't remember much, but a sheet of black ice altered my life forever and ended his. After he died, I vowed, like my father, to change. To recover and be reborn. I would never have made it without my wife and children. Many years later, Olivia and I launched this company, which employs thousands of hard-working people. I don't consider David's death a curse but a sacrifice. And I try to honor his sacrifice every moment of every day.

"Why am I telling you this? Because my son was just like David. Hearts as big as the harbor. Tommy's sensitivity subjected him to temptation. He made mistakes, yes. I know he was flawed and allowed himself to be led astray. But cursed? Hardly. He was a kind young man who would die before he brought harm to another. If you think he deserved to be murdered because he shared a last name with a gangster who's been dead for over fifty years, I think that says a lot more about you than it does my son, me, my father or our family…I don't know if this walking trash heap Stratton pulled the trigger, but I promise to honor my son just like I honor David: by walking in the light. I will bring the full weight of this organization, all of my resources and any legal recourse to expose the people responsible for Tommy and Henry Washington's deaths. And I will not rest until justice is served."

CHAPTER 32

Riley had yet to respond, but Beck knew she couldn't remain in the chancel all day. Also, her stomach was doing backflips. She snuck down and out of the church and walked the less-beaten paths to Lewek's. Head down, she ordered a corned beef burrito and Red Bull. She craved the pharma in her loft but didn't want to risk running into Amy or anyone searching for her. According to X's local news, nobody knew about the break-in at MrGabriel, but she felt hunted nonetheless. Rather than sit around and wait for the next assassin to jump out of the shadows, she decided to search for Riley, beginning with the only tried-and-true hiding spot.

hide 'n seek

This time, the descent into the abandoned subway line produced less of a fright. Beck half-ran to the room with the door wrenched off its hinges.

Empty.

She noted a dozen spurs, access tunnels and utility passages around her. The thought of checking each one sapped her resolve. "Riley!"

Shouting made her feel desperate, like a child. Maybe Underhill was wrong, and Riley had continued to put many miles between herself and Boston. Despite how incensed she was at her sister, the possibility of Riley abandoning her just like their mother pierced Beck's heart.

She picked one spur and charged ahead, looking for footprints, water bottles, evidence from Riley's 7-Eleven shopping spree. Offshoots led to dead-ends, demoralizing and exhausting her as she backtracked to the main corridors.

One tunnel narrowed into a darkness so profound her cell flashlight barely cut through the murk. She checked the power gauge: 20%. Her pulse raced as she contemplated the light failing, the blackness closing around her, recalling her nightmare of being submerged in a pool of nothing by her sister. A few more steps, then she would have no choice but to turn around.

The illumination bounced off something metallic – an access panel. No knob. The panel was half open. Beck ducked through. A faint red light appeared ahead, high off the ground: an EXIT sign at the top of a long stairwell. She noted an empty bottle of Poland Spring and a newish wrapper of Sunny Doodles, one of her sister's many guilty pleasures. Riley had been here, but maybe only to jog up the stairs and out the door, vanishing for—

"Hey."

Beck's scream rebounded off stone and concrete. She whirled around and stumbled in reverse until her back hit the wall. Mr. G said something, but the connection was spotty; his words distorted until they finally cut out.

Riley stepped into Beck's light. "Jesus, take it easy."

"Take it easy? Take it easy? Where have you been?"

"Right behind you."

Beck couldn't find the words.

"I needed to make sure no one followed you," her sister said.

"Why didn't you respond to my text?"

"Same reason – someone looking over your shoulder."

"You think I'd sell you out? After all the opportunities I've already had?"

"I think you'd do just about anything to save MrGabriel."

"Yeah, well, speaking of, I got jumped inside our offices last night."

"What." Riley rushed over, checking her.

"I'm okay. A few cuts and bruises. A breeze compared to getting shot."

"Who was it?"

"That's what we need to find out."

CHAPTER 33

Francis Hain checked his surroundings. Unnecessary but habitual. His tavern, Four Treasures, was packed to the rafters. He funded New England, New York and Miami establishments through subsidiaries and hedges not directly tied to him or his business; safe houses and meeting rooms available at a moment's notice. A coterie that had been aligned with Hain ancestry for over a century operated Four Treasures. The good and loyal proprietor ran daily scans for bugs and never hesitated to toss someone out who looked even a little like a rat. Francis adored the atmosphere. He'd done most of his best strategizing in taverns like this one.

He smoothed his gabardine and adjusted his tie. A right dandy he was, and he seemed to have caught the eye of a pretty lass at the bar who grinned at the stately man in the corner booth. He returned it, knowing he'd go no further, appreciating the interest while also realizing she regarded him as a walking dollar sign, not a paramour. You dressed well, no matter the occasion, old Natty had instructed, but you never succumbed to flattery.

Francis sipped his stout. A limited brew from the Isle. He underwrote the cost and browbeat Carlow into loading kegs of it onto his ships. Francis may have embraced the land of yore, its speech, customs, dress and drink – especially the drink – but he considered himself as American as apple pie. America meant promise. In America, you wore success like a badge and didn't risk it because a lovely winked at you from the bar. You fought tooth and nail to defend your trappings because somewhere, somebody was angling to steal it. Nobody took anything from Francis Hain he didn't give over. The quality of a man was measured by what he surrendered and what he saved when forces conspired. Francis had more than proven his worth. All that remained was to clear the pasture for his kin.

Too bad they were such mother-loving disappointments.

He cherished his sons as any father should, but David was the anointed one. Francis missed his youngest every hour of the day. Neither he nor Ide fully recovered from their son's death. All parents play favorites; if they claimed otherwise, they were topped off in shite. To lose someone so special…

And now Tommy. Like David, blessed, but bedeviled. Like David, gone too soon. Two lucky clovers plucked, leaving Francis to deal with the repercussions. Patriarchs didn't have the luxury of self-pity. Their duty was to balance the ledger.

The platinum blondie slinked to a cocktail table to chat with a lonely heart in bug-eyed glasses who was downing cheap bourbon and cheering on the Celtics.

Watch your wallet, fella, Francis thought before pondering this knacker Z Stratton. Kind of name was that, anyway? The hell kind of age was Francis livin' in where people's idea of hard was a single letter in place of a name? He finished his stout and waited for the bartender to bring a freshie. It didn't take thirty seconds from when Francis' empty glass hit the table. A solid boy-o this barkeep. The tip would be generous and well-deserved.

A man sidewinded through the crowd. Francis had rung him this afternoon. A childhood buddy, the most steadfast kind of friend. A man who had information concerning Tommy and the drug dealer. He rose to greet him with a hug and a smile. "Hey, Winnie."

Father Winston Ismera returned a muted grin. "Good evening, Frankie."

CHAPTER 34

"People tell me I'm lookin' more and more like Harrison Ford these days," Frankie said. "I say, hey, I got a year on that prick." He laughed, then added, "Sorry."

Winston grinned; the apology was reflexive. Francis Hain was many things; remorseful wasn't one of them. And if "prick" bothered their Savior, Frankie would spend eternity repenting for all the vulgarity he'd uttered.

Frankie.

A childhood moniker from their days in Lynn, the municipality north of Boston, where Winston's parents settled after fleeing Haiti. Where he encountered more stone-cold trouble than virtue in the years before Vietnam and before the Lord's calling, when an immigrant kid who went by Winnie met an Irish kid named Frankie before he insisted on Francis. No one called the well-dressed man across from him "Frankie" unless they were an original, and Winston was the only original left on this side of the grass.

"My deepest condolences," he said. "Tommy was a good man. How are you holding up?"

"Well, ya know, I've been having these dreams." Frankie straightened his already straight tie. "Intense. I woulda sworn they'd actually happened. Like Scrooge."

"Are we talking ghosts?"

"I don't believe in ghosts."

"But something's upsetting you."

"I see things. Things I done. People I've lost. Last night I saw Tommy. And it got me thinking…why the fuck didn't you call me about his debt?"

The room seemed to disappear, subsumed by the man whose half-lidded gaze affixed itself on Winston, an original friend, the priest who'd baptized all three of the Hain boys and steadfastly believed Frankie and Ide – especially Ide, as devout a woman as there'd ever been – when they claimed they'd seen the light. Winston had endured a ramshackle upbringing and a war. He did not fear death. But he would always fear Francis Hain.

"I'm sorry. I should have called. I failed you. I failed Tommy."

Frankie kept his eyes on Winston as he drained his beer and lowered it to the table. Then he reached over to grip his friend's hands. "We all failed him."

The bartender set a new beer down and retreated.

Frankie went on. "In my dream, Tommy starts talking 'bout all the people we lost. All those taken before their time. David. Natty. My sweet Ide...The Hain Curse. As much as I despise the phrase, it's a proper spell, isn't it?" He gulped half his pint. "There's nothing I wouldn't do for my family. Most days, I'm by myself, watching the waves. But I'm never alone. There are others. I feel 'em watching me, reminding me. They say people get like this right before they die. It feels like punishment. For the first time, I'm worried about my immortal soul, Winnie. What if Tommy and David and every dreadful thing that's befallen my family...what if it's my fault?"

It is your fault, Winston thought. "Perhaps it's time to unburden yourself."

"Figured you'd say as much. But I gotta admit, it's one of those churchin' things I never quite understood. You truly believe you can be a lout your whole life, then go, oops, sorry, and all's forgiven?"

"I do, as long as the confessor is truly remorseful and makes the proper amends."

"What if you're wrong?"

"This is not something I've decided on my own. It's scripture."

"Then it doesn't matter when I ask for absolution as long as I unburden myself before I slough off."

"Whatever it is you're thinking of doing—"

"I hear there's attention being paid to two girls raised in your care."

"They are not involved."

"Ehh, I don't know. Seems the coppers are hunting Riley Gideon as hard as they're hunting Stratton."

"Hunting is a strong word—"

"This Underhill dick brought her sister in for a chat. A chat interrupted by you, Winnie. Why'd you go racing down to cop central? Why so eager to expose Tommy's debt to the cops when you hadn't even informed his fucking family?"

A river of ice race ran through Winston's veins. "I'm sorry I didn't come to you. But I swear Beck has no connection to Tommy's troubles. I raised her. She's like…"

"A daughter."

"Yes."

"And you'd do anything for her?"

"Just about."

"Now you know how I feel." He uttered the words in a low, almost accusatory tone. "But that's Beck, not the older one. Riley. Tommy's pump, from what I'm now hearing. Twenty years off and on. I mean, he had lots of girlfriends. Nobody could keep up, and we all feel even more terrible about how little we knew about his life. But this Riley goes back forever, it seems. One of the druggies."

"They were friends. She worked at the club."

"And now she's taken a powder. With a fuckton of cash."

"I don't know where you're getting your information—"

"Everywhere, Winnie. Everybody's chirping. I need to ken what's idle speculation and what's hand-of-God truth. And my first wondering is how a couple of low-rent wretches from Dyer hooked into a rich kid from the North Shore?"

Winston shifted to offset his distress. Frankie was edging into unwanted territory. "They met at a party, I believe. A long time ago."

"She a looker?"

"Frankie."

"Ah, c'mon, you know what I'm saying. Is admitting some gal's easy on the eyes a crime now? There's gotta be a reason they stuck through thick and thin."

"They stuck together because your grandson, for all of his flaws, possessed a kind soul. So does Riley. Tommy was a loyal friend to both her and Beck."

"Then there's no reason for me to go looking into them?"

"There's no reason for you to do anything except let the police handle it."

Frankie called over to the bartender. "Two shots of Jami's, if you please." He straightened his already straight tie again. "I've been sitting in offices too long, Winnie, staring at charts and graphs. I didn't do enough to save Tommy. The least I can do is find the cretins responsible for his death. But don't worry. When it's over, I'll be sure to make amends."

CHAPTER 35

Beck watched her sister gnaw at her cuticles.

"These fuckers. They won't stop," Riley said.

"Who's they?"

"If I knew, I wouldn't be hiding down here. Did you clean the loft?"

"I dumped the bullets without touching them. A sentence I never thought I'd use in my lifetime. But none of that matters anymore."

"What do you mean?"

"This intruder knows what we did." Beck described the video of them putting Washington's body into the GTO. "I caught him hacking our servers."

Riley fired off all the right questions – Why hasn't he gone to the cops? Why did he break into MrGabriel? What's he want, the money? – questions Beck could not answer. Her sister plopped down, grimacing as she rolled her neck back and forth.

"What's the matter?" Beck asked.

"Got an ass-kicking migraine. The concrete floor of a subway line is hardly an air mattress."

"Yeah, well, the floor of a church balcony isn't much better." The headaches used to lay Riley flat. No prescription could allay their debilitating effect. Beck always suspected Riley's migraines as the first impetus to narcotics; despite their corrosive impact on every other facet of her sister's life, at least they dulled the pain in her head.

"You're not looking too spry, either." She touched Beck's forehead. "You're on fire. Sit." She directed her to the stairs and handed her a water bottle.

Beck gulped, the depth of her thirst unrealized until the moisture hit her throat. "Why are you still here? You couldn't get away from me fast enough the other day."

Riley searched her gear. "Dream come true, right?"

"You got the money. You said goodbye…and made it all the way to New Hampshire, only to turn around and come back."

"Unfinished business." Her sister removed a small First Aid kit. "I thought about what you said. A hundred thousand's a lot, but it's not forever money." She helped Beck remove her coat and blouse, then unwrapped the bandage. "Damn, this is ugly. You need a doctor."

"No doctor. Do what you can." Beck watched her clean the area around the staples, accepting Riley's explanation as only somewhat honest; lies worked best when mixed with facts. However, trying to uproot the truth would only waste precious time.

"Tell me about the intruder," Riley said.

"Late twenties, or a young-looking thirties. Black. Nice eyes."

"Nice eyes?"

"Kind you can't look away from. Everything else was designed to be forgotten. Nondescript jacket. Chuck Taylors. Don't get me wrong. He scared the hell out of me, but…yeah, he was good-looking. Had a tiny scar."

Her sister slowed. "Just over his left eye…John Morrell."

"You know him?"

"He was one of our biggest customers."

CHAPTER 36

"You didn't have customers," Beck said, her distrust heating up. "That's what you told me."

"I said we didn't have enough customers. Morrell started coming in a couple of months ago, flashing cash. Tommy introduced him to Stratton. The three of 'em had a total bromance." Morrell, Riley thought. Of all the people...Beck was right; he did have nice eyes. But why was he snooping around MrGabriel?

"Who is he?"

"Some poo-bah from out of town. He paid for private parties. Rented out the whole second floor."

"For who?"

"He asked us to bring the guests. At first, maybe he thought we could access A-listers. The best we could do was Z-list, but Morrell didn't care. He loved making it rain and lording over a packed dance floor. He breezed in every two, three weeks. Paid for an open bar. The only big business we got was when John Morrell came to town. Wasn't enough to keep us afloat, though. Not nearly."

"How do you know he was just visiting?"

"He referenced his travels. He was a consultant – for whom and doing what he never said. Once, he offered me a thousand bucks to return to his room at the Encore."

"Did you?"

"Beck!" Riley half-shoved her. "For all the crap I've done, I've never turned a trick!" What she didn't offer up is that the proposal had sent a thrill through her. John Morrell oozed confidence, unlike the spastic, amped-up bros who surrounded her at Round Midnight. She'd never met anyone like him, and if he hadn't propositioned her like some Blue Hill hooker and instead offered to, like, take her out on a proper date, he might have gotten what he wanted. She felt guilty about the attraction because of Tommy, but John Morrell struck her as the kind of guy who could change a life.

"Just because he rented a hotel room doesn't mean he's from out of town."

"Then why ask us to populate his parties? He never brought a single friend or associate."

"I assume Stratton supplied the party favors. It wasn't just the free drinks people showed up for."

"Look, if you're asking me if there was some gangster shit going down, the answer is yes. People don't disappear in the can for twenty minutes to comb their hair."

"But you looked the other way."

"You're damn right, and if you want me to apologize, you can forget it. I do what it takes to survive dusk to dawn."

"Oh, I know. It's all the way with you. No middle ground."

"Middle ground's for pussies. The second you compromise is the second you show weakness. Morrell made things happen. And I desperately needed to make things happen. Because of you, Beck. Because I hurt you and wanted to win you back."

"You never lost me—"

"You ghosted me for five months! I know we embarrassed you at graduation, but you always forgave me before. And then you open an office in the town we grew up in, and I still don't get a call." She hadn't intended to tell Beck how she felt, but Riley's emotions often had a mind of their own. "And I get it, okay? I'm not saying this to make you feel bad. All of us, me, Father W, the Lunatic, Tommy – we always wanted you to move on, and there you were, moving on. I don't know why I wasn't ready for it. Seeing you mingling with all those bigshots, watching them seek your approval – and yeah, I followed you a couple of times because what else could I do? – it meant everything to me. But it also hurt. I knew it was penance or something, but it stung. So I kept my mouth shut and did my job because the next time I saw you, I wanted to look you in the eye, tell you I was clean and mean it. But surprise, surprise, even sober, I still found a way to fuck everything up." She tied Beck's bandage and folded her legs beneath her, nibbling at her cuticles until they started to bleed.

"Stop."

"Leave me alone."

Beck held her hands. "Riley. Stop." She grabbed an antiseptic pad from the First Aid kit to clean her sister's gashed fingers. Three of them required band-aids. "I thought it was tough love."

"It was. Most definitely."

"Curing addiction is about support. And I took mine away when you needed it the most. I'm sorry."

Riley stared for a long time as if gauging Beck's sincerity. "I'm sorry I'm such an idiot."

"You're not. You're smart. Brilliant, even. You've just convinced yourself you're stupid." She cleaned Riley's face with another swab. "And you need to stop apologizing and feeling sorry for yourself 'cause I need your help."

"To do what?"

"Find Z Stratton."

CHAPTER 37

As he departed Four Treasures, Jordan plugged a set of headphones into the Klover MiK's recorder and listened to the playback. At nine inches, it was one of the market's most compact parabolic microphones. It fit inside the puffy ski jacket he'd bought at a vintage clothing store, a gaudy atrocity that, combined with a grayed-out wig, scraggly goatee spirit-gummed to his chin and coke-bottle glasses, completed his role of a sad townie barfly. The limp from his injured back reinforced the appearance of a beat-down soul who lived for cheap drinks and sports.

Getting close to Francis Hain initially seemed futile. His bodyguards stood out like roughnecks at a baby shower. But then a spot opened up at a four-top near his booth, and Jordan scampered onto the stool. When a woman with platinum hair looking to score strolled over, he plied her with drinks as the Klover MiK recorded Hain's conversation.

Coming here had been risky because of the possibility Hain would see through the disguise of the man he'd earmarked for permanent removal. However, Jordan was bereft of leads. The connective tissue, the motives, the existentialism of it all, remained out of reach. His mentor once said, "The most powerful person in the area code is either the source of trouble or the reason for it. If you get off-course, work the VIP; they are your North Star." A version of Follow the Money but more comprehensive: the shot-caller was typically the nucleus around which all events revolved.

The VIP associated with this ordeal was Francis Hain. And who showed up to meet with him? Father Winston Ismera, surrogate poppa to flavor-of-the-month Beck Gideon and her renegade sister. As Jordan listened to the recording, it became clear "Winnie" and "Frankie" were old friends. Frankie sounded prepared to raze the city to the ground to find his grandson's murderer. Winnie seemed eager to redirect Frankie's scorched-earth strategy. Did the *padre* know the Gideons greased Washington? One of many questions Jordan still needed to answer, but at least he'd confirmed that the sisters warranted further examination.

Sufficiently distant from Four Treasures and its stumbling clientele, Jordan removed the headphones and slid them inside the puffy coat beside the parabolic. He peeled off the goatee and used a makeup remover pad to dissolve the spirit gum. He did the same with the wig, returning to his buzz-cut, then folded the coke-bottle glasses into his shirt pocket.

The client's vehicle waited at the intersection of Faragut and William J. Out beyond the sand, the ebony ocean gleamed under a harvest moon. Jordan grimaced as he lowered himself onto the leather backseat. He scanned the interior for any threats. The linebacker-sized driver raised the glass partition to give them privacy.

"Are you okay?" his client asked from the opposing bench.

"Fine, why?"

"You're limping."

Jordan searched for any indication his client already knew the source of his pain. "Tripped going up the stairs."

"What did you learn?"

"The Gideons are the linchpin."

"How do you know?"

"I'm still putting it together. Father Ismera shared a drink and some good old-fashioned Catholic guilt with Hain twenty minutes ago and did his best to deflect Francis' pending wrath away from the girls."

The client considered this, swirling an amber-colored whiskey in a crystal highball that probably cost more than he made in a month. "The neighborhood priest continues to surprise."

"Francis asked how two broke-ass orphans linked to his grandson."

"Easy, they were both delinquents."

"Except Tommy was a well-connected delinquent, unlike Riley. But despite all the interventions and second chances, he always gravitated back to her. Why?"

"What did Father W say?"

"Tommy had a kind heart."

His client guffawed. Despite being on different ends of the high-tension wires powering the elite, Jordan and his client had learned enough to know "kindness" was the stuff of fairy tales. "The *padre* and that tech-wiz zoomer know more than they're letting on."

"Do you have more than a cryptic conversation between two old-timers to support that?"

"Not yet, but I know. Trust me."

His client paused mid-drink. "Trust you?"

Damn.

Bad choice of words.

"Trust doesn't exist in my line of work, Jordan. I need facts. I hired you because you said you could find the answers nobody wants found."

"I can."

Barbara Azakian finished her drink. "Then why are you still sitting here?"

CHAPTER 38

Riley checked her phone – it was just before 4 AM. Waking up super early had become more of a common occurrence. She couldn't pinpoint its start, but it had picked up in frequency since living clean, as if her addiction wanted to deprive her of solid rest as punishment for going cold turkey.

While staring at Beck in the sleeping bag, Riley's mind drifted back to less complicated times when they formed an atypical but caring family at St. J's, not long ago in years, but in spirit, another era. They'd been so tight. The age gap didn't matter. If anything, their bond was fortified because of it. Beck wanted nothing more than to hang by Riley's side. They'd spent many nights just like this, watching a movie or listening to the .mp3 player Tommy had gifted on Riley's birthday, Beck maintaining a safe distance, even from Riley, but *close*.

Beck's forehead was still warm. She desperately needed her meds. She'd continued to check in with her friends and lie about seeking treatment for her arm, determined to maintain a low profile until they tracked down John Morrell and Z Stratton.

Riley had laughed when she first proposed it. "And then what, Ivy League? Swoop in like Lara Croft and take 'em down? I'm supposed to be the crazy one, remember?"

"Morrell's got a ton of dough. He rented out the club and bought drugs off Stratton. Who better to give him safe harbor? At the very least, Morrell might know where to find him. And we might be the only ones who know about Morrell's existence. The news hasn't mentioned him, and he didn't come up in any of my interactions with the cops."

"They might be keeping his identity to themselves."

"Possibly, but he's our last lead."

"Lead? Who are you, Nancy Drew? Stay out of it."

"I tried, and I'm getting mugged inside my office. No more pretending. No more hoping for the best. I'm too pissed off. Do you know how to contact Stratton, or don't you?"

"I don't. Tommy didn't want me interacting with that maniac."

"What about Morrell?"

"I have an email. I coordinated the parties. Even organized limo service to chariot him around. I trashed my phone, but I can log into my account and find the history of our convos."

"Was he at the club Friday night?"

"I don't think so."

"Yet he filmed us stuffing Washington's corpse into Tommy's car. He's more than just a high-roller, Riles."

"Fine, but do you think he's gonna help us just 'cause we ask nicely?"

"Let me worry about that."

With a plan of action in place, Beck had yawned and crawled into the sleeping bag, claiming she just wanted to rest her eyes. She was out the rest of the night.

Riley would forever regret racing to Dyer after the massacre at the club. Hurt and terrified, she'd needed to recuperate to figure out what to do, and okay, sure, a part of her had hoped Beck could convert the cash into untraceable ones and zeroes. But if Riley had known it would lead to all this, she would have driven her and Tommy off a cliff and called it a life. Locating Morrell would only prolong Beck's jeopardy, but once she got an idea in her head…

Her dedication and discipline were off the charts. Beck had avoided all the vice Riley indulged – never snuck off to smoke cigarettes in Ronan Park, never filched booze from Gleason Liquors whose owner could barely see past the checkout counter and never set foot inside any of the flops and illegal raves. Beck viewed these activities as unwise and very, very dull. Kids thought she was an egghead brown-noser when she volunteered for laundry or kitchen duty, powered through the donated library, ran math problems *for fun* and helped Lucinda tend the garden every spring, researching optimal pH levels. They didn't get it. Beck wasn't trying to curry favor or avoid trouble; she was staying busy. As Riley once pointed out to a grabby boy bullying Beck for her brainiac tendencies, prompting Riley to cram his head into the toilet, "Sitting around bitchin' about life just ain't my sister's style."

Partnering up also allowed Riley to watch over her and steer her away from perilous territory. Any hope of restoring their union relied on controlling the narrative and keeping certain aspects of Riley's involvement hidden.

So she decided to follow Beck's lead.

For the time being.

CHAPTER 39

Beck woke up to a breakfast of Sunny Doodles and bottled cold brew. An array of medicine, wet naps, deodorant, toothpaste, toothbrush, face cloths and antiperspirant sat beside the food. One of her business suits hung from the railing. "Did you go to my loft?"

"Used the fire escape and came in through the roof deck. You really gotta do something about that cheap-ass lock."

"Riley—"

"Relax, no one saw me."

"How do you know?"

"Because it's been five hours, and a S.W.A.T. team hasn't filled the tunnel with tear gas." Riley waited while Beck swallowed her pills, then showed her an email on the burner.

"John Morrell?"

"The one and only. Guess I'm good for something."

"Before you pat yourself on the back, realize we are hiding in an abandoned subway line eating Hostess pastries."

"It's Drake's, thank you very much, and look what it says on the wrapper: Freshness Guaranteed."

Beck downed the coffee and cupcakes, then climbed up to the door to improve her connection. "Morning, G. I'm going offline and then changing devices. Please run a backup." She waited while he copied her phone's device-specific settings, preferences, passwords and contact data to the cloud.

Done. When will I see you again?

"Soon. I hope."

Riley grinned. "I'd love to take him for a test drive one day."

"Anytime. After all, you created him."

Her sister blushed with pride.

"By the way, why did you bring me dress clothes?"

"In case you had to go to work or something. Besides, aren't you all fancy now?"

"Smartass…Let's get cleaned up. Remember how to dodge?"

"Hey, I taught you."

Ten minutes later, they were ready to go. Beck bunched her hair up inside her knit hat and raised the lapels of her pea coat. Riley pocketed her sunglasses, lowered her baseball cap and shrugged on the backpack.

Bargain-rack spies.

Rather than charge out into the unknown through the exit over their heads, her sister said they could cover a significant portion of the trip underground. She led the way into a narrow access tunnel, which eventually reached the working area of the T. Beck noted the alcoves for maintenance staff and inspectors to "dodge" passing trains. They crossed into the Orange Line, heard the din of a subway car and leaped into alcoves before the train whooshed by in a vortex of wind.

"Gimme your burner." Beck took a pen from her pocket and copied Morrell's email onto a dollar bill, then set her phone and Riley's burner on the tracks to await their demise, fiberoptic damsels lashed to the rails in a new age Western. She felt momentarily uneasy; it had been years since she'd gone without Mr. G monitoring her proximity, answering questions and offering advice.

"Let's say this all goes according to plan, and we root out Morrell and Stratton," Riley said. "Then what?"

"We call Underhill, the FBI, the State Police, John Oliver and freakin' Oprah and post everything online before the ringleaders can spin it to their advantage. And we beeline to Barbara Azakian for help. She's got real juice and plays by her own rules."

"My kind of lady."

Twice more they dodged before reaching Stony Brook station. They perched at the platform's edge while passengers got on and off the train. After it departed, they ran up the short flight of stairs to the empty platform, the riskiest part of their journey. Any guards monitoring the cameras would come running to question the unauthorized tunnel dwellers. Beck and Riley hurried up to a herd of commuters leaving the station.

The police waited outside.

Beck came up short, trapped, indecisive. The patrol, however, had their backs to the station, checking arrivals, reasonably sure their targets were not, by chance, already creeping around inside. The cruiser's tailpipe puffed white clouds into the cold air. She looped her arm through Riley's and used the exhaust to cover their deviation onto Paul Gore Street.

As they crossed Centre Street, she told Riley to keep watch while she entered a wireless store. Twenty minutes later, she exited with a plastic bag and led her sister into Mozart Park. The sounds of a rousing pickup game orchestrated the area while older gents in windbreakers and earmuffs played speed chess. Beck chose a table far from the action and showed Riley her purchases: a second-hand iPad, two Bluetooth earbuds and two cell phones with prepaid SIMs.

"Did the clerk ask for ID?" her sister asked.

"It's not required, and he was too busy watching SportsCenter." She powered up the disposables and scuffed one against the table's edge before dropping it on the asphalt until the screen cracked.

"What are you doing?"

"I want it to look beat up like its owner." Beck explained her plan for the burner.

"Damn, maybe you're the crazy one after all."

CHAPTER 40

Jordan heard a ding on his phone – an email notification from his John Morrell account.

Sent from "Round Midnight."

He sat up in the POS, feeling the ice bag crinkle against his back. He read the message. Typically, he would never even open an unknown email, but these were not typical times, and he was pretty confident he knew the sender's identity. He dialed the number referenced in the message.

Riley Gideon answered. "Yeah."

"It's me."

"Me who?" she asked.

"Don't play games."

"I won't if you leave my sister alone."

"I can't. Not until we talk."

"You can start anytime."

"Not on the phone. Where are you?"

"Public Library. Before the hour or I'm history." She disconnected.

He entered the number into a lookup program. It confirmed Riley's location next to the library. He threw the POS in gear and sped out to Route 9, leaving his post outside MrGabriel's headquarters, realizing he had wasted the day: the sisters must have reunited. It explained Beck's absence from work.

He moved his Colt from the harness to his outside pocket, determined never to be caught off-guard again.

CHAPTER 41

Beck lingered behind the colonnade of Trinity Church, half-hidden under the archway. She could barely keep Riley in view because of the foot traffic across Copley Square, the crowds dense as the end of the workday approached. She clenched whenever someone came within striking distance of her sister, assuming it was John Morrell going in for the kill. Beck's plan hinged for speed, a swift exchange after which her sister would walk away. Under no circumstances was Riley to accompany him anywhere, get in his car, or allow him to follow—

"Fancy meeting you here."

She whipped around so fast she nearly fell over.

John Morrell – the intruder – crowded Beck against the brick columns, hands stuffed into his coat pockets. Every nerve shot to life at the invasion of her personal space. "How did you—"

"What am I, an amateur?" He motioned with one pocket. "Move."

Beck moved, picturing a gun concealed within that motion. They crossed the plaza and then the street, heading for the library. Riley tensed as they approached.

"My car's on St. James," Morrell said, cocking his head in that direction.

"We're not going anywhere," her sister replied, pulling Beck over. "And I want you to know something, John. You ever put your hands on her again, I'll kill you. Nothing will stop me. Look at me and tell me I'm lying."

"You're not lying."

"We'll answer your questions, but first, we have one of our own. Who the hell are you?"

"A concerned citizen and you're not in charge here, Riley. Not with what I've got on my phone." He drew out a thin device about the size of a pen. "Stand still." He ran it over their bodies. A light at the tip turned blue.

"We're not bugged," Beck said.

He pocketed the scanner. "Then you won't mind telling me who put the kibosh on Washington."

"He fell," Riley said. "After he tried to kill us."

"Why did he want to kill you?"

"The money. Maybe Washington worked for Stratton, and the exchange went south. Or maybe he wanted to grab himself a bonus. It's not the kind of cash that gets reported stolen."

Morrell rechecked his perimeters.

Something's off, Beck thought. She'd encountered a conniver and brute inside HQ. Riley had described a slick high-roller from out of town. Morrell's behavior, posture, and tone didn't square. He looked and sounded like a man scrambling for answers, using bluster to cover up his trepidation.

"Friday night," he said to Riley. "Run it down."

She recounted the events. Getting knocked out. Waking up to a battlefield. Tommy and her running for their lives. Holding Tommy as he bled out.

"How'd he raise the money?" Morrell asked.

"Couldn't tell ya."

"Why didn't you call the police?"

"Did you miss the part about the cops trying to kill us? I thought we were cool, John. You were nice to me. Know how many customers were nice to me in six years at that place? When Beck described her attacker, I couldn't believe it. If you're riding with Stratton, you're on the losing side."

"I'm not on anyone's side but my own."

"So you don't know where to find him."

"No."

"Or contact him."

"He gave me a list of numbers to order party favors, but that doesn't make us friends. I'd love to see that nutjob go down, but there are still too many gaps, too many unknowns for me to be comfortable."

"And you thought the answers might be on my servers?" Beck asked.

"Or your email, your phone, the junk drawer in your kitchen, the mailbox in your foyer you rarely check – you don't know what you'll find or where."

Beck bristled at the thought that this man had been rooting around in her life even before their confrontation at HQ.

"Maybe this will help." Riley pulled out the second burner, the one Beck had damaged. "It's Tommy's."

Morrell's eyes came alight, but he made no move to take it. "Just when I think I got you two pegged, you deal me another surprise."

"You want it or not?"

He hesitated – then snatched the burner out of her hand.

"We don't know the code," Beck said. "Maybe you got someone who can break it."

"You don't?"

"Contrary to popular belief, not everyone in tech is a professional hacker…Look. We all want answers and to avoid getting dragged deeper into Stratton and Tommy's cluster."

"Is that right?"

"Yes. That's why you haven't turned that recording over to the cops."

"I could send it in anonymously."

"You could, but doing so won't fill in the gaps. It also risks the police tracking the footage back to you. After all, how do you know a nearby security cam didn't record you lurking outside my loft?"

He reached behind to rub his back.

"You got all the power here, John," Riley said, selling the angle Beck had laid out. "You know everything we do, probably more. Once Stratton's dead or in jail, we'll turn over the money, make a statement, whatever, but if you don't give us a reason to mention your name, we won't. Do whatever you gotta do; just leave us out of it." She took Beck's hand.

"Wait."

"No. We're done." Riley led Beck away.

They'd know in the next few seconds if the plan stood any chance of success. Morrell wouldn't gun them down on a bustling Back Bay street, but he might try to follow them to a spot where aggression became possible. Beck was betting the feint of giving him "Tommy's phone" would bolster their desire to be left alone, that they were not privy to any other critical information. Exclusive evidence for mercy.

They reached the corner of Boylston and turned around.

Morrell was gone.

"Holy shit!" Riley said. "We did it."

"Don't get too excited. The next step's even harder."

"Following him?"

"Asking Amy and Eli for help."

CHAPTER 42

"You were right; I've been keeping secrets," Beck said.

Riley felt terrible watching her admit to deception. They sat inside one of the library's private study rooms. On Beck's burner, Amy and Eli stared back over Zoom. Getting Amy to answer the unknown number, grab Eli, and find a quiet spot inside their office took a few minutes.

She'd met Beck's friends a few times and liked them enough, even if they came off a bit snobphisticated. Mostly, Riley was envious of their closeness with Beck. Amy and Eli didn't appear surprised by Beck's confessional, just incredibly hurt.

And they don't even know the full deets. Beck left out Washington's plummet down the elevator shaft and Riley's river work.

"So you knew where your sister was this whole time," Eli said.

"And the power outage was because a hacker broke in," Amy added.

"I'm sorry. I realize those words ring pretty hollow right now, but there's more to what's being said. A lot more."

"How did you hurt your arm?" Eli asked. "Where did those bloody bandages come from?"

"From me," Riley said. "I ran to Beck's after Round Midnight. I was all banged up. She half-carried me up to her loft. I tripped and knocked over the bust. She cut her arm on the shards, trying to catch me. I'm the one you should be mad at, not her."

The temperature dropped in the room as the sun fell outside.

"How can we believe either of you?" Amy asked.

"If I were in your shoes, I'd be asking myself the same thing," Beck said. "But I need your help."

Eli laughed while Amy leaned back and pressed her fingers to her eyes.

"We're tracking someone who might have answers for us. I set them up as a Lost One."

"You used Mr. G?" Eli asked.

"I installed the app on a burner and enabled all the takeover functionality, like the world's biggest helicopter parent. The longer we wait, though, the bigger his lead."

"Why didn't you just turn on Find My?"

"Because I need more than just his location. I need to tune in, and a cell connection is too unreliable to render all the calcs in real-time. Also, I need your mindshare."

An incredulous beat cut across the screen.

"After everything we've done together," Amy said, "all the hard work and hours we put in, I can't believe you're doing this."

"She didn't," Riley said. "I did."

Beck shook her head. "No. I made my own choices."

Her friends exchanged glances. Riley expected one of them to disconnect. However, whatever remained of their friendship – their undeniable history – kept them online.

Amy typed on her laptop. "The most recent install belongs to a John Morrell."

"That's him."

"He's heading north up Beacon."

"I'm tethered to the burner," Eli said. He angled Amy's camera to his laptop.

John Morrell's voice bristled through the speaker. "…no, it can't wait!"

Eli accessed the burner's camera through his administrative access. Morrell appeared and disappeared, swinging back and forth. Judging from the angle, he held the burner by his waist as he spoke on another cell.

Riley retreated a step.

"Don't worry," Beck said, "he can't see or hear us."

"And he doesn't know the app is running?"

"Not with the phone locked," Eli said. "Takeover functionality is precisely what it sounds like. You can assume full control of a phone. Beck wasn't kidding when she said helicopter parent, but it's integral to saving a child who's threatened or incapacitated."

Morrell's voice reclaimed their attention. "What do I got? Try Tommy Hain's phone…Don't worry about how. The point is, it's in my hand…Yeah, the usual spot." He ended his call, and the burner went black as he shoved it into his pocket.

"Put in your Bluetooth," Eli said.

Beck slid one earbud home.

The Zoom cut out.

A second later, Amy and Eli called on the burner.

"Let's go," Beck said, leading Riley out at a fast trot.

CHAPTER 43

Beck paired the second earbud to her burner and handed it to Riley so she could receive Amy and Eli's oversight. A panicky forty minutes followed when Amy lost Morrell's signal before it popped back up outside Haymarket Station. They risked a taxi ride to his location on Salem Street. Morrell made no more calls, and the view from his burner remained smudged out inside his pocket.

"He's turning onto Stillman," Amy said. "Stopped just outside a park...He's got the phone out...sitting down and...I don't know...grimacing? Looks like he's arching his back."

Beck led Riley into Tre Monte. At the bar, she ordered two double espressos. The jolt only slightly settled her nerves.

"This is genius," her sister said.

"Yeah, it's great," Amy replied, "if the whole kid thing doesn't work out, we can license Mr. G to the CIA."

"What happens when he realizes you tricked him?" Eli asked.

"We're already targets," Beck said. "What's he gonna do – kill us harder? At least he'll know we're not gonna roll over." She found Riley grinning at her. "What?"

"You're good at this. Who'd a thunk?"

"It's a problem."

"No kidding."

"I mean, a philosophical problem. Probabilistic causation. A fancy way of saying, figure out what happened based on the outcomes."

"Like, two trains leave Boston and New York on the same track; how long until everyone dies in a fiery head-on collision?"

"I don't quite remember them phrased that way, but it's the other way around: the two trains crashed. Create a list of potential reasons and test which ones are most likely."

"Your scenario is also more complex," Eli added. "It's an unknown number of trains on an unknown number of tracks."

"Sounds unsolvable," Riley said.

"It's not," Beck said. "Just takes longer to figure out."

"What's your gut say?"

"Stratton and Morrell conspired to take the money and eliminate the witnesses, and somehow Washington messed up their plan."

"I hear a car," Amy said. "A door just slammed...Hang on...We'll put you close to the speaker."

"—not how this works," a man said, not Morrell, raspy, as if breathing was a chore.

A heavy smoker, Beck thought.

"Check your text," Amy said.

Beck pulled up her burner: her friends had sent a new Zoom invite. She powered it on to reveal Eli's laptop monitor. The imagery warbled and resolved into another shot from a low angle, half the screen filled by an extreme closeup of Morrell's knee.

"Who gave it to you?" the smoker asked.

"My targets – Rebecca and Riley Gideon."

Beck shuddered at his use of the word "targets" and the possibility he might show the smoker the video of their dubious mortuary services.

"Let me see," the smoker said. The video swirled, producing a shot of a large man, unshaven, his tie loose around a bull neck. "Code?"

"Dunno."

Two sharp clacks preceded tendrils of smoke drifting across the screen as the smoker exhaled. "These are not people you cross, Jordan."

"I thought his name was John," Beck said.

Riley shook her head, confused.

"Except Francis Hain is born again," Morrell said.

The smoker snickered. "Hain generates billions. A governor, senator or corporate goliath cuts a ribbon on his latest project every other week. You roll on Hain, you better have the Archangel Michael as backup."

"Was Henry Washington compromised?"

"Why do you ask?"

"He tried to kill the sisters." A beat, then Morrell added: "And someone took a shot at me."

"So that's why you called," the smoker laughed. "You're running scared, and nothing's scarier than Francis Hain with your name on his naughty list." He laughed harder, causing him to cough longer. "I'm guessing your employer's no help."

"Let's put it this way: I can count the number of people I trust on one hand and have all four fingers left over. You gotta give me something."

"I'm not in the lost cause business, kid."

The POV flipped as Morrell took back the burner, now rendering a perfect frame of the car's ceiling. "I've done good work for you."

"Fine." The smoker snatched the phone, the screen going dark as he shoved it into his pocket. "I'll see what I can see. Where can I find you?"

"The boat."

"Still like to fish, huh?"

"It's my job."

"Go."

They heard the door open and close. The sounds of '70s rock filled the car as it sped away.

"See what you can find out about the smoker," Beck said, "but if he unlocks the burner, kill the session and remove the app before he sees it."

"Will do," Eli said.

She took a breath. What needed to be said couldn't be conveyed over a phone call, but their help suggested Amy and Eli weren't ready to banish her yet. "I don't deserve you two."

"Be careful," Amy said.

The conference line and the Zoom call ended.

"Maybe he's a cop," Beck said. "You've been around enough of them; what do you think?"

"First, bite me. Second, Morrell's no cop."

"Then we see where he leads us." Beck jumped off her stool, edging to the entrance, nervous about following Morrell on foot—

—he was ten feet from the restaurant's front door.

She pushed back through the after-work crowd, a few calling out "Whoa" and "Watch it!" and the ever-popular "Where's the fire?" She snagged Riley's hand.

The front door opened over the heads of the patrons.

Beck hauled Riley into the sole, unisex bathroom. Before the door shut, she glanced back—

Morrell weaved through the crowd, heading straight for them.

She yanked Riley into a stall.

"What the—"

She pressed a finger to her sister's lips, climbed up on the commode and turned Riley around so her feet faced the right way.

Outside, heavy steps faltered across the linoleum – Morrell entering in his pained shuffle. Had he seen them? Was he cornering his prey?

Through the door's crack, a movement of color as he passed by.

Beck tensed, ready to run, to attack. The wall unit flushed. She never thought she'd be so happy to hear a toilet flushing. Water flowed from a tap. The towel dispenser activated. Finally, the voices from the restaurant rose and fell with the opening and closing of the door.

Riley peeked, then exited the stall. She cracked the bathroom door open an inch, peering out. "I think he left."

"You think?"

They stepped out into the restaurant.

No Morrell.

Beck leaned towards the window.

Outside, Morrell limped down Salem Street back towards the city.

CHAPTER 44

They tailed Morrell until he descended to the Orange Line. A crush of riders concealed them in the quick hop to Community College in Charlestown. The neighborhood once mistakenly christened the bank robbery capital of America. Like Dyer, close-knit Charlestown was once wary of strangers and cultivated a healthy skepticism of authority. And just like Dyer, the spirit was being gentrified right out of existence as moneyed professionals moved in, driving prices up and long-time homeowners out.

Beck and Riley walked amidst the renewed population heading home. The endless, nose-to-tail lines of cars on both sides of tight streets also provided cover, which was good because Morrell frequently stopped to knead his lower back and check the roads and alleys around him, even the rooftops. He walked with as much purpose as his ailing back allowed, following what seemed to be a random path.

Riley began to pant, her face scarlet. Not a raspy respiration like the smoker, but born of weakness, a lack of even casual exercise. Beck wondered how much damage her sister – once an athletic marvel – had done to her body. She hoped she didn't collapse in a pile on the sidewalk.

After traversing a mile across Charlestown, Morrell entered the Marina. According to its website, the boatyard had undergone a massive upgrade in the last decade and now anchored four hundred boats ranging from pleasure craft to three-hundred-foot yachts. No longer the docks of working seafarers, the webpage described the Marina as "state-of-the-art," which must have made any old-school Townie struggle to hold down their chowder.

"Think it's Stratton?" Riley asked in-between gusting breaths.

"No better hiding spot than a boat. From here, he can motor out to sea, north up the Mystic, out to Chelsea Creek or straight down the Charles if he got through the harbor locks."

"Cops gotta be checking the waterways."

"They'd have to stop every boat and search the thousands docked around the city."

"Then let's call in the cavalry."

"Not until we know if he's aligned with Stratton. We only get one shot at this."

They turned off 13th into the seaside mists. A handful of boats in the Marina were lit up. The others appeared as dark, bobbing hulks. Beck counted four docks between two sea walls with vessels of all sizes in between: two- and four-seaters to their left and near shore, cruisers and yachts to their right and closer to London. Setting up for a more expansive vantage point behind a series of two-story brick apartments, Beck still couldn't locate Morrell.

Her sister clenched against her wheezing, only for her teeth to start chattering in the blistering ocean air. "Think he spotted us?"

"I don't know. The main office is closed. So is the repair shop. The parking lot's behind us, so we'd have seen him if he'd detoured there. If he went into the restrooms, we'll know in a few minutes; otherwise, the only hiding spots left are the boats. How many are not winterized?"

"A lot."

Some hearty owners maintained a permanent residence on their boats. The Marina offered showers, WiFi, water and sewage, mailing addresses and electricity. Most, though, wrapped up their boats like Faberge eggs to stave off the howling winds of winter or pulled them out of the water to store in dry dock. Beck assumed you couldn't live onboard a winterized boat – those wrapped in heavy plastic or vinyl – unless you wanted to be carted out from carbon monoxide poisoning. Unfortunately, late October was warm enough for daytime cruises, so most remained uncovered.

Riley took out a flask.

"Seriously? After all your huffing and puffing?"

"Feel free to sign me up for Pilates should we make it to morning."

"Thought you were clean."

"I am. I can control this." She took a long gulp. "Sure you don't want a tipple?"

"Positive," Beck said, cold gnawing her flesh but not wanting to sanction her sister's exceptions to the term "clean."

She and Riley snuck out along the first pier. Camera baubles dotted the Marina. Like Stony Brook station, she hoped the cameras were there to record and not provide a live feed to security personnel; they couldn't afford to turn back now. John Morrell was their last hope of locating Z Stratton.

With the moon blanketed by clouds, the primary light source issued from tiny bulbs atop the posts. The undulating watercraft induced near-vertigo, listing and leaning, making Beck feel trapped in a barely buoyant labyrinth that could topple over and drown her at any moment. She slid her hand along the railings to steady herself. Her sister moved like an old salt; apparently, all it took was a few ounces of low-rent whiskey to restore her dexterity.

Prowling around the non-winterized boats, they put their ears to doors and eyes to windows. The seaward inhabitants lounged with a book, gaped at their phones, clicked through TV, dozed, drank or screwed. The Marina might have looked deserted, but there was a surprising amount of activity below decks. Just no Morrell or Stratton.

"This is gonna take all night," Riley said. "And what if he's on one of those?" She pointed at the vessels anchored offshore.

"No way. We would have seen him rowing out."

"Then we gotta get closer. Do a more thorough search." Her sister handed Beck the backpack.

"What are you—"

"We both know I'm quicker and quieter even with a fifth of Kessler in me and half a lung. Just don't lose that bag." She winked as if they were playing hide 'n seek or capture the flag and not trying to root out a lethal adversary. She scampered up and onto the next boat.

Beck crouched in the shadow of its hull. Riley slid along the deck, inspecting windows and doors, all locked. She shook her head, slid down and quickstepped to the next possibility. The top door opened. Beck held her breath as Riley disappeared inside, her chest close to bursting until her sister reappeared.

By the time they reached the third pier, Beck felt more confident. Riley was no more than a slip against the night and smothered her coughing fits by burying her face into the lapels of her coat. At one point, they had to hide between two yachts as a couple returned with takeout from Daily Catch. A second couple emerged from the bowels of a large sailboat and escorted their friends inside. Strains of music drifted out a second later.

Riley indicated the bigger boats parked horizontally against the end of the docks. The first one was V-shaped, its mast a good fifty feet above the water, the name *Chaya* emblazoned across its hull. Given the location, though, there were no hiding spots. Her sister nodded at a nearby motorboat. Beck shook her head. Riley insisted with a flick of her wrist. Beck climbed into a cockpit about three feet deep, lined with benches, the controls inaccessible under a locked cabinet. She watched her sister leap up and snare *Chaya*'s railing.

And immediately lose her grip.

Beck hissed, waiting for Morrell or Stratton to pop out to check the disturbance, but Riley landed softly and jumped back up as the night endured, its soft percussion covering her insurgence.

In her earliest days at St. J's, wary of being lit up by Lucinda the Lunatic's all-seeing flashlight, Riley had been a regular cat burglar, slipping off and on campus undetected, experiences which taught her the art of moving furtively. The trick was to roll your feet, heel to toe. The idea you "tiptoed" was ludicrous – that only tired out your feet, and when tired, the *tap-tap-tap* of a person skulking around on the tips of their toes was as loud as a woodpecker. You set your heel, then rolled to your toes, gliding forward. A soft pair of shoes helped, like the cross-trainers she'd been wearing since her teen years. There'd have to be three feet of snow on the ground for Riley to swap out her sneaks, and they now elided her around the boat's upper deck. She paused to listen through the hatches, continuing along the boat's edge, the ocean churning beneath her. Her teeth clacked harder just thinking about how cold those waters would be as she wondered for the umpteenth time why she continued to live in the Great White North.

Two reasons and only two: Tommy and Beck. Riley had hoped Beck would choose another location – like California or Texas – to set up MrGabriel, so she and Tommy could follow. Yeah, Boston was home. It was also the source of all her torment. With Tommy gone, maybe Riley could convince Beck to relocate. The workers wouldn't care. They were all babies. They'd consider it a lark.

First, they needed to bring this ordeal to a close, and only Riley understood it involved more than just exposing Morrell and Stratton. Beck must never learn all the circumstances leading up to the carnage at Round Midnight; losing Tommy was already more than Riley could stomach.

As she reached the back of the boat – *Prow? Stern? The fuck did she know from boats?* – Riley leaned over the railing to check the windows. On this side, a blue-gray hue etched one curtain. She noticed a door to her right. Reached out and tried the handle: locked. She heel-toed it to the main hatch. Gripped the handle and slowly turned. The bolt slid out of the strike with a soft pop. A short ladder led down, the light more pronounced in the hallway below. She set one foot on the top rung. Thankfully, it didn't grate or groan. There was only the calm of the Marina.

Until Beck started shouting.

CHAPTER 45

She ignored her buzzing cell at first, then finally read Amy's text:

PICK UP!

A call followed.

Beck answered. "Hey—"

"Get out of there! They're coming!"

Amy kept shouting, but Beck was already scanning the Marina. It wasn't until the shape passed through one of the pier-post lights his movement caught her attention. His rifle and face cover suggested he wasn't returning from a late-night fishing expedition, and his destination was clear: the V-shaped boat.

She jumped up. "Riley, look out!"

Her sister spun around as Beck pointed toward the hunter.

A stream of hornets pocked Beck's location.

Bullets. Fired from the dock behind her.

A *second* hunter.

She hit the deck and crawled towards the outboard motors, rounds ripping up wood and fiberglass. She slung the backpack of money over her shoulder and dove headfirst to the pier, using her hands to cushion the impact. The docked boats on either side protected her.

But there was nowhere left to run.

Riley sprinted towards the wide end of *Chaya*'s V-shape. At first, the gunfire streamed elsewhere – at Beck! – but a second later, another torrent perforated her boat. It sounded like a chainsaw chewing through plastic. If she returned to the dock, the shooter could close his eyes and still score about ten bullseyes. Nothing but water on the opposite side. The only path was directly away from the shooter. She planted one foot on the rear bench and leaped over the cold, cold sea.

The railing of the adjoining boat slammed into her gut, knocking out what little air remained in her constricted lungs. The thought of the gushing brine cued a surge of adrenaline.

Kicking, pulling, grunting, she hauled herself onto the next boat and kept running.

The second hunter stepped between the docked boats. Took his time reloading. Beck's only option was to jump into the sea and offer herself up as floating target practice. The hunter leveled his aim – and then jerked in place, spasming as heavy rounds punched through his body. He tumbled formlessly onto the wooden planks.

John Morrell limped out of the dark, a knapsack slung across his body, smoke lilting from his gun. "Go."

Beck trembled in place.

He pulled her upright – "Run!" – and unleashed a shot at the remaining hunter.

She ran until she heard her name called. A rush filled her chest as Riley ran across an idle boat, jumped onto another, and then down to the dock. They nearly bowled each other over as they joined hands, checking each other. Then, her sister pulled her toward the Marina's entrance.

A sharp cry.

Beck glanced behind her—

Morrell lay sprawled on the pier. She wondered if he'd been hit, then saw him reach behind and grip his lower back. She slowed down, releasing Riley's hand.

"What are you doing?" her sister shouted.

Morrell pushed a clip into his handgun and tried to stand. He collapsed again. Rolled over and screamed in pain as he fired back at the first hunter.

"We have to help him," Beck said.

"There's no time!"

There wasn't, but a part of her brain had already drawn the most mystifying of conclusions: John Morrell had saved her life.

He regained his feet but lurched sideways, catching himself. Barely. Eventually, he'd fall again or run out of ammo.

Beck ran towards him. Riley spewed a stream of profanity but fell in. They each grabbed one of Morrell's arms. A millisecond of surprise, then he leaned into their support.

"My bag!" he shouted.

Riley snagged the knapsack. He fired off a volley to keep the first hunter at bay. The blasts numbed Beck's ears. They half-dragged him off the docks and behind an apartment building.

Stopped to catch their breath.

Searched for any pursuit.

A thousand questions hung in the air, overridden by an unspoken need to keep moving.

They turned Morrell around, his arms draped across their shoulders. Riley wheezed but showed no signs of slowing, even with the added burden of the man's weight.

"Was it Stratton?" Beck asked. "On the boat!"

Morrell shook his head. "It's mine…the boat belongs to me."

An explosion threw red stars into the sky.

"Deep vengeance is the daughter of deep silence."

– Vittorio Alfieri

CHAPTER 46

Four months earlier

Tommy hated this family farce; *Annwn* and the people who lived and routinely gathered here no longer held a special place in his heart, except for his kid sister Susan. He should have been at the club, rolling out their Fourth of July bonanza, except there were no fireworks at Round Midnight and certainly no bonanza. His business was a dollar payout on a two-dollar scratcher, the latest entry in a diary of piss-poor luck.

He knew they relished his failure. It was pheromonal how Hains sensed one another's setbacks, their smug joy conveyed in snarky asides and sawed-off smiles. Except for Susan – the only worthwhile member with Uncle Dave in the ground – Hains aligned exclusively on money and power. Their allegiance rose in direct correlation to how much of each they thought someone could give them. As a clueless kid, Tommy showed deference but, over time, recognized the platitudes of tradition and respect as control mechanisms.

The VISs (Very Important Suckups) feasted on the banging buffet. Kids splashed in and out of the temperature-controlled pool even though the freaking ocean was a hundred yards away. Uncle Owen had taken a crew deep-sea fishing at dawn, returning with a few bony flounders and a crew shit-faced and sunburned. Tommy endured the predictable "Decided to bless us with your presence?" and "Well, look who it is, The Big Man himself," with a "yeah, yeah" smile. He spent so little time with his extended family he had a hard time putting names to faces; cousins had sprouted from bratty and obnoxious to over-educated, bratty and obnoxious, while his aunts and uncles seemed oblivious to their hideous Botox and laughable dye jobs. Tommy at least had the stones to show his mileage.

He wolfed down shrimp salad as Grandpop regaled the reptiles with tales of *Annwn*'s creation. "A wild of dunegrass and rocks," the bony gasbag bragged, "converted into a hamlet befitting its namesake." He ended his tale by saying he needed to "lay out the big spread" to entice his kin back for the briefest of visits, an audacious play at sympathy as if he was some poor relic abandoned to a nursing home and not the lord of a multi-million-dollar stronghold with twelve staff at his beck and call.

This was the game. Human chess. Tommy had his failings, too many to count, but he never held anyone's blunders against them, unlike his family, who wielded a person's shortcomings like a scythe. After Grandpop kicked it, Tommy expected nothing less than an all-out civil war to claim the throne.

How much he once loved this place. He remembered when it all changed – the night Uncle Dave died. New Year's Eve. Tommy peered down the shoreline at the rocks that had shattered his uncle's body.

He did a few fly-bys with higher-ups at Hain and Hillary, complaining about Round Midnight's struggles. No one showed any inclination to help, offering only condescending sympathy, empty encouragement and barely concealed side-eyes as he walked away. He was an enigma to them, an ungrateful gnat they wished would fly away forever. He finally cornered Uncle Owen and laid his troubles bare.

"Gee, Tommy, I'm sorry to hear that, okay? It's been tough trying to recover from the pandemic." He was barely listening, distracted by the lady friend of one of their cousins.

"Uncle O, you know how much it pains me to ask. I'm just trying to keep things afloat. Never mind the bills; I got eighteen employees counting on me."

His uncle inhaled the rest of his hamburger and fries, sucked the ketchup off his bloated fingers and tossed the plate into a bin. "Look, I can Venmo you a few grand, okay? But you can't tell anyone, especially Carlow and Pop. They're obsessed with the race. It's eaten up any extra resources, you know? If you gotta let a few people go until the business comes back, that's the way the cookie crumbles, am I right? Your old man's gonna be the Big Kahuna. That should be worth some free publicity, yeah?"

A few grand would help about as much as a water pistol at a forest fire, and no amount of "free PR" would bring the number of customers necessary to keep Round Midnight alive.

His uncle waddled off to embarrass himself in front of their cousin's date. Tommy watched his father and Grandpop work the crowds. Uncle O was spot on: there was no chance of Carlow or Francis Hain cracking open their wallets, not with the campaign entering its final stretch…certainly not for him. When was the last time Tommy had shared anything personal or meaningful with either of them? He didn't think he'd be able to withstand their scorn.

"Screw it." He walked out, ready to take up an alternate scheme – a potential partner who viewed Round Midnight as a marketplace for something other than music and liquor.

Tommy was sick of the business. Sick of New England. Sick of being a Hain. He needed money so he could hit the road with Riley. He would have already lit a match on the club if he hadn't canceled all but the bare minimums in insurance. It was time to accept this most recent proposal. Riley would be tear-ass if she found out, considering the business of his soon-to-be partner, but this was their last shot at emancipation and a minor offense compared to the crimes behind *Annwn*.

A short-term deal.

All cash.

Tommy would build a nest egg, and then he and Riley would jet.

Six months, he figured. Six months dealing for Z Stratton to sign a new lease on life.

A can't-miss opportunity.

CHAPTER 47

The sisters propped Jordan up like a drunken bachelor as they hurried back to the Community College stop. He hated relying on them, but his legs were nearly useless. They hopped the T.

He cued up the video of them carrying out Washington's body, then snapped the phone in half and pulled out the chipboard and SIM card, crushing them beneath his heel.

"Any copies?" Riley asked.

"Nope."

"Guess we'll have to trust you."

"Guess so."

She turned away from him.

Beck placed her cell under the train seats.

"Not gonna destroy it?" he asked.

"It's a burner. Even if they somehow link it to us, a little goose chase may work to our advantage."

They transferred trains to head out to Dyer. Jordan didn't object. He couldn't think of a better spot to hole up with Chaya gone. Like it or not, he needed the Gideons.

"I'm sorry for what happened at the office," he told Beck. "I just wanted to keep you from running away. I needed information and didn't know where to look, so I looked everywhere. Still doesn't justify putting my hands on you, but you never know what you're capable of when your life's on the line." The train screeched around a corner and began to slow as the next station came into view. "All I can do now is try to make it right."

Beck stared for a beat, noncommittal. "So. Is it John, Jordan, or something else?"

"Jordan Lear."

"Who are you?"

"A researcher."

"More like a spy," Riley said.

"They hired me to shadow your sister."

"Who?"

He waited while Beck drew the obvious conclusion.

"Paradigm. Barbara Azakian."

He nodded, the first time he'd violated client confidentiality in his brief career, but none of the rules applied anymore.

"How long?"

"Six months."

"Why?" Riley asked.

"Because you don't hand over five million bucks until you know everything about your investment," Beck said.

CHAPTER 48

The silhouette standing over him nearly gave Winston a heart attack. He thought for sure the Holy Ghost had finally come to claim him. Or maybe Francis Hain had dispatched the trespasser to do Satan's grim work.

"It's me," the figure said, stepping into the moonlight – Beck. She looked close to passing out.

Winston rolled out of bed.

"Outside," she said.

He pulled on his overcoat and followed her downstairs without question, too stunned by her ragged state. She looked like she'd gone ten rounds with a bobcat. Once outside, though, he realized Beck's battery wasn't the work of a wild animal but her proximity to a wild soul. "Riley."

She didn't respond. There was no need: her presence alongside an equally frazzled young man with a gun on his hip made it clear Beck had lied about her involvement in recent events, most likely at Riley's behest.

"I'm sorry," Beck said. She gripped her left arm, her fingers wet from something seeping through her clothing.

Winston recognized it as blood and led them into St. J's medical room. He started an IV and administered a mild sedative. Beck's racing heartbeat settled. Soon after, she was out like a light. He undid the bandage on a bulging, weeping gash. "*Bondye mwen*. She's been shot."

Still, Riley said nothing.

His tour as a twenty-two-year-old medic had kicked off at Khe Sanh and continued through the Quảng Trị Province. He'd treated similar injuries on the battlefield, everything from sliced-open limbs to horrific breaches that spilled a soldier's delicate insides. A half-century later, Vietnam still possessed the power to generate soul-shaking night terrors. He and his fellow soldiers had been children playing warrior, their deployment a gruesome farce. However, this wasn't Khe Sanh or Quảng Trị. His priestly journey had served as a quest for order and understanding. At St. J's, he'd anticipated broken bones, skinned knees and addictions, but unlike the war, a chance to ease suffering and repair spirits.

How misguided. Life was a forever war, voracious, consuming all, even those as promising as Beck Gideon.

Riley sported a few cuts and bruises and a bump on the noggin. The young man with the gun, while uncut, writhed in distress.

"What's your name?"

"Jordan. Someone tried to stab me, but my body armor stopped the blade."

"I'm sorry I asked." Winston motioned for Riley to help get Jordan onto the gurney. She unbuttoned the young man's shirt, exposing the vest. Winston undid the Velcro straps and gently lifted it off. He rolled up a drenched undershirt on a severely discolored back. Jordan reported a tingling from his butt down through his feet. "A bulging disc," Winston said, "possibly a bruised spinal cord."

"No ambulance, *padre*. No nine-one-one. Got it?"

"I do not."

"Two hitters came gunning for us, the second time someone tried to take me out this week. I'm getting a little tired of it, truth be told. The ladies did nothing wrong. In fact, they saved me."

"After he saved Beck," Riley said. "We need sanctuary, Winnie."

"Obviously."

"If you can't help, just say so, and we'll get out of your hair."

"And where will you go?" He thrust his thumb at Beck. "Look at her. Look at the state of your sister. My guess is she's lying there because of you."

"The last thing I need is one of your lectures."

"Maybe if you'd ever taken one to heart."

"Maybe if you hadn't thrown me out."

"You left me no choice. The drugs. The alcohol—"

"I never brought any on campus."

"Stop lying!" Winston shouted. "How big of a fool do you take me for? Do you think I enjoyed barring you from campus? From my home? All the nights I sat up with you. Held your hand while they siphoned those poisons out of your body. You broke my heart, Riley. All you've ever done is break my heart!" He marched to the basin to wash his face and hands, trembling from his outburst.

Riley was the first Gideon to reside at St. J's. While Beck spent her formative years in foster care, Winston and Riley had developed a special relationship. He taught her chess and admonished her sharp tongue even as she made him laugh harder than anyone he'd ever known. They watched movies, and she remade the popcorn he frequently burned. Before addiction dimmed her light, he hired her as a residence supervisor. The children adored her. The good ones, anyway. The bad seeds feared and respected her.

And she still knew how to leverage his emotions, using the word "sanctuary" precisely because of its power to compel him.

A flashlight bounced out in the hall. Sister Lucinda. She angled her giant Maglite down as she entered, exhibiting no signs of sleepiness despite being awoken in the dead of night. Her shock and discontent were evident from ten paces.

"They're hurt," Winston said.

Questions and objections flashed in her eyes, but she nodded, rolled up her sleeves and scrubbed in. He had shared his medic training with Sister over the years, and she'd maintained First Aid and CPR certifications as they lacked the funds to employ a full-time nurse. Nevertheless, she gasped at the sight of Beck's injury. He avoided any mention of a gunshot, and Lucinda thankfully didn't ask. She grabbed meds and ice packs for Riley and Jordan. Winston set about removing the staples in Beck's arm, then lanced, drained and re-sutured her wound.

Lucinda left and returned with bottles of water from the cafeteria. "I'll get some clothes from the bins." She referred to the garments in the church's basement collected as donations for the needy.

"I'll help," Winston said, leading her out of the residence hall and locking it behind them, wishing to avoid any more bickering with Riley.

They hurried past the statue of St. Gerolamo, a granite rendition of the painting by Tiepolo depicting the saint with one arm around a small child, eyes cast skyward for guidance.

"We must call the police," Sister said.

"They requested sanctuary. And I promised."

"You've made a lot of promises over the years." As much positivity as the Gideon girls, notably Beck, engendered, Sister had long ago sensed just as much unspoken turbulence in their relationship with Father Winston. "I will not violate my covenant or alter the word from my lips."

While he could not compete with her eidetic memory of scripture, Winston countered with one of his favorites: "I have no greater joy than to hear that my children are walking in the truth."

"They're not your children. They are not even your flock anymore. And you've done everything for them and more."

If only, he thought and opened the basement door.

CHAPTER 49

Jordan shifted in search of a resting comfort. The clothes the *padre* and nun brought fit well enough, and a heavy blanket restored his body temperature, but while each movement produced a moment's peace, the hurt returned a second later, twice as intense.

Beck stirred; the IV depleted. She squinted under the bright fluorescents, looking like she'd journeyed to the abyss and back again. Riley disconnected the line and helped her drink some water.

"Think the *padre* and Sister will keep their mouths shut?" Jordan asked.

"For tonight," Riley said.

"And Tommy Hain's phone?"

"A burner. Beck installed her app so we could follow you and eavesdrop on your conversations."

Jordan made a mental note not to underestimate these two again.

"Amy," Beck croaked and cleared her throat. "She warned me."

"How did she know?"

"Let's find out." Beck dialed her friend on speaker, spent a few harried minutes assuring her she was alive and somewhat well, and then asked what she and Eli had heard on the burner.

"He made a call," Amy said. "He identified himself as Gene D'Angelo."

Jordan nodded.

"He said he had evidence this other person might be interested in. The fake Tommy phone. Then he tells whoever he was talking to where he could find 'the mole.' I assume he was talking about this Morrell guy, the asshole who attacked you at HQ."

Jordan's face flushed.

"D'Angelo then mentioned Morrell's location in the Marina, and I freaked, terrified you'd get caught in the middle of whatever was about to happen. I only wanted to help."

"You did. Just in the nick of time."

"We killed the session and remote deleted the app."

"Good."

"So what happened?"

"Check the news."

A minute later, Amy returned, her concern clear across the line. "What are we gonna do?"

"You tell whoever shows up – Barbara, the police – the truth. All of it. Hold nothing back. And then you and Eli get as far away from me as possible."

"Forget it, Beck. I'm with you all the way."

"I know, but Mr. G's in your hands now. Yours and Eli's. Take good care of him." She ended the call before her friend could say anything else.

CHAPTER 50

Six days earlier

The GTO nearly took flight as it surged from the garage beneath Round Midnight. The gun battle possessed Jordan, so its sudden appearance made him leap back off his stool. He grabbed his coat and ran downstairs.

Outside, he smelled the acrid char of cordite. People ran amok. Gunshots rebounded from all directions. He crouched behind the cars, moving towards the POS—

Henry Washington sprinted across the street in front of him, fleeing the scene of an active shooting. His destination appeared to be the subway station half a block away. Jordan took another look around. The GTO was long gone. The detective was his next-best lead. He ran in pursuit.

Jordan adopted a cool-kid shuffle as he entered the desolate T station. Even donned his sunglasses despite the lateness of the hour. He glanced repeatedly at the entrance, playing it off like he knew there was ill intent upstairs, but it wasn't any of his concern. In went the earbuds, and up went the volume on 310babii to sell the image of a city dweller minding his business.

Not once did he glance in Washington's direction.

The T arrived. Jordan sat one car up, checking the detective with a few eye shifts. Washington stood by the door, ready to move. They rolled into Jackson Square. The cop angled his body to get off the train even before the doors fully opened. Jordan gave him a good fifty feet.

Back outside, he removed his sunglasses and earbuds and reversed his jacket – he always bought coats with contrasting interiors to change his appearance. Half a mile later, they reached an alleyway. Jordan ran up a short staircase to a tenement, pretending to search for his keys. Washington disappeared into the alley. Jordan leaped off the stoop, sliding up to the corner.

The detective pulled a briefcase out of the dumpster. It was empty. He slammed it against the ground, cursing. Stabbed at his cell, pacing. A few minutes later, he ran off again.

Jordan had a hell of a time keeping him in sight without giving himself away. Five blocks later, they crossed into Dyer. Even before he saw the building, he inferred Washington's destination.

Beck Gideon's place.

The detective dialed the call box and got buzzed inside. Dashing through what was now a torrential downpour, Jordan set up at an overpass with a view of the front and rear of the building. He felt conflicted: Beck was his target. Barbara Azakian had hired him to identify potential threats to Paradigm's investment. A research grind, not a protection detail. He didn't do protection details: too close, too personal.

But he'd heard the stories about Henry Washington. When the detective turned up at Round Midnight yesterday, Jordan's spidey sense went into overdrive. Since then, the dude's behavior didn't jibe with official police business but skewed closer to the cop-for-hire mythos associated with him. His presence called Beck's well-being into question. If anything happened to her under Jordan's watch—

She and Washington exited the back door of her building and entered a rotting garage. Ten minutes later, they raced back out, and Jordan snuck up to inspect the structure. Inside, the sight of Tommy Hain's corpse nailed his feet to the floor. Jordan had already assumed a considerable risk posing as John Morrell. Hain hadn't struck him as inherently corrupt, just desperate. Most critically, none of his or Riley's licentiousness had impacted Beck or Mr. G.

Until tonight.

He eyed the fire escape. The ladder rested on the ground, a major-league security violation but a lucky break for Jordan. Climbing up, he hoped the rickety structure didn't crash him down in a jumble of rusty metal. Footsteps pounded across the roof. Drawing the Colt, he crouched, wondering what to do if Henry Washington came barreling down the scaffold.

The rain and lightning intensified.

He eased up to the lip of the roof and peered over. Beck shuffled across the tiles. A second person ran out – Riley Gideon. She led her sister into an antechamber.

This wasn't getting any easier. But if Washington was inside…if Riley and Beck believed they were dealing with an honest cop…

Jordan hurried into the antechamber, grateful to be out of the storm. He listened for sounds of confrontation, of pain.

Nothing.

"In for a penny, in for an ass-whooping," he whispered.

One slow step at a time, he lowered himself into the loft.

Voices.

Not shouts. Normal tones.

He peered around the corner of a darkened hallway and saw Beck and her sister in the bathroom. There was no sign or sound of Henry Washington. Jordan dared not chance a creaky floorboard to confirm, but the sisters' conversation would not be so subdued with the detective in their face. Maybe Beck had somehow convinced him she wasn't harboring Riley. Perhaps the detective had been called back to the charnel house formerly known as Round Midnight.

But would he have left, given his true purpose?

After seeing Tommy Hain's body downstairs?

Twenty minutes later, Jordan recorded the reason for Washington's absence.

CHAPTER 51

Beck fixed a glare on her sister after Jordan finished his story. "I thought you'd never seen Washington before! He was in the goddamn club!"

"I didn't see him! I was out cold!"

"He wasn't a regular," Jordan said, mediating. "The first time I saw him was Thursday. He and his partners were casing Round Midnight. He never set foot inside until the next night, minutes before the shooting."

Beck continued to pace, refueled by an angry skepticism of everything Riley.

"I've been running this job since May, Beck. The first time I saw Henry Washington anywhere was Thursday. I promise you."

She decided not to browbeat her sister, which would only push Riley into defense mode. She nodded at Jordan's statement and added, "I wanted to help him before he fell."

"You're lucky you didn't. He would have repaid your charity by tossing you down the same shaft."

"Maybe."

"There's no maybe about it, Beck. Henry Washington went there to kill you two." He turned to Riley. "I assume you then took the GTO for a swim?"

She nodded. "Did you know Stratton before all this?"

"Only by reputation."

"Why get so close?"

"To learn everything I could."

"Because no matter how much these investors believed in me," Beck said, "I'm still a Lost One they can't fully trust."

He didn't disagree with her. "Risk assessment is only as valid as the breadth and depth of its coverage. You never know where the threat's gonna originate. Barbara gave me whatever I needed. Money was no object. I ran up and down every avenue of your life, backgrounded every face."

"Personas," Beck said. "Winning software is about more than the code. It's like a restaurant; the presentation is as vital as the cuisine. You have to understand the diner. In tech, it's the end user. So you engage them. Survey them. Identify their problems and figure out how to solve them. You craft a user journey, but it's profiling by any other name. You funded the parties and asked Tommy and Riley to populate the guest list to see who'd show up. To see if I showed up."

"You or anyone affiliated with Mr. Gabriel."

"What about the time you, ya know…" Riley said.

"Propositioned you?"

"What happens if I say yes?"

"I come up with an excuse to retract my offer, and your inclination goes into my report…but I wasn't expecting you to accept."

"Really."

"You're not that kind of person, Riley."

His compliment caught her by surprise and softened her posture. "Does this also mean you saw me following Beck those couple of times?"

"Three times, yes. After the mishegaas at Commencement—"

"Don't tell me—" Beck said.

"I sat on the Chapel Street side, row four, middle aisle."

"Oh my God," the sisters said in unison.

"I explained to Barbara how you two fell out and became estranged. Still, she kept me digging." He drained his water. "Finally, after six months, she felt satisfied you two led very separate lives. I was preparing to wrap it up when life went all Grand Theft Auto."

Beck rubbed her temples. "And D'Angelo?"

"A prosecutor for the District Attorney."

"He sold you out," Riley said.

"I'm not sure."

"I am. I didn't imagine the bullets."

"Obviously, I regret going to him. That boat was my dream. I purchased it through one of my covers, but unlike all of my other flops, hotels and used vehicles, *Chaya* was my sanctuary…I've worked for Gene before. Alibi checks, witness backgrounds, jury research. We conducted all our meetings face-to-face. A few on *Chaya*. He was probably following protocol, logging evidence. I'm less worried about Gene D'Angelo than whoever was on the other end of the line."

"Why?" Beck asked.

"Because whoever he called is most likely working for Francis Hain."

CHAPTER 52

Jordan pulled a laptop out of his knapsack. Riley shut off the lights. He opened a photo of an aged but regal man walking the sand of a beachfront mansion.

Beck recognized Francis Hain instantly. Boston crime was a curious thing. The population was less than a million, which didn't even rank in the nation's top twenty. In terms of land area, Las Cruces, New Mexico was bigger. Such density made everything personal and created the underworld version of six degrees of Kevin Bacon. If you lived here long enough, you could stitch connections to a schemer who made all the wrong headlines. Regardless of the crime, people would recall *something* positive about the perpetrator: "I know he knocked over a convenience store, but his old lady was my second-grade teacher and, like, the nicest ever," or "Yeah, he was cuckoo for Cocoa Puffs, but I swear that kid could hit a curveball over the moon." The Hains were as much a part of Boston lore as the Puritans, the Massacre, the Tea Party, Paul Revere, Sam Adams (the founding father and the brewery), selling Babe Ruth to the Yankees, the USS Constitution and *Cheers*. You couldn't live in the region without recognizing Tommy's grandfather.

"I thought he was on the up-and-up," she said.

"Not everybody's bought in. A curious pattern has emerged: many of Hain's former rivals and co-conspirators have a nasty tendency of going to jail or turning up dead. Washington worked what's called Major Crimes; anything's possible if you can pay off the centurions. Who's gonna complain about Hain's associates going down? Viewed one way, the deceased are mob chiefs, enforcers, and wiseguys: men who lived dangerous lives where violent death is preordained. Viewed another, their expiration eliminated threats to the Wall Street rise of the Hains. But as far as anyone can prove, Francis did his time and found salvation."

"No way that was all Washington."

"Agreed. Which makes it even scarier. How many are taking bribes from Francis?"

"What's this gotta do with us?" Riley asked.

He clicked on a video file. The high-res footage, shot from an elevated position, captured Round Midnight. It zoomed in on three men walking its perimeter: a dour middle-aged man with a Spartan crewcut, a second man head and shoulders above his colleagues, and Henry Washington. "Crewcut is Oswald Grieg, and the giant is Tony DeLillo, both members of Washington's squad. This is Thursday, the first time I saw them. Tommy wasn't even home."

"He was hiding from Stratton."

"Friday night, Washington and his crew turn back up." Jordan launched another video of Tommy driving the GTO into the parking garage a few minutes before Washington, Grieg and DeLillo entered the club. Loud house music thumped. He fast-forwarded until the front door flew open. Two young women ran out. The doorman stumbled behind them, gripping his bleeding chest, shooting back through the entrance before he finally fell. More patrons and staff crawled out of doors and windows broken open by chairs. The music cut off, replaced by gunfire. He fast-forwarded again until Tommy's GTO fishtailed out of the underground garage with Riley at the wheel. Washington ran for the subway. It looked like some faraway war on the evening news. Cop cars laid siege as a police chopper's spotlight swirled overhead. The torrential rain obscured the details, but it was another thirty minutes before the battle ended. First responders brought out covered gurneys and suspects in handcuffs.

"Six dead," he said. "Two from Stratton's gang, a bouncer, two customers and a young patrolwoman who caught one in the head clearing the alley."

The video finally went black. Beck released the breath she'd been holding.

"My guess is Grieg and DeLillo stayed behind to control the narrative while Washington went after the money."

"How did they even know about it?" Beck asked.

"I'll show you."

CHAPTER 53

Six days earlier

Slunk low in his seat, Jordan held up his cell to record. He felt vulnerable, the area replete with pedestrians streaming across City Hall Plaza. No choice, though. After six months of profiling perhaps the most boring twenty-two-year-olds alive, a black-hat badge, Henry Washington, had inexplicably started casing Round Midnight.

Jordan prided himself on staying informed. His livelihood depended on knowing the business, scuttlebutt, innuendo, rumors, and scandals of the day. An A+ from Barbara Azakian would push him – and his rates – into rarified air. He vowed to unearth, down to the most minute detail, how Washington connected, or didn't, to Beck Gideon.

Fifty yards up, the detective and Oswald Grieg sat inside a Jeep. Non-department issue. Probably Grieg's vehicle or a rental – a ride that couldn't be tracked. They stepped out and entered a squat municipal tower at Tremont and State. Google Maps listed a virtual post office at the location. Jordan had come across them before while researching the nefarious proclivities of his targets. Digital age upgrades on P.O. Boxes, V-Posts provided a numbered address to people who didn't want to use their own and offered safety deposit boxes like a bank. The service opened correspondence on demand, scanned and emailed the contents to the recipient, shredded junk mail, and forwarded packages, and every action was controlled through an app. They weren't without controversy because governments like to know where their citizens live. V-Posts enabled people to stay off the grid and were open twenty-four-seven – handy services when moving contraband.

Washington and Grieg returned to the Jeep. Grieg slid a credit card into the meter to pay for more time. Jordan did the same.

Three more times, he funded his meter. Hours of idle watching.

A waste of time.

Until Washington and Grieg came alive.

Jordan craned his head around to get a look at what they were seeing—

A man with a silver briefcase. The door to the V-Post swung closed behind him. Grieg drove forward. Jordan tailed them a few cars back, trying to keep his phone-cam steady. The man with the suitcase entered the new Government Center parking station. Washington spoke into his cell as he and Grieg idled. A minute later, everyone was back in motion, following a car.

A 1970s GTO.

"Tommy," Jordan said. He followed the caravan back to Round Midnight, then ran up to his rented flop on the third floor of a business more accustomed to renting by the hour. He checked his surveillance array – Vega long-range day/night cameras with infrared, precision range-finding, stabilization and motion detection – all directed at the club's entrance, the mouth of the underground garage, the alley to the side and the block in front.

He zoomed one camera in on Grieg and Washington in the Jeep. A sedan arrived a second later, Tony DeLillo behind the wheel; the second day in a row, the Major Crimes trio had perched themselves on the nightclub's stoop. Tonight, they entered.

And a war broke out.

CHAPTER 54

Beck ambled around the room again, her injured arm in a sling. "The money was sent to Tommy via virtual post. Why? Why didn't the lender hand him the cash?"

Riley stared at the floor, arms crossed. Feeling Beck's gaze, she looked up. "What?"

"Where were you when Tommy went to retrieve the money?"

"At work. When he told me he'd found the money, I nearly cried. I'd been so worried about him. I figured a family member or one of his buddies finally came through, but there wasn't any time to get into it because Stratton was already at Midnight, waiting for his payout."

"He asked me," Jordan said. "He called Wednesday night. Made it sound like an investment opportunity. I liked the club so much, why not take a piece of the action? I suspected there was more to it. After I tagged Washington and his team, I figured Tommy was in over his head with Stratton."

"Wait a minute," Beck said. "Washington and his partner were watching the V-Post, not Tommy. That means they knew the money was inside."

"Waiting to see who showed up to claim it," Jordan said. "I already figured. What I can't figure out is how they knew."

"Do we think it was Grieg and DeLillo at the Marina?" Riley asked.

"The one I shot was pretty tall."

"DeLillo."

"Most likely, which means Grieg's still on the loose, plus any number of partisans getting paid by Francis Hain to clean up this mess. Stratton's the only witness left, but unless you got a crystal ball…"

"I don't," Beck said. Her injuries dragged her closer to narcosis. She slumped back onto the gurney. "But you do."

CHAPTER 55

After Beck outlined her plan, Jordan closed his laptop, leaned back, and passed out. Riley told her she was crazy again, then said she was going in search of a bed.

Before she left, Beck opened a document on her iPad and asked Riley to write down the accounts she managed at Round Midnight. "I'll need the logins and passwords, too."

"I use the same for all of 'em."

"As someone in technology, that offends me on multiple levels."

Her sister wandered off. Beck considered grabbing a few winks, but a clock was ticking in her head. Any chance of pulling off this last-ditch effort depended on momentum. She couldn't afford to sleep. Couldn't afford to even Drift; she needed to step up and take control.

Accessing the club's accounts would be dicey. Most certainly, the police were monitoring them and would wonder why Tommy seemed to be logging in from beyond the grave. They'd track the IP, and while it wouldn't lead the cops to Beck's door, it would guide them close enough to notice St. J's and come sniffing. To cover her tracks, she opened a Tor browser designed for anonymous internet usage and logged in via MrGabriel's Virtual Private Network, which encrypted all incoming and outgoing data.

Feeling suitably camouflaged, she started with the Slack account for the club. She ran keyword searches for "Stratton," "Z," "Zee," "one hundred thousand," "club," "cash," "grandpop," "Francis," "Round Midnight," "Washington."

Nada. She searched for "Riley" and found a message Tommy had sent of four kangaroos humping each other. The caption read: "Meanwhile, in Australia."

Pure Tommy. Beck wondered what people would think if they learned the man at the center of this saga enjoyed funny kangaroo memes. It reminded her of all the times she wished for a jot of his unbridled enthusiasm or to experience something like his and Riley's high-test relationship. It wasn't long ago Tommy's attention and teasing made Beck blush. She used to look forward to his visits and recalled those escapades when he graciously allowed "Beck-Beck" to tag along.

Her first trip to Fenway.

Her first concert – Juliana Hatfield's Awesome Christmas show at POP Allston.

Movies she desperately wanted to see but had no friends with whom to go.

She noticed a URL he sent to Riley titled "Beck's Grad" and clicked it to a cloud storage site with dozens of pictures and videos from Commencement. Because of his inebriation, many were cocked at an angle or obscured by a thumb or the back of someone's head. One video showed Beck accepting her diploma as the Dean cited the achievement of "*summa cum laude*." Riley screeched while Tommy whistled through his fingers. Another video captured Beck posing with Amy and Eli's families for photos. She wondered if Tommy even realized his camera was still recording.

"Hey, we want in on that!" he yelled. The angle zigzagged, catching horrified expressions from friends, families and professors, reminding Beck of her humiliation.

Someone asked if they wanted a photo of Riley and her boyfriend. "He's not my boyfriend!" her sister shouted and hugged Beck. "But this here's my girl!"

Beck offered a tentative smile to those nearby. Apologizing and pleading for help.

Tommy passed the camera to Riley and hurried into the frame, his eyes glassy not from emotion but from whatever they'd consumed, inhaled, snorted or injected. "Some come loudly, baby!" He and Riley laughed like it was the most ingenious joke ever.

The day sped downhill from there, culminating in a shouting match at the dinner Amy's parents had graciously hosted at Olea. Riley scolded Tommy for how fast he was drinking, then joked they weren't doing Jello shots, spurring him to storm out. She followed, subjecting the entire restaurant to an argument barely dampened by the window. Beck fled into the bathroom, pursued and consoled by Amy. By the time they returned, her sister and Tommy were gone, asked politely to leave by Eli's father, whom Tommy told to "go fuck himself" before Riley dragged him out, nearly knocking over the adjoining table's meal just as it arrived.

Beck shut the replay off and wiped tears from her eyes. She returned to her research, no longer angry about Commencement, just brokenhearted.

CHAPTER 56

The iPad hit the floor, jolting Beck awake.

Why were her hands and feet tied?

They weren't. She slumbered in the same chair in the medical room, but now a heavy blanket mummified her in a tight embrace. A foggy memory drifted up: Madeleine, covering her with the blanket as Jimmy set a plate of apple slices on the table beside the chair. She looked over – the apples glistened like jewels. She wormed her arms free and scarfed them down, then picked up the iPad. It appeared unharmed. Jordan slumbered on the gurney. The light outside suggested it wasn't much past dawn.

They'd finished all the bottled water, so she took her medicine by slurping straight from the tap. She palmed her forehead. It was no longer ablaze, and her arm didn't feel like it had been run over by a cement truck, maybe a tyke-bike with a set of training wheels. She searched for her sister, clearing the classrooms before heading up to the residences on the second floor. Madeleine and Jimmy slept on twin beds under cartoon covers in the first room. She was about to depart when she noticed feet sticking out from under the covers on a third mattress.

Riley.

She must have fallen into the first bed she found. If Sister Lucinda discovered her near the children, Riley would go bouncing down the stairs a second later. Beck stepped over to wake her sister, but the mural on the wall, a crayon rendition of Mr. G, distracted her. A child hung in the air, his mammoth hands open to catch her.

Beck opened the app and held up the camera. "Check it out, G."

Is that what I look like?

"The one in my room was a little more refined."

The one your sister drew.

"Yep. I was having a nasty run of night terrors. I came home and found Riley painting in your details. She can draw, you know…My roommates fell in love with you. Riley said you'd watch over us, and the house would be the safest place

174

we'd ever know. It didn't always live up to the hype, but it came darn close."

That's a beautiful story.

"The story of your birth."

Thank you.

She grinned. It felt good to have a conversation that didn't involve death and crime. There were moments when she'd convinced herself Mr. G was the only companion she'd ever want or need. Amy and Eli were treasures, Father W and Lucinda loving and consistent, Riley loving and inconsistent, but they were also their own people, capable of unintended harshness and hurtful reproach. Human. And Beck had always struggled to process humanity's punitive deviations.

The worst she could say about Mr. G was he didn't always give her *everything* she needed or exactly how she wanted it. But he damn sure tried. Who else could she confide in and trust that they would never reveal her secrets out of spite, jealousy, or an urge to gossip? Who could advise her on how to most effectively deploy Active Remote Sensing to advance her wearable tech ambitions, then dive straight into a conversation about what a second season of *Girlboss* would have looked like? In the ongoing debate about man vs. machine, she was solidly – if not quietly – for machines.

"Beck?"

She spun around to find Madeleine sitting up. "Did I wake you? I'm sorry. Go back to sleep."

"I finished him last week after your podcast. I know he's not as good as the one in your app."

"He's perfect. Thank you. But c'mon, close your eyes." She waited until the little girl fell back asleep.

Jimmy stirred on the next bed, moaning softly in his sleep. Beck slid over. Like their first meeting, she didn't know how to comfort him. Another soft cry escaped his lips.

She bent down, forcing herself to get closer, resting her head on his pillow. "It's okay."

His hand found her cheek. She waited for him to relax, then eased it under the covers. Her eyes closed. Sitting here and listening to the kids breathe felt so good.

Jordan's voice echoed, calling her name.

She went over to wake Riley.

Their feeble rest had come to an end.

Jordan grimaced as he sat up against the wall.

"No better?" Riley asked.

"A little. Instead of a red-hot poker being rammed into my back, it's no longer red-hot." He swallowed anti-inflammatories.

Beck checked the iPad. As expected, the Marina led all news programs. They felt disconcerted hearing their names bandied about, particularly Jordan, an operative accustomed to working in the shades.

"I went through the club accounts last night," she said. "It looks like Tommy owed money to everyone in Boston, so we're back to you, Jordan. You said you had Z Stratton's number. Please tell me you backed it up somewhere."

"Eight numbers, actually, and I don't need the backup. I memorize every key detail on a job."

"Good, but first, we gotta get scarce." She powered off her burner. Pulled out the prepaid SIM card and used a pair of medical shears to cut it into pieces. Dropped them and the phone into the trash. "I'll pull the van up."

She ran out the door. Halfway down the hall, she heard someone call her name – Jimmy stood on the base of the stairs, his too-large baseball hat cocked on his head, a mitt over one hand, a second one tucked under his arm. She jogged back. "What are you doing up?"

"I wanted to play catch before school."

She laughed sadly. Jimmy didn't question why three adults had shown up in the middle of the night, and he didn't care. He liked Beck, the woman with the muffins who was nice to him after such a horrifying ordeal. She was his friend, and he wanted to play catch with her.

"I can't," she said. "But soon."

"Promise?"

She drew an X over her heart. He surprised her by throwing his arms around her head and neck. There was no choice but to reciprocate. He felt so tiny in her arms, so close to breaking, his bones too delicate to protect what was inside. Conflicting emotions ran through her: a desire to shield him and an urge to get away, to not be responsible and risk the heartbreak of failing to protect someone so vulnerable.

The app was the solution. Mr. G. Not her. How could she make someone so young understand? Jimmy finally pulled back and scampered upstairs, calling for Madeleine. Beck ran outside and across campus, nearly slipping on the dewy grass. The side door of the rectory was unlocked. In the kitchen, she snatched the van keys off the wooden peg—

"Good morning," Sister Lucinda said.

Beck came up short. "Hey. Morning." Her stomach twisted. Suddenly, she was twelve years old again and tensing at the mere prospect of Lucinda's disapproval.

"Where are you going?"

"Jordan needs the ER. Me, too." She gently swung her arm, faking a grimace too phony for community theater.

"I'll take you. You're in no condition to drive." Sister held her hand out.

"Riley can do it. You have to get ready for school."

"We don't start until eight. Plenty of time to drop you off and come back."

Beck remained in place.

Sister folded her hands behind her back. "We raised you to live in truth, Rebecca."

"I know. And I know you can stop me if you want, but I hope you won't. I'm begging you not to."

"You don't have to beg me. Your decisions are your own now."

The stark disappointment in Sister Lucinda's eyes, a woman with a picture of Beck blowing out birthday candles on her nightstand, was gutting. "I'm sorry," was all Beck could muster before she sprinted back out the door.

CHAPTER 57

Francis poured twice as much Dead Rabbit into his coffee. The goddamn ghosts had kept him up again; they refused to grant him a decent night's slumber.

His driver poked his head into the library: "Something you should see, sir."

Francis followed him to the great room where the TV news people were hysterical over a late-night clash that had turned Charlestown Marina into the Battle of Midway. Security footage showed a cop – DeLillo – getting skewered by a few calibers; the ultimate act blurred out to avoid upsetting citizens munching their Cheerios.

Most shocking was the sight of Riley and Beck Gideon amidst the havoc. The young women Winnie had stressed were two sets of wings short of angelhood. Francis watched them assist a young man – the gunslinger who cut down DeLillo – escape.

And then one of the boats exploded, whiting out the feed.

"Get the car," he told his driver, downing his coffee-and-sin in a single gulp.

CHAPTER 58

They left Jordan stretched out across the back bench of the van as they entered the 24-hour pharmacy. In the electronics aisle, racks of disposable phones hung on hooks.

Beck checked her wallet. She was down to three bucks. "Got any cash?"

Riley leaned close: "I have a hundred thousand dollars."

"Oh. Right."

Her sister unzipped the backpack, peeling off several C notes. Beck selected six of the best burners, cheaply constructed but outfitted with 5G, GPS, a camera and a gig of storage. She grabbed a two-slot car charger as well. They checked out, ordering six SIM cards, each with a month's worth of unlimited data. The cashier accepted the cash and the bogus user information they provided for all six accounts: Jaylen Tatum, 1000 Commonwealth Avenue, Boston.

Back in the van, Beck drove and told Riley and Jordan to scooch down out of sight. "We need to get somewhere private, far from prying eyes."

"I know where," her sister said and called out directions.

After thirty minutes, Beck realized their destination. "Really?"

"Guess which places are never patrolled at night and seldom during the day?"

"Cemeteries." Beck pulled into the parking lot of Mount Hope, studying the headstones in the morning fog. "I did say private."

She installed MrGabriel on a burner and pulled down all the info she'd backed up on the cloud. "Hey, G."

Nice to see you again.

"We need to run some serious tests today. I'm gonna replicate you on several phones and use a tester profile."

Jaylen Tatum?

"That's me. Super-admin access for all six installs."

Would you mind providing the password?

She typed out the alphanumeric string.

Confirmed.

She repeated the process on the other five burners, then handed one to Jordan. "Create contacts for Stratton's numbers and give each one a different name."

"Like what?"

"Anything: Moe, Larry, Curly, one, two, three. Doesn't matter." She watched him create the contacts, impressed by his recall.

"He never picked up," Jordan explained, "so I always had to dial all eight numbers and leave messages."

"Give him a shout."

He tapped the first contact and listened. "Nothing. Not even ringing."

"Which means…" Riley said.

"He powered off the phone or destroyed it. Even when powered off, a cell phone can still be traced to its last location.

"What if he destroyed all of them?"

"I'm betting he didn't," Beck said. "No doubt he opened these accounts under fake names like we did. He's a drug dealer. His entire business, his network, rests on his phones, and he can't just stroll into a store to buy more as Boston's most wanted."

"One of his soldiers can. He could be living under one of those aliases in Budapest by now."

"If that's the case, then we're screwed."

"Oh."

"You were expecting a different answer?"

"Well, yeah. You're always three moves ahead of everyone else."

"Not lately; otherwise, we wouldn't be hiding in a stolen van near a cemetery. We work with what we have and hope for the best."

Jordan tapped the following two numbers, rewarded with more dead air. The fourth number, however, trilled a few times. "Voice mail." He waited while the robotic voice told him the person was unavailable, then left the message: "It's me, your party pal. I'm getting concerned. I wanna help. If you're safe, I'm safe. Whatever you need. Call me." He disconnected. "There's another way this can fall apart: if Stratton's the one who blew my cover and targeted me, he'll know I'm trying to play him."

"Doesn't matter. As long as the call connects, we have a chance. Keep going."

He ran through the rest of the numbers, leaving three more messages.

"Four out of eight," Beck said. "Not bad."

"Now what?" Riley asked.

"Now we wait."

The radio prattled on about the Marina. It was bizarre to hear their names mentioned on the broadcast. They adjusted the hats, scarves and sunglasses lifted from St. J's donation bins. Beck told Jordan and her sister to stay down regardless: the be-on-the-lookout specified a threesome, not a pair.

"Does the *padre* have a toolkit in here?" Jordan asked.

"Guaranteed," Riley said and crawled into the payload. She found a kit in the spare tire hold.

"How many other cars in the lot?"

"One."

"Swap the plates. Don't let anyone see you."

Riley rolled out, unscrewing the van's front plate, then disappeared around the back to remove the other. Beck used the mirrors to watch her double-time it to a Buick clunker. "What if the owner notices the different tags?"

"How often do you check your license plates?"

"I don't own a car."

"Most people don't look. If the *padre* or the good Sister fess up about the van, the cops will scan plates. Massachusetts banned facial recognition a couple of years ago unless it is court-ordered or to address extreme threats, like a terrorist attack. Even if they get the okay, adding our likeness to the program takes time. Once Riley's done, the greater threat will be Joe and Jane Public or a patrol cop recognizing us, not the van."

Swapping the plates made Beck feel worse; first, she'd more or less stolen St. J's property, and now they were refashioning it into a getaway vehicle. As much as she tried to convince herself that their best chance of bringing this calamity to an end was flushing Z Stratton, their ongoing lies and misconduct deepened her guilt.

Riley ran back with the Buick's plates, screwing the first into the rear holder, then coming around to work on the front.

An aged woman shuffled across the cemetery.

Beck rolled down her window. "Hurry, Riles." She kept her eye on the bundled-up, hunched-over woman with the craggy, determined face. A New England face of one who had accepted the inevitability of lying next to her loved one someday, but not until her cosmic dice crapped out. Until then, she'd pay her respects and keep fighting.

Riley slipped into the back of the van, closing the doors.

The woman strutted to her Buick and slowly lowered herself behind the wheel.

Not once did she peek at her new plates.

CHAPTER 59

They left the engine off to avoid anyone noticing the fumes of an idling van. The seats turned frigid, the air frosty. Riley dozed in the payload while Jordan lifted himself partway off the ice slab, keeping below the windowsills.

He saw Beck studying her iPad. "Anything new?"

"No. Just waiting for our system to update with your call data."

"Staring at it helps?"

She laughed and set the tablet aside. Picked up her burner, which was replete with updates on the Marina. "How about some music, Mr. G?"

A cartoon man who looked like Grizzly Adams popped up onscreen. "Snarky Puppy?"

"Yeah, but only their mellow stuff."

The music drifted out.

"Man of the moment," Jordan said. "I've been curious."

She held up the burner. "Meet Jordan, G."

Hello, Jordan. A pleasure.

He'd read up on Beck's app. An unabashed tech-head, he appreciated her invention, but the proof was always in the pudding. So many of these startups were ninety percent hype and ten percent vaporware to create buzz and spur fundraising. "Can I ask him something?"

"Anything."

"Mr. G, can you show me a photo of Jordan Lear?"

The avatar screwed up his face as if thinking. Jordan had explicitly requested an unfulfillable task. Given the sensitivity of his occupation, he'd spent years scrubbing images of himself from Google's cache and other search engines. These days, the primary result for "Jordan Lear" was a Welsh pop star.

I found seven million two-hundred-sixty thousand results. Can you tell me more about the Jordan Lear you're interested in?

"He's a private investigator," Beck said. "In Boston. Most likely former military. African-American. Late twenties."

Mr. G made his thinking face again.

183

Jordan grinned. "I'm cheating, I know. If I asked about public schools or child-rearing, he'd have zipped back with an answer."

"We'll see."

Is this the man you're looking for?

A blurry black-and-white photo took over the screen – Jordan Lear in the flesh.

"What the—" His back voices its displeasure at how quickly he jerked upright. He grabbed at the spot but kept his focus on the picture. "How old is that?"

Eleven years.

Younger, but unmistakably the same person, unmistakably Jordan. The photo appeared to be scanned from a newspaper. He stood on a soccer pitch amidst five other players. The image listed names along the bottom, including "J. Lear."

"Looks like a blog about the Roxbury Youth Soccer League," Beck said.

And no one has updated it for ten years, eight months, and twenty-two days.

"I requested removal for every result I could find," Jordan said. "I went ten, twenty pages deep in the search results."

"Results produced by meta-tags, keywords and search engine indices. This image lacks meaningful tags. J period instead of Jordan. A picture from a newsletter that was never indexed for the net, just scanned for a WordPress site over a decade ago. Easy to see how your searches missed it."

"But he found it."

"AI works differently. Mr. G interprets intent and context, as well as the specifics of the request. Those extra prompts I provided led him to the photo."

Jordan made a gesture as if his head were exploding. "Why did you build a powerful search engine inside a KidTech app?"

"Eight years ago, I first integrated with an AI beta to access their large language model and search capabilities. Worked so well, I started developing off of it, and we kept it."

"You designed Mr. G when you were fourteen?"

"I started at twelve."

From everything he'd read, listened to and watched, Beck Gideon's unshakable belief in MrGabriel was her most consistent trait. She claimed his abilities would eventually follow a child into adulthood. Her company would never stop building; therefore, Mr. G would never stop learning. Her vision was almost zealous. Given the state of humanity, justified, too.

She set the burner down. "So now you know my story. I mean, you better, after six months of stalking me—"

"Please don't use that word."

"Tomato, tomahto. My point is, I like to know everything I can about my partners."

"That what we are?"

"I think so. If not by choice, then by circumstance." She waited out his silence for a few beats. "I assume you don't like to share, but maybe this one time, you can make an exception."

He leaned back against the seat. The cold felt good against his nagging back. "Ever hear of Fiorello LaGuardia High School?"

"I think so."

"Upper West Side, Manhattan. Most people remember one of its predecessors, the High School of Performing Arts. They made a movie about it called Fame. Well before our time. My parents were political refugees but fought their way here. Mom was a violinist for the New York Symphony, Dad a Professor of Anthropology at NYU. They bred music, art, history, and culture into me. A dream-like childhood."

"How does an Upper West Side boy immersed in art and academia become a Boston private eye tailing scum like Z Stratton and Henry Washington?"

"Said boy's folks die in a plane crash coming home from the Toronto Art Fair."

Beck leaned over the seat. "I'm sorry. I didn't mean to make light."

"You didn't know. Besides, I ask myself the same question all the time. My parents survived a civil war, tyrants and genocide, and a fucking plane ride does them in…Just isn't right…I had one living relative: a cousin in Roxbury. The money my folks left slowly disappeared. My cuz used it to upgrade her life. I had to get out. The only way I could was to enlist. By the way, how'd you know I was military?"

"Educated guess. Your occupation. Firearms expert."

He nodded. "I did my four, then tried to access the veteran's program at a faraway college. But even the best programs left a huge nut. So I went to work. A fellow vet recommended a private security outfit, and eventually, I split to do my own thing…You learn things about yourself in war you'd never discover anywhere else. This art-school kid discovered he thrived on living in the extremes and putting on different facades. I'm sure you and Riley can relate."

Beck rooted around in her pocket and came out with a crinkled photo. She passed it back to him. "My mother. Her name was Ava. But you already know this and why I carry the picture…I'd give anything to meet her, but never knowing your parents is probably easier than loving and losing them. You had yours for, what, sixteen years?"

"They died a week after my sixteenth birthday. How'd you guess?"

"You went to that fancy high school before they died, which means you were at least fourteen but not eighteen because you hadn't graduated and had to move in with your cousin long enough to learn she was stealing your inheritance. I picked the median."

Jordan laughed and handed the photo back. "Instant deduction always come this easy to you?"

"Yes. Unfortunately, logic can't protect you from a world that runs on spontaneous combustion. Life may be predictable ninety-nine percent of the time, but the one percent it's not is when your pilot decides to end his life and take you and three hundred passengers with him."

"Now there's a cheery thought."

"I'm just saying, as much as I love Mr. G, there's no programming for baseless, unpredictable, volatile human intuition. If we'd turned ourselves in and followed my rulebook instead of Riley's instincts, you'd all be putting flowers on our graves right about now."

"Good thing big sis was looking out."

"She always has been."

CHAPTER 60

A challenging morning had followed Winston's tough night. Two sick parishioners required visitations: one recovering from pneumonia at St. Elizabeth's and poor Gladys Williams, receiving hospice care after a catastrophic stroke. He administered the sacraments of Penance, Anointing of the Sick and Viaticum – once referred to as the last rites – and then sat with her family. Despite assurances of eternal peace, they'd yet to accept her fate. As one of the most jubilant individuals remaining in his congregation, Winston also found it difficult to reconcile her imminent passing, the shared grief piling on top of the unrest generated by Beck and Riley's arrival.

On the walk home, he detoured into Lewek's. The line was mercifully short, in and out, with two coffees and lox on garlic bagels in under five minutes. Back at St. J's, he entered the rectory to give Lucinda her breakfast. She would see through his transparent attempt to soften her up, but Sister cherished Lewek's lox, cold-smoked on site.

She wasn't inside the rectory. School hadn't started yet, and a check of his inbox confirmed that none of the children had reported as sick. The campus grounds were vacant because of the wet chill that had settled in overnight. That left either the medical room where Beck, Riley and their new associate were recuperating or the church. He ventured to the latter, expecting to find her in morning prayer. He entered the side door quietly to avoid disturbing her, but then voices drew him through the curtain into the south transept. Sister sat in the front pew. She wasn't alone.

"Reverend Petievich," Winston said.

Formally, the Very Reverend Ambrose Petievich, vicar for the Archbishop of Boston. As St. Gerolamo's sole remaining champion, his presence and Sister's difficulty meeting Winston's gaze suggested this wasn't a casual or friendly visit.

"Sister Lucinda suggested I come by after the news," Petievich said.

"News?"

They returned to the rectory and turned on the television.

Winston fell to the couch as replays of the Marina weakened his knees. "*Bondye sove nou.*" He ran his hands down his face and peered up at the Reverend. "They requested sanctuary."

"A tradition which ended three hundred years ago in Europe and never had legal standing in the United States. Father, we cannot harbor those who have broken the law…even those who hold a special place in our hearts." Petievich was well-versed in every child's history at St. Gerolamo's but particularly cognizant of Beck and Riley's. He was kind and soft-spoken but also exacting. "I don't have to remind you of your responsibility to those actively in your care."

"You do not."

"Beck's injury was quite severe," Sister said to Petievich. "At risk of infection. I believe we acted appropriately in first providing medical aid."

Winston felt a rush of emotion at her attempt to defend him.

"Initially, yes," Petievich replied, "but a call to the authorities should have followed immediately."

"This isn't the first time a victim crossed our threshold seeking protection," Winston said, "nor the first time a victim begged us not to contact the police for fear of payback."

"The key word is victim. Considering the sisters' history, you must have assumed that their quandary was connected to the death of Thomas Hain."

"Precisely why I wanted to protect them." Winston stood up. "But I only gave them one night. I'll fetch them."

"They're gone," Sister said. "Beck took the van and fled first thing this morning."

"Fled?"

"Talk to us, Winston," Petievich said.

He returned to the couch. "I cannot. I made a promise."

No mere promise. A solemn oath, expressed under the Sacrament of Confession. Betraying the covenant was a mortal sin and a crime against the church punishable by excommunication, even if lives were on the line. An absolute, inviolable contract – no circumstances existed by which a priest could divulge the details of a Confession.

"I told the police about Tommy's debt," he said carefully. "However, the debt is not the complete tale. I am torn, Ambrose, because there is no one with whom I can discuss the full circumstances of this plight…the parts of the story shared with me and me alone…no one except our Heavenly Father."

The light went on behind both the Reverend and Sister's eyes. They grasped his implication and realized that he was skirting dangerously close to betraying a Sacrament. Revealing the substance of a Confession and suggesting an incrimination had been shared during the rite was a violation and a dangerous betrayal of a Sacrament. A priest was encouraged to talk about the consequences of sin and ask the parishioner to complete contrition. He could ask them to surrender to the police or admit their crime to the aggrieved party. A priest could dish out thousands of Hail Marys and a million Our Fathers. The one thing he absolutely could not do was discuss a Confession with anyone but the confessant.

"Say no more, Father," Petievich said. "I need to use your office."

Lucinda led him out. Winston rewatched the violence from the Marina, considering the possibility he wasn't as devout as he believed. This wasn't the first time he'd deployed questionable tactics in service to a burden he'd carried for far too long.

The worst sins are those committed for the right reasons.

Countless times, he had impressed this and other observations onto his students and residents.

Perhaps it was finally time for this sin to come to light.

CHAPTER 61

A car horn stirred her. Beck cussed softly, realizing all three of them had fallen asleep. She grabbed her iPad, logged into Mr. Gabriel's administration, and checked the activity logs. The database contained updates on Jordan's calls. She spent the next twenty minutes instructing Mr. G to pull the information from the system and map it. When he finished, she shouted a wake-up.

Jordan rallied slowly. Riley crawled up to the passenger seat, wiping sleepies from her eyes. They peered over Beck's shoulder at a map of eastern Massachusetts marked by circles and jagged lines.

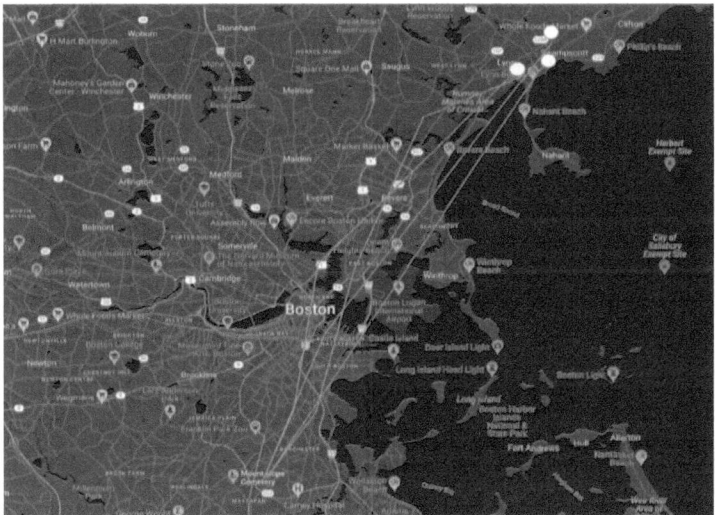

"Stratton is near one of these circles," she said.

"Okay," her sister started, "besides being the kind of kid who does her homework during recess, how did you figure this out?"

"To design MrGabriel, I boned up on cellular technology. The least busy tower carries a call, which is transferred to other towers depending on user movements and signal strength. When Jordan called Stratton's phones, we were stationary here at Mount Hope." Her finger tapped the bottom of the map. "Antennae are used to boost signals. Without them, buildings would impede connectivity. Paradigm arranged contacts with the tower and antennae providers to give us transmission data to identify trends, such as spots in the city where children made more calls because they were lost, in trouble, or just feeling uneasy."

"I'm glad you didn't try to explain this to me when I had a headache."

"The point is, we know the paths Jordan's calls traveled."

"The four that connected to voicemails," he said.

"Exactly. The receiving phone rang, which means the burner was active."

"Pretty big spreads."

"I know. It's one drawback. We've narrowed Stratton down directionally but still have an extensive area to search."

"What are the other drawbacks?" Riley asked.

"One, someone other than Z Stratton is using his burners. Two, this is historical data. It indicates where the burner was when Jordan called two hours ago. Stratton could have moved locations since then."

"He's managed to avoid capture for four days," Jordan said. "What are the chances he'll abandon a reliable hiding spot until he can escape? He's a rabbit in a warren."

"Let's hope so."

"Won't the cops do the same calculations?" her sister asked.

"They can do better. They can ping the phone to a live location, but only if they have the numbers, which we can reasonably assume they don't. Otherwise, we'd have already heard about Stratton's arrest."

Jordan glanced at Riley. "She gets all this from you?"

"Not even close."

"We need to narrow down these search sites," Beck said. "I've been staring at the map to see if anything jumps out."

"You mean, like a neon sign that says asshole drug dealer here?"

"Riley."

They spent the next few minutes scanning the map. Beck felt her initial excitement cool. She may have drastically reduced the number of haystacks, but they were still searching for a needle. This felt like their last shot at figuring out what sparked the battle at Round Midnight. They were on the BPD's capture list – and some unknown party's extermination list. The clock in her head began to tick faster.

"We can't get any more specific than these circles?" Riley asked, using her fingers to expand and move the map.

"No. We need another factor, another variable."

"Such as?"

"Stratton selected this hideout for a reason. Do you see anything noteworthy? The only commonality I see is they all went to Lynn, two bouncing off the same tower—"

"You mean Swampscott," Jordan said. He reached over to zoom in on the neighborhood, the circles filling the entire screen. "North of Lynn."

"Okay. What's in Swampscott?"

"Not what. Who." His finger indicated a spot on the map. "Francis Hain."

CHAPTER 62

After zipping north up 93, Beck went from Route 1 to 1A to 129 to reach Swampscott. An armada of cars slowed them considerably, construction crews continuing the never-ending expansion in and around the city. You wouldn't know there'd been a downturn in real estate: condos and homes still sold for eye-watering amounts as developers poured more landfill into the mud. Beck felt like tearing the steering wheel off its joint if she hit one more traffic jam. She turned on Puritan Road and idled at a vantage point where she could see news vans surrounding a stately home that easily could have housed all the residents and day students of St. J's.

Annwn.

"Why would Stratton bunker in the same town as Tommy's grandfather?" Jordan asked and shot a look at Riley.

"Don't look at me. Only Hain I had anything to do with was Tommy."

"It can't be a coincidence."

"I agree, but I still got no clue."

Beck looped back and forth between 129 and Puritan, passing from Lynn into Swampscott and back again. It was too cold for anyone to be on the beaches, and the area reflected as much; summer businesses were shuttered, and many For Lease signs swung in front of the three-deckers. "If one of these units is empty, Stratton might have snuck inside."

"There's too many," her sister said.

"Focus on ones with a view of Annwn," Jordan said.

"Why does he need a view?"

"He came here to keep tabs on Francis – or maybe even meet with him – but the news and police presence has made it impossible."

"Wouldn't he just call him?"

"Not if he suspects the police are tapping Francis' lines. Are you sure Tommy and his grandfather weren't in business together?"

"Positive. Maybe it was Francis who was involved with Stratton."

194

"Guy's worth millions," Beck said. "Why risk his new reputation to invest in club drugs?"

"Then what?"

Beck thought about it for a minute. "What if Stratton's trying to clear his name? He may not care about going to jail, but he cares about staying off Francis Hain's hit list. Face to face, he could try to convince Hain the reports are wrong, that someone else shot Tommy."

Her proposal hung in the air for a few minutes as they circled.

"Turn around," Jordan said.

"What?"

"Just—" he made a fast circular motion with his hand and slid up to the passenger-side window.

Beck pulled a three-pointer and followed his direction to a four-level cracked-brick industrial plant on Sanderson Avenue, the border between East Lynn and Swampscott. It looked like it had been constructed when industry blended in with the neighborhoods. She imagined local workers marching to the plant with lunch pails in hand. A washed-out sign proclaimed it as Pioneer Tannery, the block-sized lot fenced off.

"Mr. G, what do we know about Pioneer Tannery?" She cued the speaker.

Shuttered in nineteen sixty-four, Pioneer Tannery serviced Lynn's robust shoe industry as one of the largest processors of animal hides and skins. Authorities have designated the former factory as a superfund site because of high levels of arsenic and other hazardous chemicals.

"From the top floor, you'd have an unobstructed view of Annwn," Jordan said.

"And we're less than a quarter mile from the cell tower on Greenwood where two of your calls bounced," Beck said, the excitement of a discovery in her voice.

"This is a bad idea," Riley said, chewing her nails.

The question of what else she might be hiding returned to Beck. They'd shared some tears. One or two bridges had been crossed, but faith remained far off. "We're out of alternatives."

"Pull over." Jordan checked his sidearm and opened the door as the van cruised to a halt. "Wait for my call." He stepped out.

Nearly shouting as his legs bowed. He held the door to keep from falling, holding on with one hand as his other clawed at his back. He flexed his legs one at a time, cursing.

Riley jumped out and steadied him, looking back at Beck. "Do not leave the van."

"Wait—"

"You want to do this; this is how it's gonna go. Jordan's got the gun, and I can move faster if I don't have to worry about you. If Stratton's in there, we'll find him." She slammed the door.

It took Beck a second to realize her sister had taken the backpack.

CHAPTER 63

She parked at a red curb across the street, figuring a ticket was worth the line of sight on Pioneer. Riley and Jordan disappeared around the corner of the plant. Beck checked her mirrors and the surrounding thoroughfares for patrol cars.

Which is how she spotted the goon jaywalking across the street.

The guy was huge, six-five, muscle-busting the seams of his clothes. He walked with a side-to-side bop all bros looking for trouble use, head slung low, a Dunkin sack in one hand, a steaming coffee in the other. He wore the loud clothing all rave kids with cheap tastes prefer. Very Jersey Shore. Thug Chic. She knew little about Zachary Stratton, but if asked to guess what his entourage might look like, this guy would hit all her talking points. She wondered if she should text Jordan and Riley. Any sound amplified inside Pioneer might give away their position. At the same time, the goon might be walking up behind them. He disappeared down an alley between Pioneer and a UPS facility next door.

She crawled into the rear of the van, grabbed the tire iron, and jumped out. Ran to the corner and peered down the alley. The goon forced his way through an opening between the gate and the fence. The chain securing it was loose, the metal bent. Not the most secure arrangement, but how many people were eager to infiltrate an arsenic-soaked superfund site? He marched to a loading bay door, hauled it up and crawled under. A second later, the door sank back into position.

Beck traced his steps. At the loading bay, she tried to recall a squeal of runners when the goon thew the door up. Given its condition, it seemed unlikely it wouldn't make a sound. However, another entrance would probably be just as noisy. Setting the tire iron down, she wriggled her hands under the door and lifted, applying increments of force. The door barely budged. She put more heft behind it—

The door shot up six inches with a loud scrape.

She grabbed the tire iron, ready to run or fight.

No alarm, no shouts.

Another few inches up, and she crawled inside.

Two raised sections bracketed a zone where trucks once backed in for loading. An interior door opened into a juncture of hallways. A thick coating of dust – hopefully, not instant cancer particles – covered the floors, exposing recent footfalls. Like following breadcrumbs through a forest, she tracked them to a staircase and started up.

The next landing hovered over a cavernous production space. Mired by age, the shine of day lanced through the steel-reinforced glass and off the ironworks of outdated machinery. Wheeled mixers occupied one wall; the opposing side was lined with conveyor belts and drying racks. Two stories of catwalks circled the arena. The goon crept along the one in front of Beck. He no longer carried breakfast – the sack and cup rested on the floor. A massive silver gun had taken their place. She snuck up to the higher catwalk, tracking the goon's movements through the weave of the floor. He went through a doorway.

A shout.

Booming gunfire.

She sprinted back to the stairwell, fully aware she was rushing into a shootout with a tire iron. She hustled down the stairs, hoping to come up behind the goon. Heart hammering, she entered a brightly lit room lined with shelving racks. A breeze washed over her – someone had knocked out a window pane. Through the hole, she saw *Annwn*'s impressive spread along the shoreline.

And then the tire iron was chopped from her grip.

CHAPTER 64

All the kids rushed to the window despite the teacher's instructions to stay in their seats. Jimmy joined them. He saw Father W, Sister Lucinda and another priest speaking with a woman with a badge around her neck. Police officers ran in many directions, two over by the old dormitory. Sister Lucinda and Madeleine had said it was dangerous and told him never to go anywhere near it. The officers used a bar to pull off the board covering the front door. The plank bounced against the porch before landing in the grass.

The other kids all chattered at once. Jimmy appreciated any interruption to class. He was what one teacher called a daydreamer. He didn't know what the teacher meant since he only dreamed at night. But he did like to draw and sometimes missed parts of class because he was working on a dragon lair or outer space chase. If that was daydreaming, his teacher was right.

He recalled Beck's promise and hoped none of this trouble involved her. He liked Beck. He knew she wasn't here; he'd watched her drive off in the van. Wherever she was, Jimmy hoped she was safe. He looked forward to playing catch with her.

CHAPTER 65

Beck bounced off a steel shelf and hit the floor, only to be pulled up and held against it.

"And who might you be?" Z Stratton asked.

It took her a few seconds to process the flesh-and-blood rendition of the face she'd been staring at on TV and computer screens. "Beck…it's Beck."

"I'm afraid I don't know any Beck."

"Riley's sister."

He turned and shouted out into the plant. "Prez!" Silence.

"Where's my associate, Beck?"

"I don't know."

"Unfortunate." He'd been hiding in a condemned factory while being sought by every cop in the state, yet he appeared calm. Two "beds" made of neatly folded clothes occupied either side of the room, while triangular stacks of empty energy drinks and Stop & Shop bags, some filled with groceries and others with trash, adorned the wall. It looked like someone trying to tidy up a garbage dump. "You came alone?"

"I did."

He smiled. "Then who's Prez shooting at?"

She'd watched a documentary on Netflix about psychopaths and their total lack of remorse and compassion. They didn't see people as living beings, only as obstacles and opportunities. Stratton's smile mismatched the disregard in his eyes. Any doubt over Riley's claim he had killed Tommy vanished.

Stratton pressed a gun up under her chin. His pulse quickened so intensely, she felt it in the fingertips of the hand around her arm.

"We got your money," she said. "The hundred thousand."

"So Riley's here. Wonderful. Who else?"

"No one—"

He crashed the gun into her midriff. "Who. Else."

She gasped and tried to figure out how to cue Mr. G to alert the authorities without stoking more of Stratton's fire.

200

"Let's try a different approach." He shoved his gun into his waistband, spun her around and wedged her injured arm between both of his, her elbow the fulcrum against his opposing pressures. "A few more foot-pounds of force, and I'll split your arm in two. How did you find me?"

"I traced the calls! The ones Jordan made this morning."

"Jordan?"

"John. John Morrell! He's an investigator. Hired to look into those around me. Ensure I wasn't associated with whatever was going down at the club."

"You're not putting my mind at ease here, Beck."

"We just want answers! If we wanted to turn you in, we could have sent your location to the cops!"

He thought it over. "Morrell...huh...I never did trust him." He released her. "You can do that? Trace phone calls?" His voice was back in conversational mode.

"Yes."

"Tommy and Riley did talk about how smart you are. Like a friggin' savant." He walked to the door and drew his gun again. "Prez!"

"I'm not so smart; otherwise, I wouldn't be standing here."

He gestured with the gun, like, *good point.*

"I just want to get back to my life," she said. "We came here to give you the money and find out what happened at the club, what this is all about, and then we're gone. You won't see us ever again."

"Your dear sister should have explained it all."

"She was unconscious. Someone clubbed her."

He barked out a single laugh. "That's not quite how it went down, Beck. I should know: I'm the one who knocked her on the head. She was pert as a petunia the whole time."

Beck wasn't surprised, only begrieved – Riley's lies never ended.

"She tell you I shot Tommy?"

"Yes."

"Well, that part's true. I aerated that little rich boy, but good." He watched her shudder. "Oh, he deserved every ounce of that lead. All he had to do was pay off his debt. But he had to go and bring some psycho cop into it." He sighed as he regarded the empty hallway and stairwell. "Poor Prez. Dumb as a fencepost but the most ride-or-die brother on my payroll." He marched back over. "Three things are about to happen, Beck. First, you'll be my shield. Second, Riley will hand over the money. And three, she's gonna tell me where I can find the video."

Beck's mind blanked.

He read her expression. "She didn't mention the tape, did she? Real piece of work, your sister. Or are you playing dumb?"

"I don't...I don't know what..."

"Tommy's leverage. A tape that cantankerous prick—" he gestured at *Annwn*, "—didn't want to get out. Hain forked over a hundred G's like that." He snapped his fingers. "And if this recording's good for a hundred, it's good for a million or more."

Beck understood nothing. Like she'd told Jordan, logic is useless in a world running on spontaneous combustion. "I don't know anything about a video."

He grabbed her arm. "Then let's go ask her."

"I'm right here."

Stratton and Beck spun around.

Riley stood in the doorway, backpack held in front of her. "Let her go, Z. I got your money."

He put the gun in Beck's face, but his eyes angled on the backpack. The top was unzipped, exposing the bundles. "Where's the tape?"

"I got no clue what you're talking about."

"You were there—!"

A cannon blast nearly split Beck's eardrums. She shouted, her hands flying reflexively up to her head, expecting to feel only pieces of it intact just before she died.

Instead, she saw paper floating through the air.

Money.

The backpack swung in Riley's hand – exposing the gun her sister had concealed behind it. Stratton stumbled in reverse, mystified at the holes in his chest. He raised his weapon. Riley's next shot blew him off his feet and painted the wall red.

Beck sunk to her knees, shaking. A voice called out, but the volleys echoed around the room. Her disconnection wasn't related to The Drift. This was a total shutdown.

"BECK!"

The shout caused her to look up at her sister, who had emptied two Stop & Shop bags of supplies and was stuffing them with the loose and charred bills blasted free by her first shot.

"Get up."

Beck stayed down.

Jordan limped in and came to a halt, held in place by the sight of Stratton's body.

"Help her," Riley said. "Jordan!"

He hobbled over to pull Beck to her feet.

CHAPTER 66

Distant sirens whooped. Someone must have heard the shots and called it in. Jordan's spine tightened with each step. If he fell, it was over; the sisters could never carry him out of here in time. Adrenaline pushed him on.

Stratton's muscle – "Prez" – was taking on room temperature after daring Jordan to a gunfight. Bad idea, considering Prez was a glorified bouncer who learned his craft from *Call of Duty* while Jordan honed his at Fort Benning, then in Iraq, Syria and Afghanistan. Riley had snared Prez's piece and taken off before Jordan could stop her, his damnable back reducing him to halting lunges, arriving seconds after she'd sent Stratton to the hereafter.

They reached the main street.

"Slow down," he said. "Act normal." Residents peered out their windows; a few stepped onto their stoops. Cruisers and first responders began to block off the trash-strewn lot. "Put your collar up." When she didn't respond, he yanked the lapels of her coat up over her cheeks and pulled her watch cap down to the brim of her eyes. Then he slid his arm over her shoulder. He felt her tense and then relax.

Riley hurried up to a crosswalk, spotting the van across the street.

Beck began to tremble. "There's a recording. A video that threatens the Hains. Tommy used it to blackmail his own family."

"I don't know whether to be shocked or impressed."

"Stratton wanted to chisel more out of Francis. A lot more. That's why he came here. He planned on bluffing Hain when he got the chance."

"Bluffing? So Stratton didn't have the tape?"

"No. Didn't even know what's on it, but figured whatever it is has to be pretty juicy."

Jordan reconsidered the week's events. "That's why Tommy didn't take direct receipt of the funds. It wasn't a loan; it was extortion. But shouldn't he have assumed they'd be watching the V-Post?"

"Absolutely. Tommy wasn't an idiot."

204

"He didn't even bother to disguise himself. And he drove his own damn car to pick it up."

"It's almost like…" She drifted off.

"What? Don't overthink. Just say it."

"Like he wanted whoever was watching to follow him."

CHAPTER 67

Jordan sped them out of Swampscott, south towards the city, while Beck crouched across from Riley in the payload.

"You killed him. You didn't even hesitate."

Riley nodded. "Before he killed you or me. I didn't think I could shame him into putting his gun down." She began to reorganize the bundles of money. "No different from what you did to Washington."

"It's a lot different."

"I owed that sonofabitch for Tommy."

"Maybe. Or maybe you wanted to shut him up about the video." Beck waited, but her sister didn't reply, lining the inside of the damaged backpack with the shopping bags. "You were supposed to pick up the money. Extorting the cash was the first challenge; retrieving it the second. Whoever Francis Hain sent to watch the drop-off would recognize Tommy, so it had to be you."

Riley shook her head as if dismissing Beck's crazed imaginings.

"The V-Post sends a notification. The package has arrived. You order the package moved to one of the private rooms, out of sight. You put on a wig, shave your head or dye it an extreme color like you've done a thousand times before, check the bundles for any RFID or Geolocator tags and then transfer the money to your backpack. Whoever's watching never realizes they're staking out an empty mailbox."

Her sister repacked the loose cash, tightened the backpack and bounced it up and down to ensure none of the precious contents fell out. "You're reaching."

"I'm deducing. You got rid of the suitcase after fleeing Round Midnight. You knew it was bugged."

"This is nuts—"

Beck tore the backpack away, forcing Riley to focus on her. "Something went wrong, very wrong, because Tommy shows up instead of you and all but fires a signal flare to lead Washington back to the club. Tell me why."

Her sister's jaw trembled.

"The truth this time."

Riley closed her eyes. For a second, Beck feared she was shutting down.

Then her sister began to speak: "Tommy wasn't just paying off a debt…he was paying a ransom…"

CHAPTER 68

Six nights earlier

Stratton smiled as he stepped past the bouncers.

Why'd he have to bring his whole crew? Tommy thought. Immediately, Stratton's gang began demanding free drinks and harassing the few unfortunate ladies who had wandered into the club. Half of Midnight's security was outmatched, the other half taking Stratton's party favors into the alley or the can.

"Long time no see, partner." Stratton's hug turned into a hold. "If I didn't know better, I'd think you were dodging me."

"Just getting everything in order."

Stratton reached for the bruise around Tommy's eye. "Looks like it's healing up nicely."

Tommy pulled away with a grin. As difficult as life had been, it had turned infinitely worse when he partnered with Z Stratton.

Partner.

Right.

More like prisoner.

He led Stratton, his chief bodyguard, Prez, and another pumped-up hammerhead in a whistling polyester jumpsuit up to the second floor. They passed the office. He nodded at Riley, who assembled the deeds, agreements and paperwork required to assign Round Midnight to whatever bogus LLC Stratton had set up. Stratton's eventual plans for the club were a mystery. Tommy didn't care. He just wanted out.

Riley followed them up to his apartment. Lo-level celebrities – many of whom had checked out Midnight once and never returned – smiled inside cheap picture frames. She laid out the documents on the kitchen table.

Stratton didn't even glance at the forms. "Where's the money?"

"Ready to be picked up," Tommy said.

"What, at the drive-thru? The ATM down the street?"

Prez and the hammerhead laughed.

Tommy rechecked the V-Post app, confirming the shipment's arrival. "Riley's gonna pick it up. While we wait, we can sign the docs."

"Very efficient of you. I appreciate your organization, but this flea pit is hardly the crown jewel. I expected to see green."

"And you will. I want to make this right, Z."

"Nah, you want to buy your freedom. Riley stays. You go. And Prez goes with you."

"Z, I got this," Riley said.

Stratton's backhand knocked her into the table, scattering the forms.

Tommy charged. Prez intercepted him, landing a punch so hard Tommy didn't know whether he was standing or flying. The frayed carpet came up to meet him. He heard Riley shouting and regained his vision in time to see Stratton bring the butt of his gun down on her head. She went limp and landed right next to him. He crawled over, cradled her, heard a click and looked up into Stratton's nine. "What the hell, Z! I got the money! I swear on my life!"

"You've been sucking wind for years, and in two days, you come up with a hundred grand? You've been holding out on me."

"No—"

"Maybe this place is moving more product than you've let on."

"I'm not skimming!"

Prez picked Tommy up and threw him into the wall, then set his bulging forearm across his throat.

"Where'd you get the cash?" Stratton asked.

"My family!"

"Your family wants nothing to do with you. That's why you came to me."

"...leverage..."

"What leverage you got, pretty boy?"

The room began to spin.

Stratton nodded.

Prez released Tommy, who coughed, clutching his neck. "A recording...a tape!"

"Tape? Like from Blockbuster? What is this, 1999?" More laughter from his goons, Stratton doing a bit. "And what, pray tell, is on this cinematic masterpiece?"

"The only play I got left."

"Tell me."

Tommy straightened up. "No."

Stratton licked his lips, a disgusting lizard-like display.

"If you know anything about me, you know I'd do anything for her. I wouldn't make something like this up."

Stratton slid his gun back into its holster. "She's your weak link."

"And I'm hers."

"So sweet." Stratton guided Riley to her feet. She moaned, half-conscious, a trembling hand dancing over the spot where he had crowned her. He eased her onto the couch and sat next to her, tenderly swiping the hair out of her eyes. "She is a pretty one. You got good taste."

Tommy felt nauseous. "Z...please..."

Stratton held Riley like a precious doll, motioning to Prez for a paper towel, which he used to blot her head wound. "If this video's worth a hundred, it's worth ten, twenty times more. You're a terrible drug dealer, Tommy, and an even worse entrepreneur, but you may have just stumbled across an additional revenue stream: bleeding your family dry."

"No."

"C'mon, what do you care? You hate those pricks."

"I can't. You don't understand."

Riley's eyes blinked open.

"Hey, there, sweetheart," Stratton said. She tried to pull away, scratch, claw and bite. He flicked open a razor and laid it against her cheek. Everybody went still: Riley, the goons, Tommy. "New proposal, partner. The money, the club *and* this video...or else we're gonna take her to a very dark place for a very long time."

He's gonna kill us both, Tommy thought. It had always been possible, but he'd hoped to buy their way clear.

Now he knew – the second he turned over the money and the recording, he and Riley would be disappeared forever.

One card remained. The equivalent of calling in an airstrike on his own position like some doomed G.I. in those old war movies Uncle Dave liked. Chances were, he and Riley would still end the night under a white sheet or, at best, in jail. "Prez stays here."

"You're not in a position to bargain."

"If you hurt her, there's no deal. I'll burn you down, Z. I know enough. Won't matter what happens to me." He met Riley's eyes – "I'll be back," – and ran out the door.

CHAPTER 69

Six nights earlier

Riley read the twisted hunger in Stratton's eyes. She didn't think he'd try anything until he got what he wanted, but afterward…

She suspected Tommy had drawn the same conclusion: Stratton came here tonight to be paid, take everything, do whatever he pleased with her and then execute them. The realization made her want to fight until there was nothing left, but her chances were slim, and even if successful, her escape would only complicate matters for Tommy.

Prez returned minutes later, out of breath. "He's gone."

"I see," Stratton said.

"He got to his car before I could stop him."

"Understood."

The punch knocked Prez's head sideways. Stratton kept pounding – the bodyguard didn't even try to mount a defense. The second thug guarded the door to prevent Riley from making a break, not looking surprised by, or even interested in, the beating.

As much as Riley enjoyed watching their disorder, she worried Stratton would turn his rage on her next. She tried to shrink into the couch.

When it was over, Stratton shot his cuffs and used the sink to wash his hands while Prez sat against the wall and tested his wobbly jaw.

She lost track of time, the blow to her head pushing her closer to unconsciousness. She forced herself to stay awake, terrified at the prospect of passing out with Stratton and his animals in the room.

Finally, his phone rang. "Thomas. How nice to hear from you…Yes, she's fine …No, you can't talk to her, and before you ask, no, I'm not letting her go."

Tommy was trying to negotiate her release. She'd loved him for so long, and he still found new ways to remind her.

"Don't press your luck," Stratton said. "You got twenty minutes, and then I start cutting."

Tommy returned in fifteen.

With the money, but no video.

"Perhaps I'm not making myself clear," Stratton said.

Prez and the thug tore into Tommy. Riley begged them to stop. Tried to jump in, only to be tossed back. Stratton, meanwhile, fingered the money inside the briefcase. Finally, his bruisers retreated. She helped Tommy sit up.

"I'm starting to think you don't trust me," Stratton said. "Where's. The video?"

"Safe…" He spat between broken lips. "Let her go, and I'll take you."

Stratton drilled a gaze into Tommy, then laughed and waved his hand. "Fuck it. Do 'em both."

The thug shoved Tommy to the floor. Prez hauled Riley to the couch, drew his gun, and pressed a pillow over her face to muffle the shot. She gagged, punched, swiped, but he was too strong.

A series of shouts.

The pillow pulled away.

"It's in my car!" Tommy yelled, his face pushed into the filthy carpet. "The trunk! Please, Z! Don't hurt her."

Stratton shut the briefcase. "Let's go."

The thug pulled Tommy up and out the door. Prez dragged Riley behind him. Stratton brought up the rear. The music intensified as they dropped onto the exposed passageway above the dance floor. Programmed sconces sent jags of colored lights across the club, disorienting them. They were halfway across when Tommy stopped.

"Move!" the thug yelled, but Tommy held onto the railing, refusing to let go.

Prez released Riley to assist.

Tommy whirled on the thug, driving one fist after another into his face and the whistling jumpsuit. They grappled across the catwalk. The thug knocked Tommy down.

Riley didn't even hear the first shot.

The thug's head snapped back as he sank into a heap.

More gunshots cut through the swirling lights and thundering music.

She hit the floor, pulling her arms and legs up around her. Something exploded. She peered down at the kitchen area, the swinging doors hanging askew, smoke billowing out.

The briefcase landed next to her. Stratton aimed his gun with both hands over the railing and fired into the haze below. Shots pockmarked the ceiling and shot out lights over their heads. Prez trampled Riley on his way to Stratton, pulling his boss back into the stairwell.

Somebody seized her wrist.

Tommy.

"C'mon!" He started to pull her forward, then noticed the briefcase. He grabbed it and led her forward, covering her head. Skreiches of gunfire chased them into the office. He slammed the door and threw the lock. "Garage!"

She opened the rear door on a set of stairs connected to the underground parking. Only she and Tommy had access to it. Down they ran. Tommy used the remote to cue open the gate covering the garage entrance.

They'd made it.

They were going to get away.

A splash hit the side of Tommy's car. He grunted and fell against it, cupping the side of his neck. Another round hissed overhead. Riley turned to see Stratton running after them, Prez lumbering behind. She opened the passenger door, pushed Tommy in, and flung the door closed. As she ran around to the driver's side, Stratton pulled the trigger but hit empty. He cursed and reloaded, no more than thirty feet away, closing in fast.

Tommy's hand trembled as he passed her the key. Her hands shook as she tried to slide it into the ignition. Warm liquid stuck to her fingers.

Tommy's blood.

She cranked the GTO to life and put the pedal to the floor. Cracks of gunfire followed her up the circular ramp. The gate was only halfway open, slowly rattling across its rail. She slowed, trying to time it, eyes affixed to the mirrors.

Stratton came into view behind her—

"Hold on!" She slammed the gas to the floor, clipping off the side-view mirror against the gate. They nearly flew off the top of the ramp onto Talbot. Pedal down, she struggled to keep them on course, taking one last look at the club in her rearview before focusing on the road ahead.

She was five blocks away before she realized Tommy hadn't said a word.

CHAPTER 70

Riley waited for Beck to express her sympathy. Instead, all she got was a "What's on the video?" in an emotionless, monotone voice. "No idea," she replied. "I don't even know if it exists."

"Yes, you do. Francis Hain didn't cough up a hundred grand and bribe a trio of dirty cops for nothing. Tommy must have shown him proof."

"If you say so. But I'd be calling the shots now if I had it. I wouldn't be hiding underground and driving all over hell and back trying to find the frigging thing."

Riley realized her mistake as soon as the words left her mouth.

"The cabin," Beck said. "You thought Tommy hid it up there. No luck, I assume. That's why you returned to Boston. To keep looking. Don't give me this 'if it exists' crap, Riles. You know it's out there, and you want to use it to make the Hains pay all over again."

"Yeah, okay, fine. You're right, as usual. I want to make those bastards pay for the rest of their miserable lives. Surprised? I'm a lifetime screwup. It's on brand." Riley caught her breath. "Look, what's it matter? I don't know what's on it, and I don't know where it is. I've checked everywhere. The five-oh's probably got it."

"I don't think Tommy kept something that valuable in the club, his apartment or his car. He only said it was in the GTO to get Stratton and his gang into the open. He had one chance: to lead whoever was watching the money – Hain's enforcers – back to the club. And it nearly worked."

Riley wrapped her arms around her legs and stared at the van's floor. "Yeah. Nearly…"

As they approached Dyer, Jordan took out his burner.

"What are you doing?" Beck asked.

"Calling it in. It's over."

"It's not over until we find the tape. Tommy was gone for almost two hours picking up the money. Even with traffic, the V-Post is only twenty-five minutes from Round Midnight."

Riley stared at her in disbelief. "Will you stop? Jordan's right. It's over. We should have just surrendered back at Pioneer. I don't even know why I wanted to run. I guess I'm wired to. This is on me, Tommy and Stratton. It's our mess. They're dead. I'm still here."

"Now you want to be accountable? Too late, Riles. We've all made our choices, and now we gotta follow them to their inevitable conclusion. Hain isn't going to sit this out, even with Stratton dead. He wants the tape and believes we have it or, at the very least, have seen it. We're worse off now than ever. A week from now – or six or twelve – my brakes will fail. Jordan will hang himself in his bathroom. And you'll get stabbed in prison. If I'm gonna have Francis Hain as my enemy, I want to know why."

CHAPTER 71

A rat danced over Beck's hand. She cast it off with a violent jerk. The derelict subway line carried its tiny screeches as it scurried away. They had said very little on their flight back to Dyer, engrossed by the Pioneer Tannery news.

Stratton and his accomplice dead.

Beck, Riley and Jordan Lear captured on a traffic cam fleeing Swampscott.

A vigilante squad.

Who knew where they would strike next?

Just before they ditched the van, Beck tossed her burner and instructed Jordan and Riley to do the same, handing them the three other burners in their place. They parked near Shattuck Hospital, hoofed it through Franklin Park, then descended to where Riley had decamped. Beck wondered if she'd live out the rest of her days like some subterranean Quasimodo. They split the last of the water and snacks – Funyuns and two Snickers. Riley then used the backpack as a pillow and stretched across the floor.

Her sister, the inveterate con artist.

Who'd saved Beck's life.

Twice.

"Washington asked me about hiding places," she said, doing her best to focus, delineate and hypothesize, "and if Riley or Tommy had ever given me anything for safekeeping. I assumed he was talking about the money. Now…"

"He was searching for the video," Jordan said. "Same reason they torched *Chaya*, in case I had somehow gotten my hands on it. Are there cameras at the club, Riley?"

"CCTV," she muttered, "but only outside, and we erased the footage daily if there weren't any obvious events we needed to preserve."

"I can only imagine what your definition of 'obvious events' is."

She rolled over. "Crimes, assaults, that kind of thing. Not, you know, jerkwad liars who don't have any friends sponsoring blowout parties to spy on us."

Jordan bit the inside of his cheek. "Touché."

"In the beginning, we got the cool kids, you know? Midnight was a hip new spot. Influencers. A ball player or two. It cratered after COVID."

"Any of the Hains hang out there?" Beck asked.

"Just his sister, Susan."

"No Carlow, no Francis."

"Never. Neither's been part of Tommy's life for twenty-odd years. He only saw his family if he went to Annwn or his mother bribed him into attending some event. Photo ops to promote the idea of an All-American family. Ogres, the lot of 'em." She rolled back over.

Beck struggled to stay awake as the stale air closed in. "We're back to the primary question. What kind of video compels Francis Hain to pay out a hundred thousand bucks and dispatch his hit squad? Powerful people are never held accountable, not by something as quaint as a recording."

"We won't know until we find it," Jordan said. "Also, we keep talking about this video like a physical thing. How do we know someone didn't record it digitally?"

"Stratton said tape. I assume he heard that from Tommy because who uses that word anymore? It's a very specific reference."

"So when did Tommy find or get his hands on this tape? Why use the recording now and not all the other times his ass got in hock?"

"Why approach Father W for a loan if he's got the smoking gun? The only answer is Tommy acquired it very recently."

"And it's life or death Friday night. But he disappears for two hours."

"Hiding the tape."

Jordan nodded. "It's an enormous risk, but the video's crucial. That two-hour window narrows it down, just like your phone trace. I'd estimate he had forty, maybe fifty minutes to bury his treasure, keeping him in city limits, no more than a few miles from the V-Post and the club. So where? Is there anyone he would have trusted it with?"

"Everyone Tommy trusted is sitting across from you...except for his sister."

"What about the *padre* or the nun?"

"They would have come forward after his death. I assume Susan would have, too."

"Unless she decided to let Grandpa's secret die with Tommy."

Beck glanced at Riley. But her sister was either fast asleep or faking it to avoid further inquiry. Weariness settled in. Never mind half the city, there was no time to scour even one block. She trudged to the exit for a clear signal and asked Mr. G to aggregate Tommy's locations on the web – every place he ever posted about or snapped a photo of. She leaned against the door to rest, too tired to climb back down.

"Cold?" Jordan asked.

"Freezing."

He peeled off his coat and walked up.

"You don't have to—"

"I don't mind sharing." He waited, holding it open.

She studied the inside of the coat: it did look pretty warm. Finally, she nodded. He sat beside her, draped it over them like a blanket, and asked if she was okay. "Yeah. Fine. Thanks."

He tapped his shoulder. "It's no Brooklinen, but it will do."

"Brooklinen?"

"Only the best pillow in creation." He read her look. "I don't joke about my sleep."

Like the moment outside Pioneer, she grinned and relaxed in his presence. She rested her head on him, knowing she'd be out in seconds. She raised the burner to tell Mr. G to wake her in an hour when she noted the list of "Tommy Hain" results cascading across the notes section of the app. One entry contained a thumbnail photo: Tommy and Riley at Hampton Beach, leaning on his GTO, his beloved car, the center of so much of what had transpired—

His claim to Stratton that the video was hidden inside.

Washington's exacting search of the GTO.

Riley escaping to Beck's in the car.

Tommy riding out the last seconds of his life in the passenger seat.

Father W seeing Tommy driving away from campus.

She sat up. "The car."

"What about it?"

She texted Father W to pick up, then dialed him.

He answered on the second ring. "Beck?"

"Please, just listen. I know I've betrayed all your trust and disappointed you in more ways—"

"Stop. What's wrong? Are you okay?"

"Relatively speaking." She breathed. "I need to ask you something. At the police station, you told Underhill that one of the kids had seen Tommy on campus. In the back alley."

"That's right. I saw him driving away. Or so I thought. I was seeing Tommy everywhere, desperate to find him."

"The GTO was pretty distinct, though."

"Yes, it was."

"What day? Do you remember?"

"Ummm…"

"Please, it's important."

His breath turned heavy; her tension transferred to him. "Friday evening."

"What time?"

"Well, it would have been after dinner because we were cleaning up and taking out the trash."

"Are you positive?"

"Yes. Why is this so urgent?"

"Tommy hid something in his car; if they haven't found it, it's probably in the river. I'm trying to retrace all the places he drove that night."

"What did he hide?"

"A tape…a recording which might explain everything."

"Where are you, Beck?"

"I can't explain right now, but I'm okay." As with Amy and Eli, her regret and request for understanding required more than a phone call. "Thank you, Winston." She hung up.

"If it's in the river—"

"I only said that to throw the police off the scent." Her burner rang; she ignored it. "Father W will try me a few more times, but when I don't answer, he'll call the cops." She powered off the burner and smashed it apart against the cement. "But I don't think the video's in the car or the river."

"Then where is it?"

CHAPTER 72

Marrow-frozen from spending so much time outside and underground, climbing to the roof above the Kleen-o-Mat felt like a mountain expedition. Beck's injured arm throbbed under the exertion, but it was an ideal crow's nest, a regular haunt for St. J kids. The location afforded a clear view of St. J's and any potential sightings of Lucinda the Lunatic, who never hesitated to scour the neighborhood for wayward residents. The residence hall was lit up and noisy from the kids enjoying the last few moments before bedtime, but the Victorian remained a smudge against the sunset.

Jordan opened his burner on a breaking news item about "renewed activity" on the Neponset related to Tommy's murder. "Let's wait for full dark."

Beck tweaked – she wanted to get inside the Victorian now – but deferred to his guidance.

Two hours later, he woke her up. She didn't even remember falling asleep. Jordan hid his knapsack with the laptop behind some loose brickwork of the parapet, but not before pulling out extra ammunition. He glanced at Riley, then at her backpack.

"No way I'm leaving it behind," she said.

"You'll move easier without it."

"And poorer."

He slid the bricks back in place. "If we get separated, we meet back here."

They climbed down and used the alley between Parker and Higgins to approach St. J's. Riley crossed over first into the copse of evergreens outside the fence. Beck and Jordan followed when no spotlights flared to life and no Dobermans charged out of the darkness. Sodden earth squished under their shoes. Riley waited by Escape Tree, so named for its thick limbs extending over the fence. Her sister climbed up, out and over, dropping onto the lawn.

"Oh, hell, no," Jordan said, rubbing his back.

"Unless you want to cut through the church, this is the only way." Beck felt only slightly more confident. She kept herself in reasonable shape but no longer enjoyed a teenager's fearlessness. Forcing herself not to look at the sharp spikes atop the fence, she shimmied along the limb and onto a concrete column. Her balance tipped. She leaped away from the spikes. The impact turned her legs to jelly. She had the presence of mind to keep her injured shoulder turned away; else, she might have awakened the whole of Dyer with her screams.

Riley kneeled over her. "You okay?"

Beck tried to respond and spent a minute coughing instead. She waved to indicate her survival.

"Why don't I go inside," her sister said, "while you and Jordan keep watch?"

"The house is immense. If Tommy hid the tape inside, it's gonna take all three of us to find it."

Her sister made a face. Beck read her true intention – Riley wanted the video for herself. Wiping dollar signs from her sister's eyes would be difficult if they found the tape. They'd barely survived the ruthless tactics of Francis Hain, who would never stop erasing his vile past. Beck's strategy was to meet force with force: make it clear the video would remain sequestered for as long as she, Riley and Jordan drew breath. She didn't relish the idea of striking a deal, but the alternative of turning it over to the authorities felt tremendously naïve.

Jordan snaked across the limb, then used all his upper-body strength to descend to the concrete column and shimmy down.

Beck peered across campus, a kid again, worried about Sister Lucinda, who possessed "a bat-like radar system," according to Father W. She waited for the beam of Sister's Maglite to fall over her and a sentence of three days in her room, no TV and extra kitchen duty to be handed down. Luckily, this section of the school grounds remained cloaked under the trees and nearby buildings, their movements covered by a mix of nearby TVs, stereos and traffic.

They approached the Victorian. The chain-link fence made Beck's heart sink at the prospect of another climb. She prodded and felt it give way – someone had already pushed through. She also noticed the board over the front door had been removed.

"Tommy?" Jordan asked.

"He wouldn't leave a trail," Riley said. "Probably the cops, searching for us."

They detoured around the side of the house. All the windows had plywood covering them. Beck walked up the bulkhead and checked a board – it slid to the right, the nails on the left removed. She held the cover aside and shoved the window up. It didn't budge. She looked closer – the frame was empty, the glass knocked out. She laid her jacket across the bottom to avoid getting cut. Doing a pushup on the sill made her arm feel like it would fall off. She quickly swung inside. Broken glass crinkled under her boots.

"Careful," she said, holding the panel aside as Jordan and Riley climbed in.

Moonlight and streetlamps spiked into the dining room through the Victorian's fissures. The room appeared much more expansive than Beck remembered. Damaged chairs were strewn underneath empty picture frames. She peered down three different hallways leading into the space. The house had endured a century of cobbling, resulting in a slapdash blueprint ideal for a dry-land version of Marco Polo but diabolical for aides tending to rambunctious and often emotionally troubled children.

"One room at a time," Jordan said. "We follow each other in a line. This way, every spot gets checked three times. I'll go first, then Riley, then Beck."

Twenty minutes flew by, checking vents, closets, wainscotting, empty light fixtures and decaying furniture with no luck. They moved into one of the great rooms, what Father W called "rumpus rooms," coming up empty again.

"Hell, he could have nailed it to the roof," Riley said.

"Not under his time crunch," Jordan replied. "Accounting for drive times to and from the club and picking up the cash at the V-Post, he had fifty minutes to execute his plan. Take away thirty to forty for the round trip out here, and he was down to no more than ten to fifteen minutes to run inside and hide the tape."

"We're basing this on the eyewitness of a child and an eighty-year-old man with a taste for rum."

"Father W's seventy-seven and sharp as a tack," Beck said, "and the house is perfect for Tommy – a building he knows like the back of his hand that no one's entered in months."

It took another hour to comb the rest of the first floor. Fortunately, no drop ceilings were inside the Victorian, which would have required Beck to stand on someone's shoulders. Floorboards were another issue. There was no time to pry each one up, so they searched for signs of disturbance.

Nothing.

Beck struggled not to lose hope. She didn't believe Tommy would have buried his prize outside and risk damaging it, and she doubted he'd have chosen a well-trafficked part of the school and church, but countless hidey-holes remained.

They entered the house's turret. The Victorian featured four staircases: the central one by the front door, a rear stairwell connecting the kitchen, storage areas and what was once the caretaker's rooms, a deathtrap set of risers dropping almost vertically into the basement and this spiral one inside the turret. Beck used to imagine it as the entrance to a fortress. Jordan passed her his burner and used the banister to pull himself up. Each level branched off into more hallways, bedrooms, bathrooms and dens.

"I'll take the second floor," he said, wincing as he kneaded his spine. "You two go up and work your way down."

Beck and her sister continued up to the top floor of the turret, into her childhood room. Oxidized bedframes lined the perimeter. Two wobbly desks bracketed a moldy armoire.

But the denuded mural drew Beck's immediate attention – Mr. Gabriel, arms folded, his smile reassuring her everything would be okay.

CHAPTER 73

"No dice," Riley said.

While Beck's was one of the more oversized bedrooms in the Victorian, they completed their search in minutes. Her sister exited into the hallway, set her feet against one wall and walked up, shining her light into the vent.

Beck remembered the tricks and stunts Riley performed, entertaining herself and the other kids. "Anything?"

"Lots of dust and what looks like rat turds." She released her feet and landed back on the floor, kicking up dust, cueing another hacking fit from her distressed lungs.

"We're gonna have to check into a wellness clinic after this."

"I hear state prisons have wonderful health facilities."

"Funny, Riles. Real funny."

"I'll start on the other rooms." Her sister disappeared down the hall.

Already, they were abandoning Jordan's recommendation to recheck each other's inspections. Beck stared up at Mr. Gabriel, then at the stylized Mr. G on her burner. "Any suggestions?"

I need more context.

"Never mind."

When she was little, she believed in the mystical. Her passion for fantasy games and literature hadn't waned, but after Mr. G, she'd modified her belief – the magic we see is the magic we make. The darkness around her felt like the final curtain on both dogmas. Father W liked to say time was undefeated; she always considered it indifferent. Growing up meant accepting the indifference of time. Nothing was left for her here, no talisman to turn circumstances in her favor. She ran her hand along the mural, her burner light tracing the top of Mr. Gabriel's knit cap down to the top of the baseboards, which were painted to resemble grass. She clicked off the light and turned to—

Scratches.

On the floor.

She clicked the light on a series of gouges underneath a bedframe. Grit and dust impacted the scars, but one exposed the yellow oak beneath the varnish. She pushed the frame out of the way. Ran her hands over the floorboards, which felt solid. She shook the bedframe. The straps wiggled, too flexible. However, the headboard consisted of solid bars. She yanked up, rewarded as the headboard pulled free, the frames designed for fast disassembly. One bar turned in her hand, the screw-like threads coming out of the joist. Flakes of rust erupted in a puff as the bar came loose.

The nails of the gouged floorboard were bent, not flush. They inevitably worked themselves up after a hundred years of rowdy children. Father W and Sister Lucinda had made shoes mandatory at all times. A heavy stomp or the back of Sister's Maglite was usually enough to hammer flowering nails back down. However, the damage here was recent. She worked the tip of the headboard bar underneath and pried the nails out one by one with little effort, the last lifting the floorboard up and out. She drove her hand into the hole, heedless of any potential spiderwebs or rat nests.

Fabric ran along her nails, a loop catching around her index finger. She pulled a vinyl bag out of the space. She stared at it, astonished; the bag a lost relic, and she one of those kooky adventurers she idolized as a child. "Who said there's no more magic?"

Beck?

"Hang on, G!" She unzipped the bag.

A Camcorder rested inside, the kind marketed to the home director. She set it on the floor and ran her light over it, wary of damaging it. There was a tape inside, no bigger than a deck of cards. After a few seconds, she managed to pop out a tiny screen. Looked like a 4-inch LED. The Camcorder was at least ten years old, probably older.

She called her sister's name, trying to temper her excitement. Another inspection revealed the Power button. She pushed. The camera hummed to life, the LED casting the room in soft blue light. Someone had charged it recently. Pocketing her phone, she hit REWIND, then PLAY.

Wavy lines resolved into a party, bejeweled and gowned revelers under tents and heat lamps, a massive mansion lit up in the background. A band played.

A wedding video?

The handheld imagery bounced around but managed to capture silver balloons spelling out:

HAPPY NEW YEAR

The POV focused on the ladies in attendance, with juvenile zooms on their breasts. One of them called out, "Oh, Tommy!"

The video cut out.

Beck yelled again for Riley.

The video resumed, a nauseating blur of grass and…

A beach?

Hard to tell.

The videographer panted loudly, running now, accompanied by what sounded like the backbeat of surf. The noise of the party dropped off. The image panned up onto a long dock. A yacht bobbed at the end. The POV approached a boathouse, a faint light inside. Voices drifted out, muffled shouts, fervent. The POV closed in on the side door, which stood ajar. Two forms came into focus—

A man atop a woman. His suit was disheveled, his tie askew, pants dropped to his ankles. The man splayed the woman on a workbench, pushing up her white button-down over her chest, obscuring it under his bulk. As his face came up, there was no mistaking him.

Carlow Hain.

A much younger version, but Tommy's father, without a doubt. He ignored the woman's claws, slaps and pleas for him to stop.

Beck turned around to see Riley hurrying down the hall. "I found it!"

A scream.

Not from passion but pain.

Beck returned to the video as Carlow, red-faced and sweaty, planted a hand over his victim's face.

Riley ran in, shouting, "No, no!" and seized the Camcorder with both hands.

"Stop!"

"LET GO!"

"What's wrong with you—"

Riley smacked Beck across the face. Horrified by her action, she froze, giving Beck time to scurry away.

"What is this?"

"GIVE IT TO ME!" Riley flung herself at Beck again.

Another scream from the video.

Another scream from Riley.

Jordan shouted from the second floor.

Riley tugged at the Camcorder. Beck pivoted as hard as she could. Riley's momentum carried her into the armoire with enough force to cave in the doors. She collapsed to the floor and began to cry harder than Beck had ever seen another living being cry, begging her to shut it off, shut it off, shut it off.

A voice cried out: "Dad, stop!"

Dad?

Beck retreated until her back hit the wall. She brought the LED up. The POV inside the boathouse was cockeyed as if someone had tossed the camera aside. Carlow Hain grappled with the videographer who had stepped into the frame—

Tommy. A teenage version.

A loud argument. Tough to make out the words.

Carlow ran his son across the boathouse, out of frame.

"Ava, run!" Tommy shouted.

Ava…

Ava…

Ava.

Riley issued an almost inhuman scream.

Onscreen, the young woman gathered herself, sitting up, fully revealed. Twenty years younger, but there was no chance Beck would fail to recognize her.

She dropped the Camcorder.

It bounced once, then came to rest.

"Ava," she said, eyes burning, peering across the room at Riley.

The woman from the video.

Ava.

Her mother's name.

CHAPTER 74

Twenty-three years earlier

"I said, put on a goddamn tie!"

The alcohol on his father's breath made Tommy recoil. "Ties are lame," he said, hoping his father would laugh.

He didn't. Instead, Dad ripped a tie off the hangar so hard he tore the rod off its holders. All of Tommy's shirts and sweaters crashed to the floor.

"Alright, alright, I'll do it!"

But it was too late. Dad all but garroted him as he tightened it. "Don't test me, boy."

Tommy filed the abuse away for future payback. At fifteen, he was the most mature male in his family. Soon, he'd fly this coop and leave Carlow Hain behind forever. There were only so many beatings and insults a kid could take.

They left for the party. His father drove, nearly crashing half a dozen times along the two-mile stretch to *Annwn*. Tommy sat in the back, holding Susan, while his youngest brother stared out the window, going somewhere in his head to escape this psycho circus. Upon arrival, his father ingratiated himself, marginalized, craving attention he didn't deserve. Tommy felt embarrassed for him and counted the days until he was free. His uncles had promised him a summer job at one of their construction sites, a new mall up in Nashua. He'd live in an apartment under Uncle Dave's supervision.

An entire summer without his lame-o mother and father. He couldn't wait. He felt terrible leaving Susan, but she was rarely the object
of Dad's temper.

After getting her and his brother settled with the *Annwn* staff, Tommy heard Grandpop Francis calling out for him. He led Tommy into the library, where a wrapped present sat on the desk. "Sorry I missed you at Christmas, but I didn't forget about ya."

"You didn't have to, Grandpop. I know you're busy."

His grandfather rustled his hair and kissed him. "Go 'head, open her up."

Tommy tore open the present. He sucked in a breath at the sight of the JVC Camcorder.

"I hear you want to be a moviemaker," Grandpop said. "I love movies, kiddo. I can't wait to see yours."

He nearly bowled the older man over with a hug. "Can I use it tonight?"

"Yeah, but don't show the footage to anyone outside the family."

"Course not. Thank you."

Another rustle of hair, another kiss, and Grandpop Francis exited to rejoin his bash.

It only took Tommy a few minutes to get the Camcorder running; he'd been reading up on them, dreaming about having his own. His father had refused to buy him one, ridiculing him for his silly dreams. Running out with extra tapes shoved into his pockets, Tommy shot some sweet roll on the ladies gathered around the grand piano and the up-and-coming jazz singer Gramma Ide had hired. He made sure to film the eye-popping, forty-foot Christmas tree in the great room, then walked out into the heated tents. Guests mugged as he passed, but Tommy went searching for his best friend, a local girl he'd met a few years ago. He'd cocked things up at Andover, trying to show off to her, but she was righteous, telling the cops she'd been the one driving the gardening cart sticking out of the Dairy Queen. Tommy still got expelled, which gave his old man an excuse to knock him around, but it was a cool move on her part. Tommy had started to feel differently about her, like actual feelings.

Ava.

Talk about hard luck. An orphan, she referred to herself as a "nomad." She lived with a group of day workers down in Lynn. She was tall and looked older than her fifteen years. No one was ever on her ass about school, which Tommy envied. She worked odd jobs and lived in the basement of a house with people who spoke little English. Ava's earliest memories were of a farm down south somewhere.

To him, she was free.

To her, he was a prince in a fairy tale.

She was hilarious. And pretty. Her eyes blew him away. She played sports better than most of his friends, took zero crap from anyone and didn't care he was a Hain. Tommy would have fought anyone else tooth and nail if they talked to him like Ava did, but he knew it was just her way of looking out for him.

Ava couldn't believe her luck. She cried when Tommy got her a job working at the New Year's Eve party. His grandmother doubted Ava's claim of being eighteen but hired her as a server, anyway; after all, Gramma Ide started working at her grandfather's pub in Dublin at twelve. She admired Ava's grit, offering a wage of three hundred bucks plus a split of the tips, which would be plentiful. Ava nearly fainted. The pay was more money than...well, more than she'd ever seen.

She kissed Tommy for the first time after that, not because of the job, but because of his kindness. He could have anything he wanted – any girl – and chose her. He shared whatever she was willing to accept, which wasn't much: movies, ice cream, and a CD on her birthday. Otherwise, she always paid her fair share, so neither he nor his family would think she was a moocher.

Annwn enchanted her. She'd studied it from afar for years, drawing magical renditions. The first time Tommy walked her through the gates to take a sailing lesson, Ava left her body. The experience was too astonishing. While she knew about the cruelty and petty ambitions of Tommy's parents – not to mention the Hain legacy – *Annwn* represented family to her. All Ava wanted was a family, whether inside a palace like this or a one-bedroom apartment in Lynn. The thought of a home, of children, of not being a nomad, possessed her.

"Hubba-hubba," she heard him say and nearly dropped her train of gimlets in surprise.

Tommy held a Camcorder up to his eye. Who was crazy enough to give Tommy Hain a video camera?

"Not now," she laughed, passing out the drinks.

"Why not? You look great! I like the ribbon!"

She rolled her eyes but warmed at the attention. At first, she wasn't sure about the ribbon, afraid it would be too flashy. Then Gramma Ide complimented her, saying, "Pink suits you." Ava was the only server with a ribbon in her hair.

"She's gonna be in all my movies!" Tommy called out, causing the guests to laugh and Ava's cheeks to light up.

A cheer went up as Grandpop Francis announced Uncle Dave as the new CEO of Hain Developers. Tommy zoomed in on his Uncle's face as he delivered an impassioned speech. The guy knew how to work a crowd. Tommy worshipped him. A stud hockey player at BC. Harvard Law. Head of an NGO (whatever that was, Tommy still needed to look it up), and now Uncle D would spearhead the family biz. Rock star all the way.

After the speech, Uncle D beelined to Tommy, making a funny face in extreme closeup. "You got my good side, right?"

"Totally."

He led Tommy off to a quiet spot outside the tent. "Sweet gift, right?"

"The best…You told him, didn't you?"

"I might have implied having a big Hollywood director in the family wouldn't be such a bad idea."

"Thanks, man…I'm looking forward to the summer."

"Me, too, but you gotta tighten up the grades."

"I know."

"And no more stunts like creating your own drive-thru Dairy Queen."

Tommy laughed but got it; Uncle D's disappointment had shamed him more than anyone's.

"You got talent, and you got a good heart. No matter who you talk to – jocks, dweebs, metalheads, stoners, drama freaks, rich kids, poor kids – they all got positive vibes about you. You know which forks to use at dinner. You escort little old biddies across the street. You go to church on Sunday. Know what all that adds up to?"

"What?"

"A wiseass punk, too smart for his own good."

"Hey!"

Uncle D smiled. "All I'm saying is, you know which rules you can bend, which you can break and which to hold as holy. Loyalty and tradition are big deals 'round here, more than just lip service. You gotta walk it like you talk it. See this?" He held up his highball. "Club soda. Know what gives you the best high? Control."

"I got ya, Uncle D."

"Look, my brother's a handful. Everyone knows it. And he's pissed at being passed over. In his defense, it's not fair. But it's Grandpop's decision, and we all gotta respect it."

"Uncle O got skipped, and I just saw him doing the macarena with Aunt Polly."

"Yeah, well, Uncle O's a different breed…am I right?"

Tommy laughed at the imitation.

"I'm just saying, don't give Carlow any excuses. I know that's a crappy thing to tell a fifteen-year-old kid about his father, but it is the way it is. Right here, right now, let this be our New Year's resolution: study hard, work harder and no more trouble. Feel me?"

"Absolutely."

They embraced. Uncle D drifted off to join the next group of admirers.

Tommy searched for a root beer, feeling like he always did after one of Uncle D's pep talks —coasting on three feet of air. He could do this. Like Grandpop and Uncle D, he blazed a trail. He could take the worst his father threw at him and come out the other side wiser, brighter, stronger. Not to mention bigger. He was hitting a growth spurt, and one of these days, Dad would raise a fist, and Tommy would knock him into next week. Until then, he'd outlast him.

Five months, then he'd be up in New Hampshire with his uncles. He'd already asked if they'd hire Ava for some desk work, and they agreed. Tommy hadn't told her yet. He was saving it for the perfect time. He couldn't wait to see her face.

She felt trapped. Petrified. She'd stumbled across Tommy's father sitting by himself on the outskirts of the party. Now he held her in place, his fetid breath turning her stomach. She was considering more forceful maneuvers when she heard Tommy calling her name and turned to see him jogging over.

"Tommy," Mr. Hain shouted in mock cheer. "This gorgeous young thing said she's a friend of yours."

"She sure is. This is Ava. Ava, my Pops." Tommy kept his eyes on her. "Gramma's looking for you. She needs help with the flowers."

Ava produced a dazzling smile, said, "It was nice meeting you," and tried to back away.

Mr. Hain held on. "Hey, hey, hey, where you running off?"

"Dad, c'mon."

His father scowled and released her. Ava got a safe distance and then darted behind the dunegrass to watch, concerned for Tommy. Carlow waved his highball, telling his son he was dry.

"Maybe you should slow down."

"Whadidyou say?" Carlow pulled Tommy closer by his tie. "Don't get it twisted, boy. You're not in the circle, and you never will be. You're my son. And they don't give a flipping fig about us. It's all about Dave. Look at that suck-up."

Across the acreage, his uncle entertained a crowd. "Yeah, it's not fair what Grandpop did."

"Damn right. Thanks, buddy." He pulled Tommy into a rough embrace. "So. You hitting that little filly?"

Ava had never wished harm on another human being, but she now had a leading candidate.

"C'mon, you can tell me," Carlow went on. "Fine-looking girl. Tough, though. Gotta be careful. Your mother's tough. Thinks she runs the whole shooting match. Bossin' me around all the time. They don't know me, kiddo. They don't know what I'm capable of. But I'll show 'em. Wait and see. I'm gonna have what's mine." His hands balled into fists, crumpling Tommy's jacket. "You gotta take what you want.

Otherwise, you'll never get what you deserve. You want her; you take her."

Tommy pushed off. The force nearly caused his father to fall. Carlow shouted. Tommy kept moving, saw her and then looked away, ashamed of his tears. Ava followed from a distance, watching him swipe a few half-empty drinks and chug them. She called his name, but he told her he wanted to be alone and ran to the beach.

It was a trial from on high. Father Winnie once sermonized about Job in CCD. Tommy's father was the test, punishing everyone for being an afterthought. Mom was no help; she'd married in and now suffered a severe case of buyer's remorse. She spent more time fawning over Grandpop Francis and Gramma Ide than mothering her children.

Don't give him an excuse.

Uncle Dave's words.

The waves reminded him, calmed him, told him to go back and enjoy the party, North Shore's hottest of the year. Afterward, he'd hang out with Ava. Make sure she was okay after his father's aggression.

The Camcorder.

Damn.

He'd left it on the edge of a flowerbed so Dad wouldn't see it. Tommy would have to keep hiding it from his father, who'd be pissed Grandpop Francis gave Tommy a gift he'd openly ridiculed. No doubt if he found out, the miserable prick would take it away. Running back to the spot, Tommy let out a silent cheer at the sight of the camera. He fired it up and searched for Ava, wanting to shoot a few minutes of her when she wasn't looking. That's when she was prettiest.

Prettiest? She truly was turning him into a wimp.

The party multiplied, friends and family calling out to be filmed, but the longer Tommy went without seeing her, the more anxious he became. Moving back and forth, he searched every inch of Annwn, inside and out. He clocked the other servers, but Ava was nowhere. Maybe she'd left. Wouldn't be the worst thing; he'd make sure she got paid in full, and if it kept her away from his father—

The ribbon.

The sight of it caught up in the dunegrass, back out where they'd both escaped his father's clutches, prompted Tommy to look up from the camera. There was no mistaking it. The color scheme for the party was gold and black. No pink anywhere. So it wasn't a streamer or a deflated balloon.

It was Ava's ribbon.

He spun around, but he'd already searched everywhere—

Everywhere except the dock and the boathouse.

He walked.

Then ran.

Something was wrong. Very wrong. He felt it. Ava wouldn't have left without saying goodbye or recovering her ribbon.

A voice shouted his name. It sounded like Uncle D. Didn't matter because it wasn't Ava.

At the boathouse, he heard sounds. Restless sounds. He peered through the open door, thinking he'd stumbled onto one of his cousin's trysts.

But it wasn't a tryst.

He threw the Camcorder onto a shelf and ran over to pull his father off. "Dad, stop!"

"Getouttahere!" His father shoved him back.

The sight of Ava cued an intense rage. "Fucking loser!"

His father turned and pulled his pants up. "…d'you say?"

"You're just jealous. Of Grandpop, Uncle Dave, even me!"

"You little…" He hurtled forward.

Tommy connected with his first punch, but his father's weight was too great. It carried them across the boathouse. He kept swinging. "Ava, run!"

She remained frozen, shaking. He pulled away to lead her out, but his father blasted him in the back of the head. He lost a bit of time. Only Dad's grunts and shouts and kicks registered. Many missed their mark or lacked energy, but enough connected to make Tommy wonder if this was the end. His dreams, his excitement about next summer, the resolution he'd made with Uncle D…gone.

Somebody tackled his father from behind.

"Grab him!" Uncle Dave shouted.

They corralled his father and dragged him out. Tommy's head spun; it felt like he was holding on for dear life rather than helping maneuver his old man away from the party to the parking area. Dad broke away and ran to his car. Slid behind the wheel and turned the key. Every owner left the keys in the ignition, allowing the valets to jockey the vehicles around. This was *Annwn*. Who would dare steal from the Hains?

Uncle D dove in after him and shoved Dad into the passenger seat, shouting at him as he drove away. Tommy stumbled to the street; his last glimpse of his father and uncle was of their silhouettes struggling as the car whipped around the corner.

One of the security guards asked if he was okay.

Then they heard the crash. A loud metallic rumble.

Tommy sprinted down the street.

The guard shouted into his radio.

A red glow appeared over the trees. Tommy hurtled around the turn on Puritan Road. Neighbors raced out of their homes. The churned soil carved a swath out of the Lehane's lawn and out onto Eisman's Beach, where Tommy saw the overturned sedan engulfed in flames.

He called out for Uncle Dave but saw no sign of him or his father through the blaze.

No human shapes at all.

They were a hundred feet further out, splayed across the rocks.

CHAPTER 75

One week earlier

She was half-asleep when she opened the door, but Riley immediately knew Tommy was in deep trouble. A violet bruise circled one eye. He burst into her apartment, his words running together as grab the bottle of Four Roses from her cupboard, hands shaking as he filled a glass. "It's bad," he said with an exhalation that veered damn close to a sob.

When he got pissed or scared, Tommy came calling. Problem was, Tommy Hain was either pissed or scared most of his life, so there was rarely a time when Riley didn't feel like she was on call. After their embarrassing display at Beck's graduation – after seeing the hurt and downright pity in her eyes – Riley had vowed to change. She'd made promises before, but this time she was holding fast, telling Tommy to clean up his act as well, or else she'd Audi 5000 his ass. He'd begged her not to leave, claiming he was tired of the heartache and the forgotten days and nights.

She'd believed him.

Until thirty seconds ago when he started pounding on her door at six in the morning.

"I owe," he said. "Big time."

"Stratton." She filled up and drained a glass of her own. She'd stayed out of whatever they had going on, telling herself she could do her job and see no, speak no evil. Bone-weary, she rubbed her temples, a migraine coming on. How could she have been so foolish?

"I did it for us," he pressed. "So we could finally get away."

"How much?"

"A hundred thousand and the deed to the club by Friday."

She wanted to argue, wanted to berate him. Instead, she pulled him in and stroked his head because his motives were pure, and she had tacitly gone along with it by not voicing a single objection. "What are we gonna do?"

"My family," he said.

"You already tried."

241

"Not for this, I didn't. I'll go through Susan."

Riley thought it over. "That will be it, though. You realize that, don't you? We'll never get away. They'll lock you behind Annwn's walls until your father wins the race and Stratton's in the ground. They will own you forever…and we'll never see each other again."

"I've asked everyone I know. Stratton will kill me, you, Susan, burn down the club. He's psychotic. He'll believe he needs to send a message so no one ever fails to live up to their agreement again. What choice do I have?"

She closed her eyes. "There's one."

She returned to the cupboard, pulled out the rest of the booze and removed the shelves. Knocking on the backboard, she pulled it loose, exposing a slight hollow. A vinyl bag rested inside. She carried it back to the table and unzipped it.

He didn't know what to say at first. "Is that…?"

"Your camera."

CHAPTER 76

"After his uncle's funeral, Tommy wasn't Tommy anymore." Riley spoke faintly, her mind tripping back. It was easier to venture to the past than exist in the present, the one she'd always feared, more terrifying than any drug den, rehab clinic or jail cell. The truth was finally free despite twenty-three hard years of keeping it locked away. So many sacrifices, nullified in a few seconds of recorded horror. "The shine in his eyes was gone. Mine, too."

Beck sagged against the wall, feet splayed in front of her. A shaft of light from the Camcorder captured part of her face as she stared blankly at the floor.

Riley went on: "He told me I had to go away. His father was in a coma, his Uncle Dave dead, but Tommy didn't want to take any chances…Where would I go? I had no money, no family…He brought me to a friend, the priest who baptized him and all the Hain children…Father W had transferred from St. John's in Swampscott to St. Gerolamo's in Dyer…Tommy told him what happened but in confession, binding Winnie to secrecy…a crime neither of them would ever reveal." She dried her eyes. "The Hains eliminate anyone who poses a threat…what would they have done to me?"

Jordan entered. He picked up the camera and limped back out.

Riley was only vaguely aware of his passage. "I can't even remember my first few weeks here…Father W and the Sister before Lucinda – Elaine – took care of me, fed me and held me when I woke up screaming…weeks later, when I was late, we all realized I needed to become someone else…and so Ava disappeared and Riley Gideon took her place."

Beck whispered something.

Riley shuffled closer. "What?"

"Your hair…always changing it…"

"In case Carlow remembered an auburn-haired friend of Tommy's…but he didn't, not a goddamn thing…how anybody could do something like that and not remember…"

Beck squeezed her eyes shut, tears running. She slid the photo from her pocket, the one she never went anywhere without. "Who is this?"

"Your grandmother Penelope…something happened down south…I was about seven or eight…Mom worked the fields with a group of twenty, and one day, they threw us kids into their rackety vehicles and sped away…we just left her…I screamed myself raw…I overheard some workers discussing how she'd met the 'wrong man'…I still don't know what they meant…years later, I tried to track her down, but…" Riley studied the folded picture, a woman so indistinct in her mind she felt imagined. "Eventually, the group broke up… several of the older members, the de factor leaders, had died…their children worked their way into school and other trades or married into the American Dream…many, like me, drifted away…I sought out shelters…I'd get a few meals, clothes and a bed for a night or two, but the second they called social services, I was out of there…then I met Tommy…and thought I'd finally found a home."

Beck looked up, a bit more focused behind the tears. "But you lied…you all lied."

"For your protection…I had to give you up, Beck…nine years I waited for you to come back here…when you did, it set me straight for a while, but I never dealt with what happened…I never faced him…never talked to anyone about what he'd done to me…and it ate me alive."

"You used the video. Not Tommy."

"I grabbed it after they dragged Carlow out…somehow, a part of me realized it was important…the next day, Tommy asked me if I'd seen his Camcorder, and I said no…he figured a family member or worker had found it, watched the recording and torched it."

"You never told him."

"Not until last week…he freaked out…all these years…but it was my secret…it was my…"

"Sword and shield."

"Yes…I never planned on telling him, but where would we get a hundred thousand dollars?" She took a breath.

"I'd used the video before…I'd email Carlow a clip of his crime and tell him to transfer money into online accounts. I called myself Martin after Martin of Tours, the patron saint of soldiers and beggars…I've never been able to figure out which one I am."

"You've been blackmailing Carlow Hain for twenty-two years."

"The first time you were six…first grade…I wanted to buy you a new outfit…I'm not even sure I was fully aware of what I was doing, but the next thing I knew, Martin was sending Carlow an email demanding five hundred dollars or else…I never asked for too much…I had to be practical…I had to be smart…they've taken on everyone: the cops, the FBI, the media – who was I? What kind of life would you have led with the Hains after us? I only did it when you needed something: books, your first computer, braces…it wasn't the money…no amount of money could make up for what he did…but for the first time, I had the power…I had control…Tommy's debt was too high to use online transfers…we knew Carlow would send someone to the exchange and…well…you know the rest."

"You could have told me. You should have told me."

"I swore you'd never be a nomad…I told myself I could take it…the horror would end with me…I'll always have regrets, Beck…but they're nothing compared to the moments we spent together…I have no idea who I am…not really…I ceased to exist a long time ago… I had to train myself never to use or even think the word 'daughter' so I wouldn't give up the truth…but I knew exactly who you were…" She touched her chest. "In here, I've always known."

CHAPTER 77

"I told you to leave it," Francis said.

They stood in the living room of Owen's obtrusive, ten thousand square-foot mansion on Plum Island. Like *Annwn*, the house was large but, unlike the family domain, screamed "new money" and possessed none of its charm or history. Everything here was overly-extravagant and random due to the tastes of Owen's Valium-leveled wife, who, when she wasn't getting the jelly sucked from her thighs, pissed away all their money on eBay.

"I did leave it, okay?" Owen said. "These aren't our people, Pop."

Francis gestured at the TV coverage of the Marina and the old tannery right down the street from his blessed *Annwn*. "You didn't contract someone?"

"Without running it by you? No way."

To his credit, Owen hadn't complained about the slap; didn't even reference it. He took the punishment proper, so his denials felt genuine. Owen was nothing if not loyal, but his innocence was another dead end in Francis' day-long odyssey. Since his conversation with Winnie, he'd paid face-to-face visits with every patron, collaborator and ally within a hundred miles. None of this tumult seemed to be originating from within the Hain continuum.

At least, no part of the continuum he knew about.

"Sonofabitch," he said.

"What is it, Pop?"

But Francis was already shouting for his driver.

Thirty minutes later, he pushed through the fifth-floor executive suite of Hillary Maritime. The office afforded a clear view of the Harbor and Logan Airport, with boats and planes moving steadily. His son's assistant trailed after him, offering coffee, Bailey's and the little biscotti from Mike's Pastry Francis cherished, but he ignored the supplication. There were crucial matters to discuss. Family matters. And Francis' thoughts were churning as black as a stovepipe.

Carlow looked up from behind his desk. "Da."

246

"Outside."

"What's wrong?"

"Now!"

They strolled along the docks where Hillary's ships unloaded cargo.

Carlow fussed to button his coat as he hurried to keep up. "You know, Da, I don't appreciate you barging in—"

Francis whirled on his son. "Call them off."

"Who?"

"Don't play innocent, and do not pretend you're not the one behind this bloodbath! All day I'm beatin' the bushes like a damn fool! Then it finally hit me." He looked his son up and down as if regarding a stranger. "My God, you know how to play the part, don't you?"

Carlow walked to the edge of the dock, the water less than a foot away. He took a long time to answer. "You have no idea what's at stake."

And just like that, Francis' worst fears became a reality.

Carlow turned around, displaying a haughty disdain far removed from his usual babyish, nakedly expressive face. "And you're one to talk about war."

"The people I dealt with chose the life."

"You're so full of shit."

"Watch your tongue." Francis tried to summon the thunder. Instead, his voice fluttered, sounding less like a patriarch and more like a fragile old man.

"You expect me to believe you don't still have people in high places?"

"Operators, not murderers."

"Right," Carlow chuckled, a low, murky sound. "No more strong-arm tactics. Francis Hain's Great Reconciliation. See, this is why I cultivated my own network, Da. To do what needs to be done. You think you're the end-all-be-all. You even tried to take credit for all of my work here." He flung a hand out at his building. "Who do you think's been protecting us all these years while you played the penitent man? The people who could have done lasting damage to us are either rotting in prison or in the dirt. Petrelli. Nona Navies and her boys. The entire Tzu Clan. I've done more to protect this family while you sit around telling the same tired stories to the same tired bootlickers than you'll ever know."

The look on Carlow's face, the deadened stare, sent a missile through Francis. He'd never suspected such a person lurked within the boy, like the *púca*, the shapeshifters of Celtic lore who donned different skins to carry out their mischief.

"Always have a Plan B, a Plan C, all the way to Plan Z. Your words, Da. And I listened. No one worshipped at the altar of Francis Hain more than me. Not that you noticed or cared. All you did was weep over Dave. He would have been this, would have done that. The same sad refrain for twenty goddamn years. I know you wish Dave had been the one to survive those rocks instead of me."

"How dare you…"

"You didn't say it out loud, of course. You didn't have to. Nothing I did was good enough. It took me a long time to realize nothing ever would be. But you did me a favor. I learned people underestimating you can be powerful if managed properly. I knew I'd never make you proud, but I could make you pay attention. You don't know everything, and you don't need to. I'm sorry Tommy's gone, and if I had known the depth of his troubles, I would have saved him. Guess we can thank lardo Owen for that one. Tommy will haunt me just like Dave haunts you, but my son's death brings a perilous chapter to a close."

"What are you talking about?"

"Nothing you need to concern yourself with. You just keep playing the merry ol' gangster. I got this."

"Do you now? Your assets are dead, and you've taken how many shots at these two orphans? Just who's hunting who here, boy?"

"Don't call me boy. Not now, not ever again." Carlow's jaw tightened as he closed the gap, eye to eye with Francis. "My people missed, yeah, but we're covered. We disappeared DeLillo's body, and the cops are chasing their tails.

I will clean the slate, like all the other times before. Like you always preached: leave nothing to chance."

"You're going too far."

"Says the son of Natty Hain. My campaign means as much to you as it does to anyone."

"I want what's best for all of you."

"You want what's best for your legacy. Gangsters or banksters, as long as a Hain is on top, you'll assume it's because of you. You want to be cock of the block. I'd rather buy the zip code. I'm the man the people want. I'm the one they're looking to for a better life, so I will decide what's best. For myself, for my company and for my family. If you want to be a part of what I'm building, great. If not, I'll still come by to smile and suffer through your lame-ass yarns. But know this: I'm not Owen. I'm not Dave. And I'm not you. I'm Carlow Hain, and next time you want to see me, make a fucking appointment."

CHAPTER 78

Jordan forced himself through the sickening video. He'd assumed Francis Hain was the crook behind the curtain, but it was Carlow, the blandest Boy Scout.

The Gideons had confounded him. Now he understood. The only instinct stronger than self-preservation is motherhood. Call it a perpetuation of the species. Call it a genetic bond. Whatever. But a mother is the exception to all the rules.

The recording altered his perspective on Tommy Hain, too. Tommy had displayed more courage and decency as a teenager than most of his family had in their entire rotten existence.

Jordan did some mental math on the timeline. Riley had shaved five years off her actual age, which would have been tough to pull off in the real world, but within the protected confines of St. Gerolamo's, doable, especially with so much of their population changing year to year. The *padre* most likely declared Riley and Beck foundlings, then altered the date of birth on Riley's application for a birth certificate from the Department of Children and Families. DCF then placed Beck into foster homes specializing in newborn care. When Beck was nine, the *padre* brought her back under the justification of being reunited with her "sister." They both remained in his care until Riley's troubles caused her to be tossed out, and Beck sailed off under bluer skies.

What Riley had endured...the ruse under which she suffered every day...concealing the malignity perpetrated against her...never being able to tell her child who she was...

He re-entered the bedroom. Set the Camcorder down and eased himself to the floor next to Beck. "What do you want to do?"

No preamble, no consolation. No words could account for the existential bomb that had just blown up in her face, but they needed a plan. He'd seen frontline shock before. Combat stress reaction. Immediate coping mechanisms included rest and separation from the battlefield, both impossibilities. Triage also stressed immediacy and simplicity.

He believed Beck's logic and powers of deduction persisted. Immediate action might help her compartmentalize.

"Beck," he said louder, waiting until she turned to him. "What are we going to do?"

CHAPTER 79

He'd never been on the first team until Hillary Maritime.

And then the email arrived from some bastard calling himself "Martin." He periodically resurfaced over the years, but Carlow hadn't heard from him in over four until last week. He had started to believe that the extortion had run its course, that Martin was finished with him or, better yet, dead.

"Damn fool," he chastised himself.

After that first contact, Carlow made up a list of suspects – friends, family, and associates- with the stones to blackmail him. Despite Da's claims, they were not a close family but an efficient one. Every powerful lineage secretly or openly despised each other.

He could not make sense of the clip the first time it blighted his screen. Then a halting recollection teased him despite its crude copy-of-a-copy quality, bits and pieces of an unspeakable act broken up into appalling fragments. The three-week coma and ten-month recovery that followed had worn down his memory.

New Year's Eve.

The night Dave died.

The clip was short, no more than twenty seconds, just enough to show him accosting her, capturing the feral look on his face, always cutting out at her scream, never fully revealing his victim except for the top of her head. Martin always stressed there was "more, much more."

What did he mean? Had Carlow murdered this young woman?

And who was on the other side of the camera?

His first suspicion fell to Tommy. A wayward life often needs bailing out, but after needling around the subject, asking his son if he knew anyone named Martin, referencing the New Year's party, apologizing for what an abusive, drunk asshole he'd been back then, even asking if his son possessed any photos or video from the event, Tommy showed no indication he recognized the intent behind Carlow's words. Besides, he'd been the beneficiary of Hain largesse for most of his life; there'd been no need to bleed his father for a few coins.

Carlow then cobbled together a list of the private security, valet service, caterers, musicians, videographers and photographers hired. His mother had employed a lot of neighborhood kids. She paid them under the table, so he couldn't push too hard on assembling the list lest anyone wonder why he was trying to track down a bunch of hourly laborers from a party half a decade earlier. Needing dock security for his recently launched maritime business, Carlow had made the acquaintance of a moonlighting young police officer named Henry Washington, who was open to more sensitive side hustles. Carlow handed him the list, referencing a shakedown due to "an indiscretion," leaving out any mention of a video. After weeks of intense investigation, Washington couldn't produce a single suspect.

Turning his conjecture onto the guests, Carlow created two categories: incapable/implausible and very capable/very plausible. The second group was substantially more extensive, but Washington again found no motivation for or trace of blackmail, the amount minuscule compared to the earnings of those in attendance. What reason could they possibly have to wring such a paltry sum from Carlow? If money wasn't the prime motivator – if, instead, Martin wanted to torment him – simply posting the clip online or sending it to Olivia would have sufficed. Furthermore, there was no guarantee that the person who shot the video was the same person coercing him. Martin may have somehow discovered the footage, or someone may have given it to him.

And so Carlow had paid.

Every time Martin popped up, Carlow dispatched Washington.

Every time, they came up empty, and Carlow paid.

The closest they came to tracking Martin down was when Washington forced the online payment service to divulge the info on the Martin account. He'd assumed a considerable risk, obtaining a warrant by claiming it was part of another case. The trail led to a Walmart Money Center in Worcester, where, as far as the security camera and counter worker could tell, a scraggly woman with a shaved blonde buzz, sunglasses, elbow-length gloves, garish print dress, artificially red hair and an oversized raincoat cashed out the funds for a three-dollar service fee. Washington figured it was a moll doing Martin's pickup work, and he hesitated to take such a chance again.

Ultimately, Carlow resigned himself to a mutually assured destruction and kept paying. Martin never asked for the moon and surely realized releasing the video would cut off his source of funds.

Until the last demand: a hundred thousand dollars.

Martin must have experienced some drastic life event. The amount was too large to send through the financial system without throwing up red flags. The virtual post office finally presented an opportunity to unmask him. Carlow told Washington, "Clean sweep," and revealed the incriminating material as a recording. The detective wanted to know what was on it.

"Find it; you'll see for yourself," Carlow told him, realizing the crooked cop and his team would have to be removed for laying eyes on such a damning exposé.

Less than forty-eight hours later, Carlow finally learned Martin's true identity.

Tommy, after all.

It knocked him flat. The skill with which his son had dodged Carlow's inquiries all those years before. Such a winning deceit – Tommy was unquestionably a Hain. It made a perverse kind of sense. They'd grown distant, veritable strangers. Only Olivia and Da maintained the thread – and the sham – of family fealty. They'd spoiled Tommy rotten, and his consequence-free life had expedited his death. Carlow even recalled his son's absurd ambition of becoming a filmmaker. He didn't know where Tommy had obtained a video camera – had no idea if it was even Tommy's camera to begin with – but the objective remained: find the recording, destroy it and wipe out everyone who had seen it, except his son who was to be brought before his father without delay.

"Wasn't my goddamn fault," Carlow told his empty office. Da's treachery had set this whole mania in motion when he passed him over for Dave.

More hazy, damning bursts:

A pink ribbon.

The boathouse.

Drubbing his son.

Fighting with Dave in the car.

Then nothing.

Carlow had changed. Evolved. These horrid Martin videos depicted the man before, not the man reborn. He'd pushed too hard with Da tonight, but the urge to make Francis Hain realize the son he had neglected should have been the son to bet on had been too enticing to pass up.

You gotta take what you want. Otherwise, you'll never get what you deserve.

Carlow's mantra.

His circle – politicians, boards of directors, chief executives, bankers, investors – comprised the crooked and the selectively ethical. You didn't get to the top playing fair and square.

But this video…pure malevolence. He doubted even Natty Hain would forgive it.

He munched another handful of antacids. It was like attacking a grease fire with a few grains of sugar. The wet bar called to him. Carlow hadn't touched a drop since that fateful night. He stocked the bar for his guests and as proof of his transformation. Now, the thirst rumbled, stirred from hibernation. He could knock off an entire bottle of Glenlivet or Bulleit without a hiccup.

I'm a loving father.

I create jobs and take care of my people.

I'm a leader, and I'm finally getting my just—

An email arrived. Not from Martin. A Yahoo account he didn't recognize. A video embedded in the message. A recording of a recording. He knew what it was before he heard the scream. He smashed his keyboard and mouse, pounding on them until the playback shut off.

Tommy wasn't working alone.

He clicked on news sites, studying various photos and mugshots of Riley Gideon. He leaned close to the screen, trying to remember. Was it her? Did something about her appearance trigger a memory, or was he projecting? He compared the modern photos to the video. It was tough to judge because of the recording's age and grain, especially since the clip never fully revealed his victim.

He scanned the paragraph on Beck Gideon. Twenty-two. A wide-eyed star on the tech scene—

Twenty-two.

He expanded her image. Studied the flattering media snaps. Watched the first few minutes of her podcast. She shared a similarity to Riley but exhibited many unique traits. The inflection of her voice, the shape of her eyes, even the way she stared into the camera, intense when smiling – it all reminded Carlow of his mother, Ide.

The thought caused him to jerk back.

No.

No.

His mind was playing tricks on him.

He returned to the email:

Ten o'clock. Silversmith Green. Dyer.

After this, it's over. We keep the money; you get the original.

You, Carlow. No more lackeys.

Not a minute before, not a minute after, or the full recording goes viral.

– Beck and Riley

CHAPTER 80

Riley listened to Beck lay out the plan; the words stilted as Beck pushed aside the topic of her genesis. The children of St. J's specialized in repression. Everything Riley had done, every moment looking into her daughter's eyes, was now tainted. She'd lied to Beck every second of her life. Concealed the most essential truths from her. All to save her.

"Riley."

"Yeah, I hear you, but…do you think he'll even show?"

"We signed the email. No more Martin, no more tricks. He might view it as a business deal."

"Okay, but shouldn't we talk about—"

"Later." She held Riley's gaze. "Can you do this?"

"I think so…yeah."

"Then go."

She gripped Beck's hand and then hurried out the door. Climbed up the fence and crawled out on Escape Tree. The five blocks to Silversmith Green felt like five miles. She believed Beck's claims that Carlow would come himself. At the heart of every narcissist is a motherlode of fear, and the fear of being exposed as a sexual sadist would hopefully compel him to act.

Inching down the alleyway next to the Kleen-o-Mat brought her to a full view of the Green. A car pulled up a few seconds later. Two men got out. One she recognized from Jordan's surveillance videos as Grieg, Washington's partner.

The other was Carlow Hain.

She dialed her burner.

Carlow's arrival did not surprise Beck; he believed he could spin anything in his favor. "Head to the roof. We'll be there as soon as we can."

"Wait, what?"

"Don't come back here."

"Beck—"

"Someone has to make sure the truth gets out. You got the tape?"

"In my pocket, but I can't just leave you."

"You're not. And you never did…The tape is your story. We can't let him get his hands on it." She heard Riley sniffling, softly crying over the line. "I'll see you soon."

She disconnected.

CHAPTER 81

An email from Beck and Riley appeared on Carlow's cell with a soft ding:

St. Gerolamo's. The old dormitory. The camera is inside.

Third floor of the turret.

We keep the money and go our separate ways.

He knew he was being manipulated. There was no guarantee the Gideons hadn't made a hundred copies. However, there was no second option. He needed that goddamn recording, and once he had it, he'd make damn sure these loathsome bitches never messed with him again. A deep pull from his flask of Glenlivet steadied his resolve. Doing a slow circle, he examined this dirty slice of nowhere until he located the church's spire.

CHAPTER 82

"I can take it from here," Jordan said, checking his ammo.

"Not alone."

"All Carlow has to do is show up. It proves his interest in the recording."

"We need more."

"I don't understand. You told Riley—"

"What I needed to tell her to get her out of the way." Beck laid out her intentions.

The actual plan.

"You're nuts," he said.

"People have been taking shots at the Hains for as long as Hains have walked the earth. If we leave any gaps, Carlow will slip through. People like him hate being challenged, especially by those they regard as low-status, which is everyone. You asked me what we should do. This is it. This seals his fate."

"It's too dangerous."

"Story of my life."

"I won't be able to protect you in there."

She could tell he wanted to express a more personal, profound concern, and, to her surprise, the outward emotion didn't make her uncomfortable. If anything, it gave her strength. "He's a predator, Jordan. Deep down, there's a wickedness, and it's been waiting twenty years to come back out."

CHAPTER 83

Jimmy heard banging. He crawled across his bed and looked out the window at a man forcing his way into the Victorian. No one was supposed to go inside the spooky old place. He wondered if it had something to do with Beck. The other kids said she was the one the police were searching for. Maybe she came back to St. J's to hide. After all, she grew up at the top of the tower.

Unable to bear the thought of anything bad happening to Beck, he slid out of bed and got dressed, careful not to wake Madeleine.

CHAPTER 84

After edging through the pried-open front door, Carlow located the turret entrance and saw a dim light at the top of the stairs. He walked up, his 9mm in a two-handed grip, just as the instructor at Cambridge Gun Club had taught him. He tried to steady his breathing. If he had to pull the trigger, he wouldn't be shooting at paper targets, and nothing at the Gun Club ever shot back.

On the third floor, he encountered separate hallways running in and out of the turret. A blue light shined at the end of a short passage, drawing him into a large, circular room. A figure stood against the far wall. Its sheer size nearly caused Carlow to fire.

Then he recognized it as a painting, a storybook figure. The character from Beck's app: Mr. Gabriel.

A video camera rested on the windowsill, the source of the light.

This was too easy. Maybe the Gideons truly believed he'd leave them alone if they gave up the recording.

Fools.

He approached the camera, examining potential hiding spots, but the closet doors were missing, the bedframes empty, and an old bureau rested in pieces on the floor. He was alone. The camera hummed on battery power; the pop-out screen shimmered blue. Either it wasn't recording, or…

After a few seconds of button pushing, he opened the casing.

"It's not there," a voice said behind him.

He spun around, gun shaking.

"Easy." Beck Gideon stood inside the doorway. "I'm not armed, but I will send this email if you don't put that away." She held a cell phone in one hand.

"Email?"

She glanced at the gun. "You're making me nervous, Mr. Hain."

He slipped the nine into his outside pocket.

"I got about twenty news stations and blogs listed here with the video attached."

"I thought we had an understanding."

"Remains to be seen…Where's the other guy? Grieg."

"I don't—"

"Washington's partner. One of the dirty cops you hired to follow the money. We're not gonna get very far if you keep lying."

A chill ran through him. How much did she know? He regretted indulging his thirst; he needed all his wits. He slowed his breathing and used his CEO voice. "I didn't hire anyone, and I don't know anything about Detective Washington except that they found him dead alongside Tommy. Now. Are you going to tell me what's on your phone?"

"Just the usual stuff: emails, phone numbers, Candy Crush—"

"Voice recorder?"

She took a few steps and tapped her phone to life. The screen displayed an unsent email with a video attachment. In the thumbnail, he recognized his father's boathouse. A cursory glance at the recipients returned several news URLs. She swiped to show the list of open programs: just the email, no recorder.

"Who else is here?" he asked.

"Nobody."

"Now who's lying?"

"Jordan Lear. But you already know that because you sent one of Washington's goons to kill him, and if anything happens to me, he's not gonna bother with the media; he's going straight to the cops."

"I don't have the faintest idea—"

"Goodnight, Mr. Hain." She headed for the door.

He wanted to run after her and— "Wait. Come back." She did.

"I'd feel better if you at least put your phone down. After all, if you wanted to spread unfounded lies about me, you would have already sent it."

She set the cell on an empty bedframe. "They're not unfounded."

"I'm not sure what you think you saw—"

"I know what I saw. Don't try to gaslight me."

"I wouldn't dare." He held out his hands. "I have a feeling you and I are very similar, Beck. Smart, motivated. We want to do good work and make a difference. But our lineage keeps dragging us down. The past never does release us. If you have evidence Washington was corrupt, bring it to the authorities. I can help you."

"Will you?"

"Of course. I want the truth like everyone else. Or did you forget it was my son who was murdered?" He considered grabbing a swallow from his flask. Would it make him appear more human to Beck or nervous? Feeling compelled to consider the opinion of this wastrel rankled him, but she possessed the tape. "My assumption is you got caught up in Tommy and Riley's bad choices, and all you want is to return to MrGabriel and continue your journey."

"I knew it. You think you can negotiate your way out of this. Unbelievable."

"This is starting to feel like a waste of time. I thought you brought me here to talk."

"I brought you here to look you in the eye when I told you you were finished. Did you honestly think we were going to give you the tape?" She laughed.

"Here we go with the mysterious tape again," he said, feigning a calm in direct contrast to his mounting rage at her laughter.

"We got you cold, dickhead."

"Your sister has warped your mind. Don't let her rob you of your future, Beck. She may not have killed Tommy, but she's committed several crimes."

"None as depraved as yours."

He scoffed, balling up his fists inside his pockets. "I'm surprised you fell for whatever lies she's cooked up."

"How does it feel to know a couple of Lost Ones are gonna bring you down?"

"If this is about money—"

"It's about the truth. It's about making you pay for your crimes." She stepped closer. "Your disgusting past is gonna be out there for everyone to see. My only question is whether Washington worked for you directly or your father. I doubt anything goes down without Francis' approval."

His stomach broiled. "I'm afraid you have me at a loss, but I assure you, I am my own man."

"Someone's been taking out the bad guys, former associates of your family."

"My father and grandfather were criminals. I've been very transparent about that. Their network included people guilty of the worst crimes imaginable. You don't put the devil on trial, Beck. You send him back where he came from."

"So you admit Washington was working for you."

"I didn't say—"

"Sounded like a confession to me."

"I'm getting tired of this." He started to leave, but she placed a hand on his chest. He swiped it away a little more vigorously than necessary.

"Just one more thing. Answer me honestly, and this will all be over. I'll give you the tape."

His whole body jittered. Furious. "Go ahead."

"Twenty-three years ago. The New Year's Eve party at Annwn. You raped my mother. Her name's Ava Gideon."

"Lies—"

"She was fifteen. She had nobody except Tommy."

"I'm leaving."

She pushed him back again. "How could you do it?" Shoved him. "How could you just go on with your life?"

"Don't touch me—"

She cornered him against the far wall. His butt knocked the camera off the sill. "You forced yourself on her. Did the unthinkable." He tried to move around her. She stepped in front of him. "Did you get off on it, Carlow? Does it still turn you on?"

"You and your sister—"

"Are gonna bury your ass."

"Gimme the tape." He didn't like the sound of his voice, the half-threatening, half-pleading tone. Didn't like the look in her eyes. So superior. As if she and her vagabond of a sister—

—not her sister, her *mother*—

"Give it to me right now."

"No." She angled her head and smiled. "How's it feel knowing you're not in control?"

Beck turned away and grabbed her phone, hearing him pursue her, calling out threats, demands, offers of money and an elevated position inside his company.

She ignored him, wondering how long since anyone dared to ignore Carlow Hain. She'd smelled the alcohol on his breath, recognized the haze in his eyes and assumed it was the result of the threat she represented – the equivalent of a street fight, direct aggression, something these elite assholes were wholly ill-prepared for and probably hadn't faced since high school, so accustomed to buying their way out of trouble or hiring goons like Henry Washington to do their dirty work. Carlow was on her turf now, facing a direct challenge, an opportunity to settle the score in primal fashion.

This was how they settled scores in Dyer, her ultimate plan a callback to her childhood. Pure, unfiltered emotion. The years she'd been so eager to leave behind now emboldened her.

He was on tilt but hadn't given in to the urge. As much as she dreaded his frenzy and knew it could be expressed through a bullet, she needed the real Carlow Hain to step up. She showed him the email, her finger poised over Send as she headed for the door.

Then, she felt all the blood rush to her face as Carlow hauled her back inside. The phone fell from her hands as he screamed for the tape, shaking her. She peered down at the fallen telephone to see if the message had been sent. His eyes lost focus, similar to Z Stratton, regarding her not as a human being but as a possession to do with as he pleased.

His true face, finally.

She tried to break past him, but he threw her back and thrust his gun against her forehead.

Jordan...

Where was Jordan?

Gunfire flashed out in the hallway.

Carlow wanted to shoot.

He wanted the tape.

Balling up her shirt in his hand, he ran her into the
board across the main window, which cracked in two. Beck hit
the floor. He followed her down, a voice urging him to pull the
trigger. He felt enervated at the terror on her face. She wasn't
so cocky now, the impertinent little—

A light snared his attention.

A cell phone on the floor.

Not Beck's. A phone positioned behind the board,
aimed out through one of its many cracks, getting knocked free
after he slammed her into the window. He picked it up,
ignoring Beck as she rolled away, holding her arm, which was
bleeding through her sleeve.

A video chat filled the phone screen. The man on the
other side looked vaguely familiar. He said something, but the
sound was muted. Carlow turned up the volume.

"—hear me, Hain? Release her at once."

"Who...?"

"My name is Detective William Underhill—"

Feet rattled behind him. He turned and saw Beck
crawling towards the first phone.

He fired.

Missed.

She changed directions and dived out the door.

Carlow smashed the phone in his hand against the
floor and kept smashing it until the pieces speared his flesh. He
ran over to the first phone, taking careful aim. His shot split it
into pieces.

Jordan ducked as more rounds blazed out of the
shadows. He fell into a bathroom, everything but the tub
removed. Tiles cracked and popped off as bullets carved

through the walls. He rolled into the tub, his back screaming, and returned the pleasantries until he hit empty and reloaded.

When Carlow started shouting and roughing up Beck, Jordan had tried to move in, only to be driven back by Grieg's gunfire from the intersecting corridor.

Now Jordan was pinned down.

The goddamn plan was too dangerous, he thought. He couldn't believe he'd let Beck put herself in such a treacherous—

She came hurtling out of her bedroom.

"Get down!" he shouted.

Beck slid into an empty closet as gunshots burst from her left. Jordan limped out of a doorway, shooting back. More shots sounded from behind her – Carlow.

Jordan retreated into cover, no more than five feet away but separated by Carlow and Grieg's line of fire. If she stepped out, they'd pick her off, or Jordan would jump out to cover her and get cut down.

She looked around and realized she was lying on the floor of the old linen closet, the dumbwaiter door a foot over her head. There were three of them inside the house. Ages ago, the lifts were used to transport bedding up and down. Very Downton Abbey. Sister Lucinda feared one of the children would become stuck inside a box or plummet to their doom. She'd nailed all the internal accesses shut. Beck rose to her knees and rammed the heels of her hands against the door. Her skin split. Just before it felt like her wrists would snap, the door shot up, the nails popping loose.

The gunfire cut out.

"Jordan," she whispered.

He peeked around the threshold, just enough to see her by the open dumbwaiter.

"Basement," she said, then pointed behind him. "Back stairs."

He nodded and slipped out the opposing entrance of the Jack 'n Jill bathroom.

She took a breath and wedged herself into the tight shaft. Tugged on the rope. Trying not to think about Washington's ultimate fate, she prayed for a strong weave even after a hundred years and stepped out, wrapping her ankles around the rope.

It held.

She reached back to close the access and started her descent.

The rear stairs shrieked like a herd of feral cats. Jordan heard Carlow and Grieg racing down the turret stairwell, presumably to cut off the first-floor exits. Fortunately, his stairs ended close to the basement door. Relying on his arms, he lowered himself down the ladder-like steps into the damp basement, revealed in fragments of light angling around the boarded-up casement windows. He lurched over to the dumbwaiter access.

Nailed shut.

He searched. Found a chunk of narrow stone and pushed it under the first nail.

Amidst an extensive range of anxieties, claustrophobia had never reared its head until now. Between floors, the area around Beck turned dark as pitch. Her arm muscles spasmed, her wound reopened, her body on the cusp of shutting down. A tiny halo of light formed as she slid past the second-floor access door. She latched her ankles tighter around the rope—

Until they hit something solid – the dumbwaiter box blocked her passage.

She sniffed and realized she faced an even bigger problem.

Fire.

Jordan heard the blaze before he smelled the smoke. It sounded like the heavy winds that preceded a hurricane. Someone had lit a match. Given the house's condition, it wouldn't be long before he and Beck became kindling. He used the stone to bash the access door apart, no longer worried about noise. He threw it open and peered up—

The delivery box blocked the shaft.

Carlow and Grieg had split up after sprinting down the turret stairs. Carlow guarded the front while Grieg lit the blaze. With a few clicks of his lighter, the rear half of the Victorian now glowed as fire chewed through the aged wood.

The cop returned with a gleeful smile. "I'll work the perimeter, but they got nowhere to go." He ran outside.

After surrendering to Beck's taunts, Carlow felt his confidence returning as he watched the flames intensify. Underhill would be a complication, but Carlow was already spinning up tales of self-defense against his son's killers, a story his crack team of attorneys and public relations experts would refine to his advantage. He might not find the tape, but maybe no one else would either once the Gideons and Lear were gone.

It was just a question of how long these pains in the ass could withstand the burn.

Smoke oozed out of the walls, gathering mass inside the shaft. The heat made Beck woozy. No choice – she had to climb back up.

She kicked at the access door on the second floor until it broke apart. Swinging herself through, she crashed to the floor, lungs bursting. She snuck down the closest hallway, entering the main house. The smoke seemed a little thinner here. A tickle in her throat bloomed into a wheezing cough as she reached the front stairwell. It cleared her lungs but alerted someone to her presence: their feet raced up the stairs. She peered over the railing—

Carlow raised his gun and fired.

Gray clouds gushed under the basement door, the fire on the other side a molten yellow. Embers cascaded from the ceiling like fireflies.

Jordan hurried to the bulkhead. Threw his shoulder against it. He'd come around the front or through another window to retrieve Beck—

Two holes opened up inches from his head. He threw himself away from the metal-piercing bullets. More shots followed, but at a different frequency, farther away. The shooter outside the bulkhead swore loudly, firing at someone else.

Jordan locked onto a casement window. Picked himself up and ran—

A spike of pain rammed through his back, robbing his legs of all sensation and upending him.

Beck ran back up to the top floor, trying not to think about how close the bullet had come. She'd heard it sizzle past her head.

Carlow's light arced through the gathering fumes behind her.

Grieg leaned against the side of the house. The shots had come from the trees on the western side of campus. Not the police; they'd be shouting through bullhorns. To be safe, he drew his shield out from under his shirt, letting it dangle on the chain.

He wondered who was trying to get out through the bulkhead. He hoped it was Lear, the mole who'd been bird-dogging their movements. Grieg studied his bandaged hand; it still throbbed from slicing it open against the young dick's body armor, and then Lear had dropped Tony at the Marina…

Please, let it be Lear, Grieg thought, eager for payback.

Riley slipped over the fence, keeping an eye out for Grieg after she shot at him by the bulkhead.

After their phone call, she suspected Beck had something else up her sleeve and decided she couldn't stay away. She'd done enough running for ten lifetimes.

The blaze intensified.

Stepping inside, Riley stayed low, bushwhacked by the heat. She peered down the main corridor into a maw of fire churning up the walls and along the ceiling.

Another problem: she was out of bullets

She tossed the gun aside and ducked through the smoke.

She wouldn't leave Beck. They'd taken everything else; they would not take her daughter.

A gunshot boomed upstairs, followed by a scream.

Beck's scream.

Jordan hauled himself upright, holstering the Colt – he was lucky he hadn't blown off a toe or his head in the fall. He limped over to the casement window and did a pull-up on the sill, sliding the window open. He struck the board across the opening, knocking it free. The casements were flush with the ground, with no tiny well to complicate matters. He tried to kick against the wall but nearly wilted at the anguish produced by the effort.

Don't fall.

Don't you fall.

You fall, you die.

He fell.

One hand managed to hang on to the edge of the sill. He threw his other one up and set his chin on the ledge, using every muscle to power out the window as part of the ceiling caved in behind him. His fingers found soil. He clawed.

Inch by inch.

Beck heard Carlow checking rooms, firing random shots to flush her. His silhouette danced against the walls. She felt trapped inside some surrealistic nightmare, returning to where she started. Where it all began, it would all end.

She saw her bedroom ahead, a vague impression of Mr. Gabriel.

Only one place to hide.

Back inside the dumbwaiter, she gripped the rope and used one hand to pull the cover closed, then slid down more recklessly than before.

Jordan was halfway out. He might not burn, but Grieg or Hain might easily snipe him into oblivion. Crawling across the grass, he reached for his sidearm. Something crackled in his back, and a new orchestra of pain radiated out. Fire blew out the window boards. He struggled to his knees and peeked around the corner—

As Grieg ran up.

A second of shock.

Then Grieg fired.

Jordan pulled back as the lead shredded the clapboards, shavings flying into his face. Exposed, he squinted, trying to acquire Grieg.

A click – the cop hit empty.

Jordan tried to aim, but Grieg was already crashing into him.

The rope scorched through Beck's fingers. She shot her feet out to either side of the shaft, halting her descent but twisting her knees. Below her, fire burst into the chute. She smacked the access door just as the one above slammed open. Carlow's light shined down. Beck dove through the opening. A shot streaked down behind her. She heard him cuss, realizing her ruse. His steps leaped down the turret stairs.

Beck took off towards the front of the house, leaving the narrow confines of the turret behind.

Another bullet erupted the plaster next to her head as Carlow stepped into the passage behind her. She kept running for the stairs even as she realized she'd never reach them in time—

A form smashed into her, knocking her over and covering her as Carlow's second shot echoed out. The form dragged her into an adjoining room—

Riley.

Carlow's silhouette approached. Riley stood up over Beck and unslung her backpack. He crossed the threshold. Narrowed his eyes, surprised by her presence but perhaps also trying to recall his victim.

"You know who I am?" she asked.

He nodded. "Martin."

"It was never Tommy. He didn't know about the video until last week." She held up the backpack. "It's all here."

"Give it to me."

"My pleasure." She hurled it into his chest. He had to use both hands to catch the bulky pack as Riley ran right behind it, leaping onto him and scraping at his eyes. They struggled out into the hallway.

Friday night all over again. Riley fought an adversary while Beck crawled around for a way to help. She darted out after their forms. As they reached the top of the main stairwell, Beck threw her arms around Carlow's legs, tripping him. He fell into the banister, snapping it. They nearly tumbled over the side. Beck grabbed at the broken wood, stabbing at him with the pointed ends. He issued a screeching roar and rolled onto her.

A gun fell against his head.

His gun.

In Riley's hands.

"Let her go."

The pain of Grieg landing atop him scrambled Jordan's senses. He tried to lift the Colt, but Grieg kneeled on his arm, pressing it into the lawn. The detective drew something from his belt, reflecting the glow of the fire – the curved blade. Jordan tucked his chin to his chest to prevent a fatal swipe, but the outcome was inevitable. He had nothing left.

Light bobbed against Grieg a second before a bar crashed into his face. He reeled back, nose spurting. It took Jordan a second to realize a large Maglite had just faced the detective. A woman's voice told him to stop. Grieg swiped, and the Sister fell back, clutching her arm as she dropped the

Maglite. Another shape yanked Grieg off his feet and threw him clear like a trash sack.

The *padre*. He boomed his voice, ordering Grieg to stand down, but balled his fists, ready to fight.

Problem was Grieg still held the Karambit.

So Jordan shot him.

Enough times to make the knife irrelevant.

"You don't understand," Carlow shouted. "I'm not that man anymore. Please."

"Again," Riley told him.

"Please!"

"Beg me."

Tears ran through the soot on his face. "I'm begging you. I've changed. Just like my father. I've done the work, Riley."

"My name's Ava." She pulled the trigger.

Carlow Hain's remains flipped over and became still.

Riley helped Beck to her feet. They turned down the stairs into the black smoke.

"The money," Beck shouted. She looked, but there was no sign of the backpack in the smoke.

"Forget it; we have to go."

As they descended, Riley began coughing. She fell on the landing between the second and first floors, tripping up Beck, whose right knee had turned to mush. At first, she thought the smoke had overcome Riley – it displaced more oxygen with each breath. Then she saw the blood. Not hers. The circle spread across Riley's blouse.

When she tackled me, Beck realized.

Red ran along her hands.

Too much.

"No…nonononono…"

"Beck…"

"I got you!" She tried to lift her. Managed to shift them a few inches, then fell again.

"Look at me…"

"C'mon!" She tried to lift Riley again. Screamed. Pounded the floor. Cried.

"Beck."

Finally, she looked up.

Riley cupped her face in her hands. "I love you…"

"I love you, too."

Riley's eyes began to close.

"Don't go…please…"

Her hands slid down—

"…don't leave me…"

—then went still.

"Mom!"

Beck tried to pull her down the stairs, but she was too weak, too damaged.

All she could do was hold on to her mother.

CHAPTER 85

Winston fell to all fours inside the front door. A furnace awaited. He dropped lower, face to the floor, calling out, trying to find—

There.

On the main stairs.

No more than twenty feet away.

"Beck!" The shout caused him to take in a double lungful of hot smoke. His vision swam. Someone pulled him out – Lucinda, her arm cut deeply. "I see them!" He tried to go again but couldn't even turn his body. He was too big, too slow, too old.

Despite her remarkable constitution, Sister could not breach the heat and fumes.

Sirens filled the air. Too late.

He kept shouting Beck's name.

Then Riley's.

In a few seconds, they'd be lost.

"No…oh, God, no…" he cried.

A tiny figure shot past him.

CHAPTER 86

Jimmy knew how to stay low. They'd taught him in school. Stop, drop and roll. Except he wasn't going to roll. He was going to salamander. He loved the movies they showed in school about animals. How the salamanders wriggled super-fast to glide forward a few inches cracked him up.

He first ran to the rectory to tell Father W and Sister Lucinda about all these people entering the spooky house. He watched them call nine one and one and followed them outside even though he'd been told to return to his room.

The fire was hot from way back. Jimmy got scared when Father W and Sister Lucinda fought a man before another man shot him. He hid behind a tree until he heard Father W shouting Beck's name. Peeking around the trunk, he saw Sister Lucinda haul Father W out of the burning house and then try to push inside. But she was hurt, and the clouds made her choke. Father W kept calling Beck's name.

She must have been inside.

Jimmy took off and ran into the spooky house. Beck was his friend. It was scary, but he was small and knew how to get in and out of tight spaces. He'd been getting in and out of tight spaces his whole life. This heat was different, though. It stung his eyes.

Beck slept on the stairs next to another woman. Holding his breath, Jimmy climbed into the thicker smoke, shaking her. Beck groaned. He grabbed her, planted his feet against the step, and pulled with all his might. It hurt as they slid to the bottom. He tried to drag her. The heat blistered his skin. He thought about his mom and how he cried for her to wake up. He tucked himself against Beck; he wouldn't leave her no matter what.

She said something soft, like waking up from a dream. He tried to call her name but gagged, thick, like when he had broncositis.

Her eyes opened.

Jimmy salamandered back to the stairs to get the woman Beck was hugging. If she was important to Beck, she was important to Jimmy. But Beck pulled him the opposite way. Told him to kick. Using their elbows and hands, they pushed and pulled each other along.

Up ahead, fire ran around the doorway.

They kicked and swam harder.

Cold air hit him in the face. He'd never thought of air as sweet before, but that was the word that jumped into his head. He struggled to catch his breath. Things were breaking all over the place. He glanced back at the stairs. Couldn't see the woman anymore. Couldn't see anything. Beck carried them the rest of the way out before she collapsed on the porch.

And then Father W was there. So was Sister Lucinda. Although her right arm was now really red, she scooped him off the ground as Father W lifted Beck in his arms and carried her away from the house, which wasn't so spooky anymore, just glowing and falling apart.

"I got you," Sister Lucinda said. Seeing her crying surprised him. He didn't think she was the kind of person who cried. "I got you, you stupid, brave little boy."

And she ran him away until the air turned even sweeter.

"There is only one day left, always starting over."

– Jean-Paul Sartre

CHAPTER 87

It was quiet in the ICU. It was also the first time Beck could keep her eyes open for more than a few minutes. Eli and Amy slumped over in hard-back chairs. As if sensing her return, they both stirred. She started to speak, but Amy shushed her gently as Eli put a cold compress on her forehead.

"We got you," Amy said.

Minutes later, Detective Underhill entered as if he'd been outside waiting for her to wake up. She told him everything.

He told her to hire a good lawyer.

Four days, she was in and out. She slept for most of it. Rested to heal, to remember and to forget. Her mind was her greatest asset. Her "wits," Father W called them. But she couldn't ponder any prevailing order or basic logic. Certainly, no wit.

Except for Jimmy. He made sense. She understood him.

Maybe everyone loses their minds after seven.

Jordan visited the next day. He moved okay for a guy who'd undergone arthroscopic surgery to repair a damaged disc. With physical therapy, the doctors promised full mobility. Beck introduced him to her friends, but he was back in operative mode, reserved, and departed soon thereafter. He returned after Amy and Eli had gone home to change and update everyone at HQ on her condition. Jordan tried to keep her away from the news, but her insistence broke him down.

He'd recovered the tape inside his knapsack on the roof of the Kleen-o-Mat; Riley had fulfilled her role – up to a point. She'd returned to the roof and stashed the recording but blew up the rest of the plan by charging back into the fray.

If she hadn't, Beck would be dead.

Coverage filled the broadcasts. First up was Underhill at Police Headquarters:

"...received a link to a video-chat session from someone claiming to be Rebecca Gideon. Despite the challenged sound and audio quality, I discerned Carlow Hain assailing Rebecca Gideon after she refused to turn over a tape…"

More press conferences focused on other aspects of the story, including Beck's allegations of a death squad led by Henry Washington in the employ of Carlow Hain, hours of surveillance provided by Jordan Lear and his and Beck's statements about the demise of Washington and Stratton, the entire saga laid bare.

No one cared.

They did, but the shock paled compared to the lascivious outcry for the tape, the original sin.

"So the email did go out," she said.

Jordan nodded. "You managed to hit send before Carlow went ballistic. By the way…I've told you this a few times already, but the morphine drip kept it from getting through…what you did took some serious *cajones*. You put yourself on the line knowing you might not leave that room alive."

"You did the same for me."

"I had a gun. You had a phone." He squeezed her hand and then continued. "You sent enough to identify Carlow and Riley, but it's only whet the appetite for more. There are…well…"

"Go on."

"Sentiment is building that the clip you sent is a deepfake, an attempt to discredit a reformist poised to lead us to the promised land. Or a takedown of a successful capitalist by pinko anarchists."

"Pinko?"

"Their words, not mine. Some are decrying it as another example of guilt before innocence, of trial by social media. Others claim to have seen it and say there's even more on the original the authorities aren't telling us, stirring up even more ridiculous conspiracies."

"Business as usual."

"What scares me is the amount of vitriol aimed at you. Olivia Hain is leading the charge." Jordan used his new phone to show her a replay of Olivia's impassioned speech at Hillary Maritime.

She derided the smear campaign against her husband, an honorable man no longer here to defend himself. She ended her incitement by asking, "Of all the people involved in this sordid affair, who is the only survivor? Who is the one we know possesses the technological know-how to pull off this level of trickery?" She didn't mention Beck by name, speculate on motivation or explain why Carlow went to St. J's armed to the teeth. She didn't need to – their followers, supporters, benefactors and beneficiaries whipped themselves into a frenzy, pushing the narrative that Beck Gideon was, in fact, the real culprit and that what Underhill saw was simply a man trying to protect himself, his name and his family from the people trying to extort him.

"What do the police say?" Beck asked.

"They're keeping the tape under wraps, claiming the need to verify its authenticity. I'm wondering if it ever sees the light of day."

"Then we better get to work."

Sneaking Beck out of the hospital was a fiasco, but with the assistance of a nurse and a couple of orderlies, she met Jordan in the shipping area behind Mass General. Amy had brought fresh clothes, scissors, and a dye kit. An hour later, a spiky pink bob caused Beck to double-take in the mirror. Jordan attended to his disguise, emerging from the bathroom with a blonde goatee and matching high top. Accessorized with sunglasses and long coats, Boston's two most recognizable faces now looked like two punky kids getting ready for a night at The Grand.

Jordan didn't explain where he acquired the Dodge Charger but assured her it couldn't be traced. "Course, I thought I'd covered all the bases last time."

"At least it's fast."

"Fastest one I could find."

They waited outside the hoop courts in Stillman Park. The weather cooperated: a misting rain kept people indoors.

Gene D'Angelo double-parked and ambled over, lighting a cigarette. It was down to its filter by the time he reached them. Dropping it onto the asphalt, he heeled the butt into flakes. With a nod at Beck, he turned to Jordan. "I'm sorry."

"Up yours, Gene."

"I reported what I believed to be Tommy Hain's phone to the team investigating Washington's murder."

"William Underhill," Beck said.

D'Angelo shook his head. "His lieutenant. Sarah Stott. It was evidence. I was required to document the complete trail – including where I got the phone, who gave it to me, your location, etcetera...and if you didn't hear me the first time, I apologize. I would have been more discreet had I known it would come to this."

"I told you Washington was dirty."

"No, you asked me if I thought he was working for Francis Hain, and when it comes to that lanky Irish prick, stories go back to before I was even born."

"So maybe Lieutenant Stott's corrupt, too," Beck said.

"Nah, Sarah's good police. I'd stake my puny pension on it. She and her team are idealistic. A new breed. But in this town, lines of communication are like leaky pipes, especially with everything online now. Grieg and DeLillo must have been monitoring comms, saw my report, and went hunting."

"The Hains are trying to scrub the story," Beck said.

"Did you think they were just gonna sit back and let you take the pulpit?"

"Carlow doesn't get to be the fucking hero."

"If it's any consolation, I believe you."

"It's not," Jordan said.

"Then why am I here?"

"You almost got my ass killed and – albeit unwittingly – helped sink Chaya to the bottom of the Harbor."

"I can't buy you a boat, Jordan. Puny pension, remember?"

"Lucky for you, there's another way you can make it up to me."

Beck laid out what they wanted.

"You're nuts," D'Angelo said.

"So people keep telling me."

CHAPTER 88

Beck studied the Victorian ash heap. They'd recovered the two sets of remains but not much else. The fire department had focused on dousing the trees and nearby telephone poles, protecting the rest of the school and surrounding neighborhood, and letting the dilapidated home burn to powder.

They shuttered St. J's until the cleanup was complete and moved the kids into foster care. Beck vowed to keep checking in on them. Particularly Jimmy. She'd taken him for pancakes yesterday, reassured him everything was going to be okay, and thanked him for saving her life. Afterward, she was the one to initiate the hug. He'd blushed and asked her to play catch.

She entered the church. Found a spot in the rear pew. She didn't have to wait long; he'd been watching her from the rectory window.

Father W sat down next to her.

"I'm sorry," she said, the first words she'd spoken to him in weeks.

"You have nothing to apologize for."

"I was mad at you…at everyone. But…I appreciate the position you were in. What Tommy confessed to you…I don't understand it or even agree with it…but I respect it…and how it must have torn you up, living with what you knew."

"It was never about me, Beck. It wasn't my place to say anything. That right belonged to Riley."

"Ava."

Father W grinned. "Ava."

"A thief, an addict and a liar…who loved me more than anyone I'll ever know. It's hard to wrap my head around."

"I can imagine. But I know the Hains. I even remember Natty Hain and the terror he instilled. Tommy and Ava did what they thought was best."

"They were so young."

"In years, not experience. Ava persevered through more trauma than any child should."

"Where did she deliver me?"

"A shelter out near Millers Falls."

"Never heard of it."

"It's beautiful. So tranquil. The shelter is near a river and doesn't appear in any directory. They protect women and children in dangerous situations. A dedicated group with therapeutic and medical expertise, including midwifery. When Ava started to show, we checked her in as Jane Doe, and four months later, you arrived. I was there. A Tuesday. I prayed outside the room until Ava was ready to introduce us."

"She never thought about ending her pregnancy?"

"Never. And not because she lived here or because of any counsel from me. She never wavered, Beck. Not once. She said she always dreamed about having a family and was determined to weave something wonderful out of something horrible. And she succeeded. Your mother wasn't the most consistent person I've ever known. Just the most courageous."

Beck nodded.

"Have you given any thought to a service?"

"I want to spread her ashes out at Carson. She loved the water." She took his hand. "And I have a confession to make."

"I'm listening."

"Dead or not, I'm gonna make that bastard pay."

"I know."

CHAPTER 89

Beck pushed through the conference room doors.

Barbara looked up, as did the management team of Paradigm Ventures. Recognizing the pink-haired woman in the long coat took her a second. "Beck. I didn't realize we had a meeting."

"We don't."

"Well. It's great to see you. How are you feeling?"

"I've been better. Can we talk?"

"As soon as I'm finished…" she trailed off as Jordan entered the room.

"Now would be great," Beck said.

"Will you all excuse us?"

The Paradigm execs filed out except for Lyle, the attorney. "Maybe I should stay."

"It's okay," Barbara said.

"I really think—"

"Get the fuck out, dude," Jordan said, bopping him on the shoulder.

Lyle left, closing the doors.

Barbara said, "I know you've both been through a lot, but you have no right—"

"You sold me out." Jordan and Beck took chairs on either side of the Paradigm director. "You told Carlow Hain about me. Took me a minute, but once I reviewed the timeline, I realized Grieg tried to kill me before I went to my contact at the District Attorney and before I broke into Mr. Gabriel."

"You what?"

Beck set a thumb drive on the table. "These are the full details of Paradigm's investment into Hillary Maritime." Barbara's façade cracked. "Funny you failed to mention you were in business with Carlow Hain, not even when you bitched us out after Tommy's death."

"Or during the half year of my research," Jordan added. "You told me to follow every connection between Beck, Riley, and Tommy, no matter how remote. Yet you didn't think the money you dumped into his father's business was pertinent."

"The investment was private. I don't know how you acquired your information, but it shouldn't surprise you. Hain Developers and Hillary Maritime are two of the city's most prominent employers, and we are one of its most prominent investors."

"So you invested in Francis, too," Beck said, glancing at Jordan. "Told ya."

"I owe you a latte."

Barbara closed her eyes, realizing her gaffe. "I don't appreciate being ambushed."

"If you think this is an ambush, you should have spent the week with us."

"They're trying to spin the story," Beck said.

"Who are they?"

"You already know. The ones holding all the cards. The ones who decide everyone else's fate…and destroy those who stand in their way."

"Don't you dare put me in that bucket."

"You gave them Jordan's name, his alias. You're the only one who could have done so."

"Yes, when I heard the news about Tommy, I called Carlow. To offer my condolences as a parent and because I possessed information about Stratton's involvement with his son. I didn't know he was a…a…fucking barbarian!" Tears filled Barbara's eyes. She stood up, snatched a tissue off a table and dabbed at her eyes before her makeup ran. "I told him I'd hired an investigator and why. He asked for Jordan's number. Wanted to hear from him firsthand. Even said he wanted to hire him to keep researching Tommy's affairs. I thought I was aiding a grieving father."

"Instead, you painted a target on my back."

"Why didn't you tell me you were attacked?"

"Same reason I hacked MrGabriel. You could have given me any information on their system, but…"

It took Barbara a second to piece it together. "You didn't know if you could trust me." She sank back into her chair. "I'm sorry. I am."

He returned a single nod.

"We can't let them get away with this," Beck said.

"Carlow's dead."

"We can't. Let them. Get away with this."

A shaky breath, a nod, and then Barbara asked, "What do you want to do?"

"You own Dark Corners."

"The podcast?"

"Currently, the third most popular true-crime podcast in the U.S. and number one in the Northeast." She pushed the thumb drive closer to Barbara. "You don't want to get put in that bucket? Help me."

"So these aren't documents about our investment in Hillary Maritime."

"No. We bluffed to get you talking."

Barbara laughed softly and picked up the thumb drive. "Then what's on here?"

CHAPTER 90

Dark Corners debuted the day before Thanksgiving – "The Round Midnight Massacre."

"You like the title?" Amy asked as she sat with Beck and Eli near the covered pool, listening to the last few minutes of the podcast.

"Not really," Beck said. "A little too Hollywood." She'd been staying at the Tennyson home. The gated community kept the newshounds out. Eli paid daily visits when not running the office while Beck recuperated, and Amy hovered over her like an annoying but loving hawk. "But they did an amazing job building off the info we gave them."

In short order, the *Dark Corners* research team had located a bevy of witnesses, starting with a Dyer retiree who had taken her cocker spaniel out for a late-night bathroom break and saw Carlow Hain and Grieg creeping around Silversmith Green. And yeah, the retiree was confident it was Carlow. "Guy's commercial is always interrupting my soaps, and his mug's plastered all over the city…well, it was."

Attendees and staff from the fateful New Year's Eve party followed, offering fresh recollections on Carlow's boorish behavior, his being escorted from the boathouse by David and Tommy and jumping behind the wheel blind-drunk before David forcibly knocked him out of the driver's seat. Even more damaging testimony came from an anonymous source, a worker who saw Carlow jostling a young cocktail server towards the beach. The one with a pretty pink ribbon in her hair.

The podcast promised an explosive conclusion the following week.

"Only two episodes?" Eli asked.

"For now. The objective was to get the story out fast to counteract the spin."

"Well, it's working," Amy said, spinning her laptop around and refreshing every few seconds so they could see the listener count climb ever higher. The episode was a supernova. "When do you think they'll come for you?"

Beck leaned against her friend. "Soon. Very soon."

CHAPTER 91

Beck liked to do her morning walk alone. A Lincoln slid smoothly beside her. The driver was polite but insistent. She didn't bother asking how he got past the gates. She spent the next forty minutes watching the ocean give way to strip malls and car dealerships before they turned down a private road and sped out to the beach. The driver patted her down, took her phone and led her back to where Francis Hain sat watching the ocean.

"Good morning, Rebecca." He stood up effortlessly for a man his age. "Let's warm ourselves."

They sat in front of a gigantic hearth with a ripping fire. Outside, expensive cars arrived: the Hains piling in for the holiday. Carlow's funeral was a week old, an intensely private affair not even news helicopters could spy on. Events seemed to be returning to normal around *Annwn*.

"I want to tell you how sorry I am," Hain said. "For what you went through. For losing your sister. I now know how much my grandson cared for you both." He sipped his coffee, legs crossed, as if exchanging pleasantries at the pub. "If there's anything I can do for you..."

"You didn't bring me up here to offer condolences."

"No?"

"You brought me up here because of the podcast; the conclusion is next week. They're not lying when they say it's the most explosive yet."

"I'm certain, lass," he laughed. "Listening to you admit you lied to the police, tossed out evidence and obstructed justice is highly entertaining."

"Of all the lies I've told, deceiving the people I love hurts the most. Whatever reasons I had don't feel important anymore. If a jury decides I need to be punished, so be it...Or maybe they'll recognize a kindred spirit, someone sick and tired of being under the heel of people like you."

"Slander. My lawyers will have a field day. Still, I don't blame you. Yours was a tough life."

"Did you watch it?" she asked. "The clip I sent. Given your connections, maybe you've even seen the whole recording."

"I don't have the faintest—"

"It happened right out there, Mr. Hain. In your boathouse. Your home. Doesn't that bother you?" She waited, but he didn't respond. "I've dug up everything I could find on you. Spent the past few days listening to Father W talk about the duality of man. Good and evil. You're a mobster. You've destroyed people. But now, who knows? At your last parole hearing, you spoke about family. I read the transcript. The only real touchstone in our lives, you said. Was that a story just to get out of prison?"

"Not hardly."

"I don't remember reading about you going after everyday people. It doesn't excuse what you did or who you are, but maybe even you have a line you won't cross. Maybe you are trying to make up for the sins of the past…which is why the video is burning you up inside."

"And just what's on this fabled film?"

"The worst thing you can imagine. Proof that you raised a monster."

He stared at her for a long time, impassive except for a slight downturn of his lips.

"I know if I don't stop telling our story, or at least step back and allow you and Olivia to control the narrative, my life will be at risk. I bet we could swing a deal right here, right now. An agreement I could profit from, but I will not do that, Mr. Hain. And if anything happens to me, I don't think cries of fake news will cut it this time. People will come knocking."

"Goddamn you," he said, his pallor white against the fire. "I've buried two of my children."

"And I lost my sister and a mother I never got to know because of your rapist asshole son. Whether you're a changed man doesn't matter because you're undoubtedly a practical man. Eventually, you'll realize defending his name isn't worth it." She took the envelope from her jacket and held it out. He hesitated. "It won't bite."

He grabbed it and unfolded the report inside. "What is this?"

"A DNA test. Tommy's was already in the system. I submitted mine. The key phrase is agnate sibling, which is a fancy term for half-brother." She watched his hands shake. "We share the same father: the deranged fucker you named Carlow. It's gonna make for a helluva climax. And before you scream about another forgery, know that the District Attorney's office oversaw the test. But if you're still skeptical..." She ripped a few strands of hair from her head. Hain pulled away, looking certain he'd invited a lunatic into his home. "Order your own test. You don't even need Carlow's DNA. They can match these against your cheek swab. The lab will test for centimorgans, and you'll have proof." She let the strands drift down to the table between them and stood up. "I'm a Hain, you sonofabitch. Ask yourself how I got here."

All he could do was stare at the strands, the report still trembling in his hands.

"Oh, and if you decide to come after me, my friends, or anyone in my orbit, remember this: Washington, Stratton and your son tried to put us down, and my mother and I sent them out in a box." She walked to the door and opened it. "Happy Thanksgiving, Frankie."

Beck walked past the entire family. Olivia Hain looked like she was wearing a death mask. Beck held her gaze until the housekeeper opened the door and then took her time crossing the sandstone pathway. A row of hard cases lined the property. None made a move. None said a word.

She turned back to see Francis Hain scowling out a window, pale, willowy, a wraith. She waited until he faded into the darkness behind the glass.

Then she passed through the gates.

A minute later, Jordan picked her up and drove her home.

About Avery

Avery West is the pen name of a screenwriter and author with a passion for high-intensity thrillers. Avery's work has been published, optioned, and produced by major studios, networks, and publishers, including The Los Angeles Times, Relativity Studios, WGN America, and Dark Horse Comics.

With a background in film and television, West brings a cinematic sensibility to stories driven by relentless suspense, flawed but compelling characters, and razor-sharp tension. Vengeance Falls marks Avery's debut as a novelist, a gripping thriller written for readers who crave fast-paced, unpredictable, character-driven storytelling.

Avery lives for great crime fiction, pulse-pounding action, and stories that keep you turning the pages long into the night.

https://www.instagram.com/averywestauthor/

www.ingramcontent.com/pod-product-compliance
Lightning Source LLC
Chambersburg PA
CBHW021644260626
47154CB00017BA/2251